Sherri Hayes

Slave

Finding Anna, Book One

First published by The Writer's Coffee Shop, 2011
Copyright © Sherri Hayes, 2011
The right of Sherri Hayes to be identified as the author of this work has been asserted by her under the *Copyright Amendment (Moral Rights) Act 2000*

Paperback ISBN - 978-0-9979049-1-8
E-book ISBN - 978-0-9909596-8-7

A CIP catalogue record for this book is available from the US Congress Library.
Cover image and design by: Sara Eirew
Layout design by: Riane Holt

Other Books by Sherri Hayes

Finding Anna series
Slave
Need
Truth
Trust
Finding Anna Boxed Set (Books 1-4)

Daniels Brothers series
Behind Closed Doors
Red Zone
Crossing the Line
What Might Have Been

Serpent's Kiss series
Welcome to Serpent's Kiss
Burning for Her Kiss
One Forbidden Night

Single Titles
Hidden Threat
A Christmas Proposal

Anthologies
Dominant Persuasions

This book is dedicated to Maria.

Chapter One

Stephan

Geno's was a small Italian restaurant about a mile from my office. They had good food and a cozy atmosphere, which made it a great place to have an informal meeting with an old friend.

The hostess greeted me at the door and let me know that my party had already been seated. She escorted me through a maze of tables to a corner booth in the back.

The restaurant was busy, but not packed. Still, getting the back corner booth with no one sitting at any of the immediate tables surrounding it told me either luck was with Daren today or he'd pulled some strings. My bet was on the strings.

Daren, my college roommate for two years, had called out of the blue this morning, asking if we could have lunch. He introduced me to the lifestyle I've lived for the last five years. Although he'd graduated a year ahead of me, we'd kept in touch through e-mails and the occasional phone call. Until I ran into him last month at a BDSM party, I hadn't seen him since his graduation day.

My mentor was always more social than me, so seeing him at a party wasn't exactly a shock. I just wasn't aware that he had moved back to Minneapolis. It had been a pleasant surprise.

After sitting down across from my friend, I took the menu from the hostess.

"Kelly will be around to get your drink orders in a minute."

I thanked her, set the menu down without looking at it, and faced Daren. He was nearly my exact opposite. Where I had brown hair, he had blond. His eyes were a baby blue, whereas mine were a vivid hazel. I was tall and lanky, even though I'd buffed up some since college. Daren, on the other hand, was four inches shorter and could have easily passed as a body builder.

Today he looked nervous, which was rather unusual for him. Not unheard of, but definitely not common either. Needless to say, it piqued my curiosity.

"So do you want to tell me what's up?"

"I will in a minute," he said, looking over my shoulder. His behavior gave me an uneasy feeling. "Do you know what you want, Stephan?"

"Yes. I come here all the time."

"Good." He sounded relieved.

And then Kelly was there asking for our orders.

As soon as she left, I raised my eyebrow in question, but he ignored me. "You're still running the family business, I see."

"Yes," I said, not sure what he was getting at. I doubted it had anything to do with why he'd called me. "I'm still head of The Coleman Foundation, but since it's a not-for-profit, I'm not sure you could say it's the family business."

He waved it away. "Same thing."

I waited, but he didn't continue so I decided to play along. "You're still consulting?"

Daren released a sharp breath. "Yeah." He leaned toward me. "Are you still looking to collar a sub?"

So that's what this was about? "If I find the right one, yes." I noticed his shoulders relax, and he sat back a little. "What does that have to do with anything?" I asked, truly confused.

The subject that I did not currently have a submissive came up during our conversation last month at the party. I hadn't played with anyone in the last six months. No one had struck my fancy, and most of them reminded me too much of Tami.

Daren had been with his submissive, Gina, since college. They were well matched in likes and dislikes and were much more open in their relationship than I personally preferred. I did not share my submissives, nor did I play with others when in a relationship. Many did, like Daren and Gina, but I'd never found it to be appealing. What was mine was mine.

Kelly came back with our drinks, so Daren waited for her to leave again before answering. "Because I found a girl for you."

"Daren," I warned, shaking my head. This was another *no* on my list. I didn't enjoy being set up. Logan, my best friend, and his girl, Lily, had tried to set me up more times than I could count. I wasn't interested.

"Hear me out. She needs your help."

This aroused my curiosity. "What do you mean she needs my help?"

"I know how much you like to help people, Stephan. I mean, look at what you do."

I was in complete disbelief. "Helping fund medical care for those who can't afford it is a little different than taking on a submissive. Is she already a trained sub? Is she looking for a Dom?"

"She's a slave."

A slave. I didn't have a problem with that, fundamentally. It was a complete power exchange. Slaves gave up all control of their lives, their bodies, to their Master or Mistress. Some women, and even some men, chose to be slaves. For most slaves it was a comfort to have someone else make the decisions in their lives for them, to give up complete control to someone else. That didn't sound like the case here if she needed my help.

"Okay," I said, drawing out the word, still not quite sure where Daren was going with this.

"I was at a party Saturday night. She was there. Her name is Brianna, and she belongs to Ian Pierce."

I knew of Ian solely by reputation. I'd never met him personally. He was well-known in the community, but from what I heard, he was into pain and humiliation. And he already had a slave. "What happened to his other one?"

"Oh, she's still there. Alex was at the party as well. Brianna is a new acquisition."

"And you don't think she wants to be?"

"No," he said firmly. "I don't."

"Maybe she's into what Ian does."

"Trust me, she's not," he said, shaking his head. "I wouldn't have come to you otherwise. And if you had seen her Saturday night, you would know it, too."

I considered this bit of information. There was no doubt in my mind that Daren believed what he was saying. If this girl didn't wish to be Ian's slave, I couldn't sit by and do nothing. How to help her was the problem. My options were limited.

"What do you want from me exactly? It's not like I can call the police and have them storm the place just on my word. Or yours for that matter."

He leaned in again, clasping his hands in front of him, but had to pull back when our food arrived. Daren took a bite, and then looked me straight in the eye. "I have a collared sub, or I'd do it myself. Plus," he said with a smirk, "you have more money than I do."

It was then I got it. "You want me to buy her." It wasn't a question, and he didn't deny it. The thought of "buying" a woman turned my stomach, but if what Daren said was true, I couldn't just leave her there.

I needed more information and ignored my food as it grew cold on my plate. "What makes you think he'd be willing to part with his property?"

Daren gave me a devilish smile. This was the Dom I knew. He could be quite twisted when he wanted to be. "I asked," he said with a shrug. "In fact, I told him about you. Said you might be giving him a call."

"You *what?*" I nearly shouted. I couldn't believe he'd told this man I might be interested in anything without talking to me, let alone the purchase of another human being.

Daren looked around us, and I followed his gaze. Everyone in the restaurant was looking at us. That was something we definitely didn't need, so I lowered my voice to almost a whisper. "Explain."

"Look, when I saw the girl, I thought of you. She has brown hair and blue eyes. I know how much you like brunettes."

I scowled, but he ignored me. "She's really pretty, *and* scared to death from what I could see," he said pointedly. "So I simply asked Ian if he was planning to keep her now that she was fully trained. He asked if I was interested. I told him no, but that I knew of someone who might be." He shrugged. "I didn't tell him you'd be looking for a submissive, though, Stephan. If you do this, you'll have to go in acting like you're looking for a slave."

My mind raced. If I did buy her, what would I do with her? What would she be like?

I couldn't just leave her there—that was certain, not if she was there against her will. It just wasn't in me. If I could help, then I had to.

Could I do what needed to be done? Could I treat a woman like a piece of meat? Buy her?

But how could I not, given the alternative?

"Okay."

Chapter Two

Stephan

The entire drive back to my office I could not stop thinking about what Daren had told me. How did she get there? And was she really, as he suspected, there against her will? What if he was wrong?

I couldn't think about that. Daren wouldn't have come to me unless he was sure.

Pushing all thoughts of this mystery girl aside, I waited for the elevator doors to open. No matter what I decided to do, I would need a clear head.

When I returned to the office, Jamie, my secretary, informed me our CFO was waiting in my office. The previous acting president had hired Karl Walker while I was still in college and before I took over my duties as head of the foundation. Karl was good at what he did, which was why he was still here. That didn't mean I liked the man.

He was rude. Not to me, of course, but to those he felt were beneath him, like Jamie. Karl was subtle about it, though; it was more sly comments than outright rudeness. Once, he'd told Jamie she was pretty good at her "little" job. The disparaging comment was a vast understatement of Jamie's duties as an executive secretary. She earned every penny she made.

Jamie had said more than once that she was very glad to be working for me and not him. Her comment was along the lines of, "If I had to work for him, I'd quit before the week was out." Although her words inflated my ego, it didn't solve my overall problem with him. Or my current problem: why was Karl in my office?

My CFO stood as I entered and waited until I took a seat before retaking his own. "What can I do for you, Karl?"

He handed me a stack of papers. "I wanted to bring you the quarterly numbers as soon as the girls finished compiling them." The look on his face was full of the arrogance I'd come to associate with Karl. And though I bristled inwardly at his words for the all-female team he'd assembled, I kept my irritation in check. My anger would get me nowhere, so I ignored his choice of words.

"And?"

"The numbers are good, but not where I would like them to be. I think we may need to ramp up the fall fundraiser to make sure we exceed our financial goal."

I set the pile down in front of me; there was no need to look at it immediately if there were no glaring issues. Besides, I had enough on my mind right now. "I'll be happy if we meet our goal, considering the economy."

"I still think we need to set our sights high," he said, pushing for more.

I was not going to argue something so stupid with him. "Fine. Meet with Lily and put together a proposal."

With that he left. I picked up the phone and dialed Lily's number to let her know he was coming. She detested Karl Walker and would kill me if I didn't warn her he was coming. Lily didn't take crap from anyone.

Lily answered on the third ring. "Stephan. To what do I owe this honor?"

I managed a smile. "Karl Walker's on his way down to see you."

She whined. "I have to be nice?"

This time an actual chuckle escaped. "Yes. You have to be nice."

"Do you know what he wants?" She sighed.

"He wants to discuss some changes to the fundraiser."

Lily's tone became defensive. "Changes? What kinds of changes?"

The fall fundraiser was Lily's baby. She took it personally. "The quarterly projections are lower than what he'd hoped."

"Ah," she surmised. "He just wants to impress the boss."

I wasn't going to disagree with her. She was probably right.

~ * ~

Ian Pierce had been pleasant enough when I'd talked to him on the phone. Daren had been correct; he was open to "selling" Brianna.

My appointment was for six o'clock Wednesday evening, and when I pulled my car up to the gated house ten miles outside the city, my stomach started churning, just as it had every time I thought about what I was going to do. *I am going to* buy *someone!*

The gate opened. My sweaty palms gripped the steering wheel as I drove my car down a long driveway leading to a house that looked like something out of a Gothic horror movie. I could only imagine how eerie it would be once the sun set.

Taking a deep breath, I put my game face on. I'd done a little research on Ian after setting up the appointment. From everything I'd found, Daren had been right about the man. Ian respected those who emanated power and detested those who exhibited weakness. I would have to mind my actions the entire time I was within the walls of his house.

Less than a minute after ringing the doorbell, a tiny woman opened the door, wearing nothing more than a tube top and a short miniskirt. Her hair was long and blond. This was not Brianna.

The woman did not speak and her gaze, after the second it took for her to see who I was, was cast down.

"I'm Stephan Coleman." My voice was firm but even.

"Yes, Sir. Will you follow me?"

She stepped back and waited for me to enter before closing the door behind me. I assumed this was Alex, Ian's alpha slave. She led me down a long hallway to a large, solid-wooden door that she knocked on twice. A stern voice answered, telling us to enter. My escort opened the door for me before following and immediately dropping to her knees.

The room was masculine, full of dark woods. The walls were

lined with bookcases filled with books. In the center of the room sat an older man, who I assumed was Ian, behind a large desk. He looked up and appraised me. I'd just come from work and wore a tailored black suit and tie with a white shirt. Classic, but it also said power, which was exactly what I'd intended.

Without looking at the woman on the floor he dismissed her, telling her to wait outside until she was wanted. The door closed behind me, and suddenly the room felt small. Ian sat staring at me, watching, looking for something. He stood to walk in front of his desk, stopped, and appraised me some more. Scrutiny was nothing new for me, but for some reason this guy gave me the creeps. I refused to let it show and stood confident under his examination.

I made the decision right then that I wasn't about to walk out of there without Brianna, so I pushed my nerves aside and stepped forward. "I'm Stephan Coleman. I'm here to look at the girl."

"Ah, yes. Brianna. Your friend told me you had an interest in my slave. Why?" His tone was even and cold.

This was a test. My response would determine if I was worthy in his eyes to own his girl. "I don't believe I need a reason."

He smiled wickedly at my response. Yep. Test. "True." He tapped his fingers together just under his chin. "Would you like to see the merchandise?"

"I would." I kept my voice flat.

"Alex!" he yelled. The door immediately opened and the woman from before stepped through. "Bring Brianna to me."

"Yes, Master."

She left quickly, scurrying out of the room, but returned shortly. The woman at Alex's side was taller than her but still petite, and wore the same tube top and miniskirt uniform. I couldn't see her eyes, but I knew they would be blue just as Daren had said. She was beautiful from what I could see. Beautiful and broken.

Brianna had medium brown hair that fell below her shoulders and curled up at the ends, framing her face and drawing attention to her breasts. Her curves were well defined, but not extravagant. In different clothing, she would have reminded me of the girl next door.

Seeing her, all my reservations vanished. Something inside me screamed that I needed to protect her. I would buy her no matter the cost.

Then Ian's sharp voice interrupted my thoughts. "Stand in the middle of the room, Brianna." She did so quickly, obviously fearful of her Master.

I knew what was expected of me. Walking to her, I circled, giving her a cursory evaluation. "Nice." And she was. She was young, and she had a subtle beauty to her. Her skin was pale with a light pink hue. There were no blemishes that I could see, which surprised me given how young she looked. I was drawn to her lips. They were a darker shade of pink, but with the expression on her face they look wrong. She was not happy, and I wondered what her lips would look like as she smiled.

Ian's prideful voice interrupted my thoughts. "Isn't she, though? She was a bit of a challenge at first, but we've taken care of that."

I nodded and cringed internally because of what I was about to do.

My hand went to her chin and pushed her face up. She kept her gaze downcast as much as she was able, but I could see the fear. Daren was right. This was not her choice. There was no satisfaction in her eyes or her posture in serving her Master.

"Open," I commanded.

She did as she was told, and I made a point of looking at the health of her teeth. I had no idea what I was looking for, of course; I was no dentist or doctor, for that matter. "How long have you had her?"

His voice was smug as we discussed his property. "A little over ten months. One of the best purchases I ever made. She has been . . ." His voice trailed off as he looked for the right word. "Entertaining." Then he sighed. "But I'm willing to part with her. For the right price, that is."

Nausea returned as I listened to him, and I was glad I'd forgone dinner.

I pushed her chin up, indicating I wanted her to close her mouth, and ran my hands down her bare neck and shoulders before palming her breasts over the thin material of her tube top. I gave them a light squeeze as if measuring their size and the feel of them in my hands. I noticed a small furrowing of her brow, but otherwise she didn't move. I tucked that piece of information away for later.

Then I knelt, bringing my hands to her narrow waist. I knew she most likely wasn't wearing underwear, so that was not what surprised me when I lifted her skirt. It was the deep bruising running up the inside of both her thighs made worse by the evidence of older bruises.

My anger roared inside me, and I had to fight with myself not to let it show. It wouldn't help my cause. I stood and continued to do what was expected.

Going around behind her, I ran my hands over her once again before stepping away.

"Do you like her? She's well proportioned. Her oral skills are quite good as well. You are more than welcome to try them out if you'd like."

"That won't be necessary. I do believe she will work." And then I uttered the words I never wanted to say again. "How much?"

I felt Brianna shift beside me. It was small, but I wasn't the only one who saw it.

Ian glared at her before walking to her side. "Maybe we should go downstairs first, and I can remind you of your place," he snapped.

She didn't answer him. Instead, her head bowed farther, showing him her submission. He seemed pleased with her compliance.

"My apologies," he said, all business again. "Now, where were we?"

The negotiation took almost an hour, but in the end I handed over a check for a substantial amount of money. Daren was correct when he mentioned that I had more money than him. He would have been hard pressed to access the sum I now freely handed over to Ian Pierce. I wouldn't miss it.

Ian removed a painting from the wall behind him and placed the check in a safe before turning to Brianna and removing her black leather collar. He laid it on his desk and asked, "Do you have something for her already?"

"I didn't bring it with me since I hadn't looked her over yet." All I wanted to do was get out of there. This entire charade was making me sick. He just nodded and then took her face in his hand, forcing her to look at him for the first time since I'd been there. I could see his fingers biting into the flesh of her cheeks. "You belong to him now. You will not embarrass me, do you understand?"

"Yes, Master." Her voice was cold, almost robotic.

His wicked smile reappeared. "I do love hearing you say that, but I am not your Master now."

With that, he released her and turned his back on both of us to stroll back to his desk. "Alex, show them out," he said with a dismissive wave of his hand.

Alex walked us directly to the door and opened it, letting the chilly evening breeze wash over us. I looked down at Brianna and her attire. A tube top and a miniskirt were not the best things to wear mid-April in Minnesota. Turning to Alex, I asked, "Does she have other clothing or a jacket?"

Ian's alpha slave looked at Brianna with what could only be described as disgust. "*She* does not own anything, Sir."

I sighed in exasperation, took off my suit jacket, and placed it around her shoulders. It was far too big for her, but it would work for now.

Brianna walked one step behind me the entire way to my car. She stopped outside the vehicle even after I opened the door for her. "You may get into the car."

After I'd given her permission, she complied quickly.

The ride back to my condo was quiet, as I knew it would be. She held my jacket close to her body as we drove. Her hands were shaking even though I could see she was trying to hide it from me. She was scared. After living with Ian Pierce for the past ten months and seeing the bruises, I had no doubt of that. Brianna lived in fear, not pleasure.

I was going to change that.

When we arrived at my building just before nine, I parked my car in its usual spot and got out. It wasn't until I was halfway to the elevator that I realized Brianna had not followed.

Walking back to my car, I opened the door for her. "You may get out of the vehicle." She did, and then stood looking down at the concrete floor. "Come." She followed.

As we made our way to the elevator and then up to my penthouse, I contemplated the new problems I had. I'd never "owned" a slave before. Brianna had nothing but the clothes on her back, and those weren't suitable to wear in public. I knew Ian might disagree with me on that, but from the little I'd seen already, I had a feeling we didn't agree on much.

We managed to reach my condo without running into any of the other tenants in the elevator, and she followed me inside.

I loved my home. When I moved back to the city after college, it was my first major purchase. It was in the heart of downtown Minneapolis, and I had a view of the city skyline from my living room. The open floor plan had always appealed to me, and of course the wood beams in my ceiling came in handy when playing. My aunt and uncle offered to let me stay with them for a while until I could find a house, but I needed to be out on my own. I was not the lost boy they'd sent off to college anymore.

Laying my keys down on the side table, I walked to the kitchen, loosening my tie. I didn't know about Brianna, but I was starving now that I'd had time to calm down after my sickening business dealings tonight.

I reached into the freezer, pulled out two French bread pizzas, and put one in the microwave. "Have you eaten dinner?"

"No, Master," she whispered.

It was not that I had a problem with her calling me Master: both of my collared submissives had at one point in time. The way she said it, though, held not respect but fear. I didn't like it, but it was too late to try and fix anything tonight. My main priority was to get us both fed and into bed.

The microwave beeped, and I took the first pizza out and slid it onto a plate. Setting it down on the counter across from me, I looked over at her. She hadn't moved a muscle. "Come eat." Brianna came.

She stood stiffly as she picked up the pizza and began eating. Her first bites were slow but soon became faster as if she hadn't eaten in a very long time. My anger for Ian continued to grow the more I observed the beautiful creature in front of me, wolfing down her dinner. Her pizza was gone before mine finished cooking.

I brought my food with me and sat on the stool beside her. She was stiff as a board and still looking down. "You may sit, Brianna."

She did.

Brianna didn't move as I began to eat. There was a mixture of both dread and excitement as I realized the task I had in front of me. She was broken, totally and completely. It would take a lot of work to rebuild her self-worth, but I knew the end result would be worth it.

All of a sudden she started jerking, almost as if she was choking. I stood immediately and moved behind her, ready to give the Heimlich maneuver should she be in need.

"Let it out," I said softly, hoping that she wasn't trying to downplay whatever was happening, fearing my response.

As soon as the words left my mouth, her jaw relaxed, and the pizza she had just shoveled down covered the counter.

I stood stunned. If I had not moved from my seat when I did, I would probably have been part of the collateral damage.

It was only Brianna's movement that brought me out of my fog. She practically collapsed onto the floor. At first I thought she had fallen, but realized it was too controlled for that.

She was on her knees, forehead to the floor. Her entire form shook with what I finally realized were silent sobs.

I stood looking back and forth from the mess on the counter to the girl shaking on the floor before deciding to leave the mess and deal with Brianna first.

Squatting down, I kept my voice calm and even. "Look at me." Her head slowly came up off the floor, but every muscle in her body tensed as if she was waiting for something awful to happen. Tears were streaming down her cheeks, and I noticed that she needed some cleaning up. "Are you okay?" I asked, concerned.

For some reason this made her cry harder, but she nodded.

I reached out, trying to offer my assistance, but she stiffened more, so I pulled back again.

With a sigh, I pushed myself up to my full height, and asked, "Can you walk?"

"Y—Yesss, Master," she stuttered.

"Follow me," I said, knowing she wouldn't move from her spot unless I told her. Leading her through the living room, I walked into the room next to mine.

This would be her bedroom. It was smaller than mine, but it had its own full bathroom. I showed her the bathroom. "Go clean yourself up. I'll wait here," I said, taking a position a few feet from the door. She lowered her head and walked inside.

I looked around the room. It had been empty for a while, since Tami. The bed was the dominant feature in the room along with a built-in dresser and closet along one wall. There were two end tables, one on either side of the bed, but other than a lamp and alarm clock they were empty. The only other piece of furniture was a plush leather chair that sat in the corner. All personal touches to the room had left with the person who used to occupy the space. Hard to believe that was six months ago.

Brianna didn't take long. She was gone less than five minutes. Her face was slightly red where she'd obviously scrubbed it clean, as were her neck and shoulders. She stood with her head bowed, waiting.

As I watched her, I wondered briefly if I should try to find her something else to wear to bed besides her current attire, but figured it wouldn't hurt her to wear them for another night. Tomorrow I'd be finding something else for her to wear anyway. "Come to bed," I said, motioning toward the queen-size bed. "This is where you will sleep."

She walked over beside the bed. But instead of getting into it, she lay down on the floor.

What the . . .

I walked over, knelt beside her, and reached out slowly for her hands. It was the first time I'd touched her since leaving Ian's, and she jumped slightly, not able to help herself. I saw her eyes widen in fear as she realized what she'd done.

"Brianna," I said in a voice that brooked no argument. "You will sleep in the bed, not on the floor."

I didn't think her eyes could get any bigger, but they did. Then she got up and climbed onto the bed, lying flat on her back, her arms down at her sides.

Her face was set, waiting for something.

I studied her for a minute before it dawned on me what she was waiting for; she thought I wanted sex.

We would get to that, but not tonight, and not with her like this. I opened the dresser drawer and pulled out a bottle of salve.

Her breathing picked up as I sat on the bed beside her, a telltale sign of her nervousness. Brianna's eyes were closed. She was mentally preparing herself for whatever I was going to do to her.

I lifted her skirt, once again revealing her bruises. They looked worse in the bright artificial light of this room, and I felt the pizza I'd just eaten threaten to come back up. Without waiting any more, I placed some of the salve on my fingers and began massaging it into her thighs.

When I finished and put her skirt back in place, she was looking at me. Then, realizing her mistake, she quickly looked away. I stood and put the bottle back in the drawer.

"You don't have to fear me, Brianna. Good night."

21

After turning off the light, I left her alone and went back out to the kitchen to clean up before heading to my own bedroom. I stripped down to my boxers and fell into bed. The emotional strain of the day quickly pulled me into a deep sleep. And my last thoughts were of a fragile woman with brown hair and blue eyes.

Chapter Three

Stephan

A piercing scream tore me from sleep. Throwing the covers off, I ran to Brianna's room to find her huddled against the headboard of her bed, looking wild with fright. Her hands were twisted in her hair, tangling it. At first she didn't seem to notice me in the dim light from the window, but when she did, she closed her eyes, tilted her head down, and began to shake.

Slowly, I walked toward her. I didn't want to frighten her more, but I felt I needed to do something. Brianna was my responsibility. She was in a strange place, alone. Although I was a stranger, I was all she had at the moment.

By the time I reached the end of her bed, she was moving. I hesitated. She nearly tripped over herself as she scrambled to the floor to kneel in front of me.

Her name was on the tip of my tongue when she started jerking. I bent down, concerned that she was having another episode, and reached out to grasp her by the shoulders. Her eyes were closed tight, and she looked like she was in pain. Scooping her up, I carried her to her bathroom and set her down by the toilet. I lifted the toilet seat and pulled her hair back. She bent over and let loose, but nothing came out. Her stomach was empty. All she had were dry heaves.

Once she calmed, I got two washcloths from the rack. After running them under cold water, I took them to Brianna. She hadn't moved, not that I'd really expected her to. Her body was unnaturally still, her eyes cast to the floor as I washed her face.

When I was finished I tossed the dirty cloth into the sink and turned back to her. Again, she looked like she was about ready to cry.

I carried her back to her bed.

Placing her on the rumpled covers, I brushed her hair back and placed the fresh washcloth on her forehead. Her eyes flicked to my face, then closed as she tensed.

She acted as if she was waiting for me to molest her. The fact that she thought I'd do so when she was obviously unwell made me wonder just what horrors she'd undergone while living with Ian Pierce.

Without another word, I stepped away and settled into the chair in the corner of the room. I'd used the chair for various reasons in the past, but a bed had never been one of them before tonight.

As I leaned back, trying to get comfortable, I watched her still form on the bed, letting myself study her. Her delicate features were silhouetted against the lights of the city coming through the window. It gave the illusion of a peace that wasn't present. She was a mystery. I had no idea of her past beyond her time with Ian, and even that was sketchy. Who was she before? Was this a life she chose that went horribly wrong or something worse?

Eventually, she seemed to relax and fall back to sleep. With a sigh, my eyes closed, and I tried to find some rest of my own.

When I woke the next morning with a crick in my neck, she was on the floor beside her bed, patiently kneeling. She had an amazing submissive presence. Her posture was near perfection. Ian had not been exaggerating on the amount of work he'd put into her training.

I rubbed the sleep from my face before addressing her. "Good morning, Brianna."

She didn't answer.

"You may respond."

"Good morning, Master." Her voice was dead, and she did not look up.

"How are you feeling?"

"Better, Master." She sounded like a robot. There was no emotion behind her words. I frowned. Was this really what Ian had wanted? Someone who just did what you told them to do without feeling? I repressed a shiver and pushed the thought aside. It would do me no good.

Looking down at her, I noticed her color had improved. Her fair skin showed a faint blush. Hopefully her stomach had also settled, but I wasn't taking any chances. "Go to your bathroom and do what you need to, then come meet me in the kitchen."

She didn't respond in any way other than to get up and walk into her bathroom. I rubbed a hand across my face, and then went to my own room to get dressed.

I decided to keep breakfast as simple as possible given what happened last night. She needed to eat something, but I didn't want to have to clean up a mess again.

As I was putting the bread in the toaster, she walked into the room. Her movements were stiff and unnatural. It was as if she were trying to be invisible.

After taking two glasses down from the cabinet, I turned to put them next to our plates only to find Brianna kneeling on the floor. I stared at her bowed head for several seconds before deciding to go ahead and finish what I was doing before addressing her.

Once I had everything set on the counter—toast, butter, and jelly, along with juice for me and water for her—I walked around the island and sat. "Come sit beside me and eat, Brianna."

She obeyed and took the same seat beside me as she had last night. When she reached for the dry toast I'd put on her plate, I placed a hand on her arm to stop her. "Slowly."

Brianna was like a statue until I turned back to my food and started eating. Then, hesitantly, she picked up her toast and took a small bite. We managed to get through breakfast without another incident.

After breakfast, I went into the living room and called Jamie to let her know that something had come up, and I would be working from home for the rest of the week. I instructed her to hold all my calls unless it was an emergency. She promised to keep things under control until I returned. I laughed, trying without success to picture my soft-spoken assistant standing up to the likes of Karl Walker. Jamie was many things, but aggressive wasn't one of them.

When I finished up with my call to Jamie, Brianna was on the floor just this side of the kitchen. I stopped and watched her.

I'd had submissives before, but this was something completely different. Sarah and I had met and talked several times before we even discussed playing together. With Tami, it had been much the same. Even with the few others I'd played with over the years I'd known them on some level before anything transpired.

With this girl, I knew nothing about her. She was obedient, yes, but that didn't tell me anything other than she was either naturally submissive, broken, or both. The fear I'd seen in her eyes a few times had me leaning toward broken.

The question was—what to do now?

I looked her over. First, we needed to get her clean and out of those absurd clothes. Her hair was still tangled from the night, and I was beginning to detest that outfit. Tami had left nothing behind, so the only option was to put her into some of my clothes until I could figure something else out.

Leaving her where she was, I went into my bedroom to see what I could find. She wasn't tiny, but she'd be swimming in most of my clothing.

Finally, I located some gym clothes I still had from college. I was a little thinner back then, and the shorts had drawstrings. They were the best option I had access to at the moment.

I walked back into the room and she was exactly where I'd left her. "Follow me," I said, knowing that she would.

When I reentered her bedroom, I smiled as I saw that she'd made her bed. Whether that was a habit Ian had drilled into her or one she'd already developed, it was a good one.

She came in the room and started to kneel again just inside the door before I stopped her. "No," I said firmly. Brianna stopped instantly. I held out the clothes to her. "Take these, shower, and put them on."

Brianna took the clothes, and I had started to leave before I thought of something. Given what I'd observed of her behavior, I didn't want her waiting around in the bathroom all day for my next instruction. "When you're finished, come find me." With that, I left her and went to get my laptop. Even though I was not going in to work for the rest of the week there were still things to be done.

I was hunched over the computer when motion alerted me that she was there. I stared openly. It was good to see her in something other than the tube top and miniskirt, but she looked even younger and more vulnerable in my clothes than I had expected. I gave her permission to watch television or read one of the books laying around in the living room. She knelt on the floor in front of the television and just stared at the blank screen for several minutes before I got up and turned it on for her, placed the remote in front of her, and returned to my work. She never touched the remote.

The rest of the day was awkward. She didn't say much. Actually, she didn't speak at all unless I asked her a direct question. Over her dinner of toast with a little bit of butter and jelly, I continued to make observations.

I had so many questions for her, but I knew it wasn't the right time. No matter my curiosity, I would have to wait.

~ * ~

Since she had been able to keep down the toast and jelly from the night before, I added oatmeal and some fruit on Friday morning. The day was again spent with me working at the dining room table and her in front of the television.

At dinner, I gave her some spaghetti with just a little sauce and made her eat slowly. She managed to keep that down, too.

Saturday we also had to address her use of the bathroom. While going through e-mails, I noticed that her face was scrunched up in pain. It made no sense to me at first since she was kneeling on a pillow in the living room at the time. When I asked her what was wrong, she quietly told me she needed to use the bathroom—Master.

After telling her to go use it I realized my mistake. Every submissive I had ever had in my home had either just gone to the bathroom when needed, or, if we were in the middle of playing, would ask. Brianna wasn't asking.

When she returned, I informed her that whenever she needed to use the facilities that she was to go and use them. She did not need to ask my permission or tell me unless we were in the middle of something. If that was the case, then she was to ask politely to be excused.

I pretty much let her be after that, hoping she'd get used to her surroundings. Food was still an issue, but I kept introducing new things and made sure she took her time eating them.

I caught her glancing at me once while I was working, but then she cringed as if she had committed a major sin and quickly turned her attention back to the television. A woman was talking about some new vacuum cleaner. It didn't seem all that interesting to me.

With her attention returned to the television screen, I sat back in my chair and watched her. She really was pretty. She had a simple beauty about her. It wasn't flashy. It didn't scream out to be noticed. But it was there all the same. Brianna was clearly trained, but I had many worries. Would she ever open up to me or would she stay in this shell forever? Only time would tell.

Brianna didn't look at me again for the rest of the weekend. I'd never insisted my submissives avert their eyes except during specified times of play. A person's eyes revealed so much about them, and I wanted that connection with whomever I was playing.

With Brianna it was different. I'd never played with someone so damaged. Of course, we weren't playing.

No matter how much I waited and watched, Brianna's personality showed no signs of emerging during the long weekend. The only real emotion I saw in four days was fear.

Chapter Four

Stephan

My alarm went off on schedule at six Monday morning. Per my normal routine, I showered and made my way into the kitchen. What I hadn't expected to find was Brianna kneeling on my kitchen floor.

We were going to have to talk, and soon.

I'd told her I would be returning to work this morning, but since she still wasn't talking, we hadn't really discussed anything. "You may stand." She complied immediately.

"Do you like ham and cheese omelets?" I asked as I pulled the ingredients out of the refrigerator.

She didn't respond right away to my question, which made me wonder just how long it had been since her opinion had been asked. Finally, I heard a weak, "Yes, Master."

It wasn't until I glanced up at her that I noticed she was still standing, head bowed. She was watching me, though, albeit covertly. I turned back to the stove to continue cooking. "You may sit, Brianna."

Her quick response threw me, but it wasn't what I'd wanted. She was back to kneeling on the floor. I sighed. After four days, I thought she would have known what I'd wanted when I told her to sit. This was going to be interesting. "Sit on one of the stools, please."

I heard her movement and knew she'd done as instructed even though I wasn't watching her. There was silence as I finished preparing breakfast and then came around to set both our plates down. She didn't eat, even after I started, until I gave her permission.

After finishing breakfast with absolutely no conversation from my companion, I took her into my bedroom and gave her another T-shirt and a pair of my jogging shorts. She took them hesitantly and waited for instructions just as she had each day since arriving. "You are to go to your room and change into these clothes. I will be leaving and won't be back until this evening. You may watch television, read any of the books in the living room, and make yourself lunch." I handed her a piece of paper. "This is my cell phone. You are to call it if you need to."

I closed the distance between us and raised her head to meet my eyes. "You will not be punished if you call me, Brianna," I whispered.

With that, I picked up my jacket and left for work.

I was late, as I knew I would be. Things with Brianna took more time than I usually allotted myself in the mornings. It was quite obvious from my observations that she had not been able to do much past breathing without permission. She didn't do anything because she was afraid. Fear had no place for my submissives inside or outside the playroom.

So, when I arrived at my office, the first thing I did was tell Jamie I needed to see Lily as soon as possible.

Lily strolled into my office less than an hour later. "You asked to see me?"

"Yes, Lily," I said. "Please shut the door."

She did and took a seat across from my desk. Her expression showed concern. "Is everything okay? Logan said he tried to call you over the weekend."

Of course, Logan had tried to call me. Not showing up to work without notice was strange behavior for me. I'd talk to him soon.

Instead of answering her, I got directly to the point. "Lily, I need your help."

"Sure," she said, smiling. "What do you need? I already talked with Karl and—"

"This doesn't have anything to do with Karl. Or work, actually."

There was no easy way to say this so it was better to get it over with. "I have . . . inherited a . . . woman. And she's . . . well, she's . . ." I grunted in frustration.

"Stephan, what's going on? Are you talking about a new submissive? You didn't say anything about getting a new sub. I mean, I know you were looking, but . . . when did you find her?"

She was rattling on in regular Lily fashion. And as much as I didn't want to have to tell anyone about this, I knew if I wanted her help there was no choice. I cut into her monologue. "I bought her Wednesday night."

Lily shot up from her chair. "You . . . you . . . *bought her*!" These last two words were said in a shout.

"Sit down, Lily," I commanded. She wasn't my submissive, but I was her boss.

After a few seconds' delay, she sat back down. "What do you mean, you *bought her*?" she said with a hiss.

"I mean, I bought a woman from Ian Pierce last week."

At the mention of Ian's name, Lily's back stiffened. After spending the weekend with Brianna, I knew Lily had good reason for her reaction. The man was obviously a sadist, and it didn't surprise me that she'd heard of him. People talk.

"Is she okay?" she asked, her voice full of concern for this girl she didn't know.

"Physically? I think so or at least she will be. Emotionally? Not at all from what I've seen. That's why I need your help."

"Anything." And she was completely serious. Logan and Lily were two of my best friends; they would do anything they could to help me.

I nodded. "First, I need you to take her shopping. She has nothing but what she left Ian's wearing, which isn't suitable. I've had her wearing some of my old things, but she needs to have clothes of her own."

"Do you know what size she is?" Lily asked, the excitement behind her eyes broadcasting her true feelings about my request. Lily loved a challenge, and this would prove to be a substantial one. Buying an entire wardrobe for a woman you've never met and knew nothing about wasn't something to take lightly, and knowing Lily and her desire to please, she would do her best for Brianna.

"No clue. She's about your size. Maybe a little taller, I'd say.

Does that help?"

"It gives me a place to start," she said, and I could see her mind already working.

"Good." I reached into my pocket, pulled out my wallet, and extracted a credit card. "I want you to take the day off, go pick her up from my place, and get her what she needs."

Her eyes lit up as she reached for the card.

I retracted my hand slightly, making her meet my eyes. "Needs, Lily. Needs."

"I'll be conservative, I promise."

With that, I handed her the card and watched her walk purposefully out of my office.

An hour later, Lily called; Brianna wouldn't leave the apartment because I had not given her permission to do so. Brianna's willingness to follow instructions to the letter would be beneficial in the playroom but having it in place every minute of the day was exhausting.

Lily put her on the phone. "Brianna," I said. "Lily is there to take you shopping for some new clothes. She'll have you back before I get home." She remained silent on the other end. "Do you understand?"

"Yes, Master."

Then the phone was given back to Lily, or more likely taken back by Lily.

"Stephan?"

"I'm here."

"I'm sorry I raised my voice to you earlier. You did the right thing."

I sighed. "Thank you. I just hope I can help her."

"You can, and you will. I have faith." Her smile was evident through the phone.

And then she was gone, leaving me once again to think about Brianna. I hadn't been doing much of anything else since my meeting with Daren last week. Lily would see what remained of her bruises today, but I trusted she would deal with it. They had lightened since I brought her home last week, in any case.

It was thinking about Brianna's bruises that led me to my next phone call. Taking her to a doctor would raise too many questions, but I did want someone to check her out. I needed to make sure the bruises were the only things I was dealing with, at least physically.

"Hello, Richard. It's Stephan."

Brianna

The minute he walked out the door I let the trembling take over my body, and my legs gave out. For the first time in months, I let the tears fall freely without worrying about the consequences.

I didn't know how long I lay there, but finally the tears stopped flowing, and I took the time to really look around. His home was nice. It was smaller than where I'd been, but less creepy, too. There were large windows all along one wall with a view of the downtown skyline.

Walking to the window, my hand came up and touched the glass. Then I remembered.

Fingerprints.

I ran to the kitchen and frantically opened the cabinets looking for glass cleaner. There under the sink was a bottle of Windex. Clutching it like a lifeline, I took several paper towels and went back to the window to wipe away my error before he came home. He'd been nice to me so far; I didn't want to make him mad.

Ian had been pleasant enough as long as I did what I was told, immediately as I was told, and I obeyed his rules. But with my new Master it was different. This place was different. And I got to sleep in my very own bed instead of the floor.

The thought of trying to escape crossed my mind, but I cowered against it. No, he'd only find me, just as Ian had when I'd tried to run.

Racing back across the room, I put the supplies back and willed the memories to go away. I didn't want to remember Ian or anything to do with the last ten months. My new Master was all I needed to think about. I had to make him happy with me.

Hearing a sound, I turned quickly and saw the front door opening. Was he home early? Did something happen? Did I do something? I was starting to panic. What did I do?

I ran out of the kitchen so that I was visible from the doorway and dropped to the floor. Maybe if he found me willing to accept whatever punishment he had in mind, he would go easy on me and it wouldn't be so bad.

But I didn't hear his heavy footfalls. These were lighter, and it sounded like the person was wearing heels. Then they stopped. When I opened my eyes, not realizing until then I'd closed them, I saw two tiny feet wearing tan pumps a foot in front of me.

I didn't know if I should look up or not, but since she seemed to be waiting for me to move first, I raised my head and found a beautiful woman with long red hair smiling down at me. "Hello. I'm Lily. You must be Brianna."

Was I supposed to answer? She seemed to be waiting again. "Um . . . yes," I said, my voice just above a whisper. Hopefully, if I wasn't supposed to answer, my meek response would lessen the retribution.

All she did was smile at me. "Nice to meet you. Stephan sent me to take you shopping."

Stephan? My new Master sent her to take me shopping? I was confused.

She didn't allow me time to ponder, though, before reaching down and pulling me to my feet. "Come on," she said. "We have lots to do today, and we simply must get you out of those clothes."

Lily led me into the room that my new Master had referred to as mine. She tossed the large bag she'd been carrying onto the bed and with hands on her hips said, "Now, let's get you out of those— things." She paused to lift the front of my shirt with the tips of two fingers before quickly releasing it as if it had bitten her. "They don't deserve the title of clothing, really."

Everything else happened in a rush of movement. Before I knew it, she had me out of the T-shirt and shorts Master had given me this morning and into a long-sleeved pink shirt and jeans. The jeans were a little big so she added a belt. The shoes didn't fit right either.

Her hands went back to her hips as she appraised me. "That color is all wrong for you, but it will have to do, I suppose." She grabbed the discarded clothing and threw it into the now empty bag. "Now to shop!" she said with excitement as she pulled me back out into the main room and toward the door.

She released her hold on my arm to retrieve a coat from a closet I hadn't known existed. That's when I realized we were leaving. I resisted, digging my heels in. Who was this Lily and did my Master really send her? What if he didn't and came home to find me gone? No. I couldn't leave.

Lily saw that I was not moving and shook her head. "I'll have you back before he returns," she said. The next thing I knew she pulled me into a hug and said, "It's okay."

Then she stepped back, still holding on to both my shoulders. I was still shaking my head, knowing I needed to speak, to explain to her why I couldn't go. Finding words was harder than I thought, but eventually I managed to blurt, "He . . . he didn't say I could leave."

She studied me for a moment, and then, putting a few feet between us, she pulled out a cell phone from her bright yellow purse, punched in a number, and put it to her ear. After a brief pause, I heard her say, "She doesn't want to go with me."

Oh no. No. No. No. No. No. I'd tried so hard to be good and something stupid like my refusing to go shopping with one of his friends was going to make him mad.

I hadn't realized I was shaking until I felt Lily's hand on my shoulder. When I looked up, she was holding her phone out to me. "He wants to talk to you," she said, encouraging me.

Taking the phone, I put it to my ear. And then I heard my new Master's voice. "Brianna, Lily is there to take you shopping for some new clothes. She'll have you back before I get home." I breathed a sigh of relief. He didn't sound upset. "Do you understand?"

"Yes, Master," I said dutifully.

Then Lily ripped the phone out of my hands and was guiding me once again toward the door. "Stephan?"

I kept my head down as we walked out the door, trying to not make it obvious I was listening to her conversation. Ian always said slaves should be invisible unless called upon to serve.

What I heard next brought my head up. "I'm sorry I raised my voice to you earlier. You did the right thing." What was she talking about? "You can, and you will. I have faith," I heard her say before she smiled, ended the call, and placed the phone once again in her purse.

"Come," she said, hauling me into the elevator. "We"—she paused for effect—"are going to shop."

And shop we did. We visited seven shops full of women who crowded us with offers to help. I clung to Lily, trying to hide.

Thankfully she didn't force me to do anything other than try on some clothes in the first store. After that, she pretty much let me be. I wasn't used to being around people like this anymore.

Two hours later we walked into a small café after Lily declared she needed to refuel.

I liked her. She was fun. Before everything happened, before my life changed, we could have maybe been friends.

It still wasn't clear to me who she was exactly. Did she work for my new Master? Was she aware of what I was?

I didn't think so. She was too nice to me and even asked me what I wanted for lunch. Trying to remember what I liked, it took me a minute to choose. In the end, I asked for a simple turkey sandwich. Lily ordered, and we took our seats.

Before taking her first bite, she looked at me. "So, Brianna, tell me about yourself."

I took my time, remembering what Master had said about eating slowly. "Um. There's . . . there's nothing to tell."

"Sure there is," she said, taking a bite of her own sandwich. "Where did you grow up?"

"Texas."

"I've never been there. I've lived in Minnesota all my life." She paused, seeming to think about something for a minute. "Do your parents still live there?"

"No." I almost choked.

"Are you all right?" She appeared genuinely concerned.

"Yes," I said, ducking my head. "I'm fine."

"Good," she said. I thought I saw something flicker across her eyes, but I could have been wrong. "Well, we still have a few more places to go, and I promised Stephan I'd have you back before five."

I wanted to ask how she knew my Master but I couldn't. Instead, I finished my lunch and followed her to the next store, both of us already carrying the bags from our earlier shopping.

By the time Lily declared we were finished, I was completely overwhelmed. It'd been a year since I'd bought anything, but even with my limited and dated knowledge, we had to have spent several thousand dollars today. For me. Real clothes. Even panties and bras.

I didn't understand. With Ian, I'd been given seven skirts and seven tube tops, one for each day of the week. That was it. We weren't allowed undergarments. He didn't like them.

The confusion I'd felt earlier began to creep up again as Lily started putting things away in my bedroom. She seemed confident in what she was doing and didn't seem to fear my Master. Lily didn't belong to him, though, so why should she fear him?

After putting away all our purchases, Lily stayed with me, and we watched television until five o'clock when she said she had to get home. Her easygoing nature surprised me, as did the fact I realized I felt comfortable. For the first time in a long while, I felt something other than fear.

As soon as the door closed, however, the apprehension returned. He would be home soon.

What would he expect?

I racked my brain trying to anticipate what he would want, but I didn't know him that well. Then it hit me. He'd sent me shopping with Lily so he'd most likely want me to be wearing something we'd bought, right?

With that thought, I went into the room he said was mine. Mine. It had been so long since I'd had anything that was mine.

Extracting an outfit along with underwear, I changed into new clothes. Lily had gotten me both pants and skirts. Although I preferred pants, I didn't want to push things, so I selected a skirt. It was still short but longer than what I was used to wearing. When I looked in the mirror, I realized I looked normal.

But I wasn't normal.

And then I heard the lock in the door turn for the second time today. This time I knew who it was. My Master was home.

Chapter Five

Stephan

Lily called as I was on my way home. She let me know she'd left Brianna and told me what she'd learned today. I was a little concerned with the response Brianna gave Lily regarding her family. If I knew she would be safe, I would try to get her home.

That didn't appear to be the case, though, and my determination to help her doubled.

Opening the door to my condo, I saw a flash of color to my right. I followed the movement to see Brianna on the floor just outside her bedroom.

I strolled over to where she knelt and reached for her hand. After only a slight hesitation, she took it with the same robotic motion as always. "Hello, Brianna."

She didn't answer. She never answered except with *yes, Master* or *no, Master*. We would get past this. And if I had anything to say about it, it would be tonight.

I led her over to the dining room table and indicated she should sit. She complied without hesitation.

After setting my briefcase down on the table, I opened it, extracted three separate pieces of paper, and handed them to her along with a pen. "I need you to fill these out. Be as honest as you can." She nodded without looking at me.

The forms were nothing special. They were the standard new patient forms one had to fill out when visiting a new doctor, asking for name, age, family medical history, etc. To be honest, I was just as curious about some of that information myself.

Brianna looked young. Very young, the more I thought about it. If I had to guess, I'd say she was no more than nineteen or twenty. I'd had a brief fear as I'd contemplated this on the way home that I'd "purchased" a minor, but I pushed it aside. If that was what she was, then I'd turn her over to social services and say I'd found her wandering the streets. It wouldn't be out of the question, given my position at the foundation. They'd never know unless Brianna told them, and in her current condition, I didn't find that likely.

I left her to fill out the forms Richard had e-mailed me today while I went to make us something to eat.

Tonight's dinner was spaghetti again. We didn't really have time for anything fancy since we had to be at Richard's office by seven, and I wasn't willing to challenge her palate when we had to go out.

When I brought the plates over to the table, she was on the last page. Brianna glanced at the plate but didn't stop writing until I took the papers and pen out of her hand. "Eat first. You can finish filling these out after you're done."

As usual, she did what I told her. While I ate, I couldn't help but look over the pages she'd already completed. She was eighteen. And according to what was on this paper and what I knew of her situation, she'd been with Ian since just before her birthday. Did Ian really buy a seventeen-year-old girl?

I continued to read, keeping my face impassive. She didn't need to see my discomfort over her answers.

Sexually active: *Yes*. Birth control: *Yes*. Type: *Unknown*.

Unknown? So she was on birth control but didn't know what kind. I was going to pass over it but then thought it might be the perfect opportunity to get more than her regular answer out of her. "You're on birth control?"

"Yes, Master."

Typical.

"But you don't know what type?"

"No, Master."

Okay.

"How do you not know?"

I saw her cringe. She thought I was upset with her even though I had not raised my voice in any way. "I . . . I wasn't told. I'm sorry, Master."

Ian. His treachery seemed to have no bounds. I could just see him taking her to a doctor she'd never met before, probably some sick friend of his, and not telling her what was being done. Maybe I could help her figure it out, though.

I tried to make my voice as gentle as I could. "Can you tell me about it? Maybe we can narrow it down." She nodded but otherwise didn't answer. "Was it an injection?"

She shook her head.

"Did you take pills? Wear a patch?"

A negative again.

That left only one option because I knew condoms weren't any Dom's contraception of choice. "Did he put something inside you?"

She nodded this time.

So that left the most likely answer to be an IUD. I made a note of that on her paperwork.

I didn't ask any more questions. She was going to be nervous enough when I took her to see Richard.

Once we were both finished eating, I took our plates to the sink and instructed her to complete the paperwork. By the time I had loaded the dishwasher, she was done.

I walked over and knelt beside her, bringing myself to her eye level. "Brianna, we are going to go see a friend tonight." She stiffened. I could feel the fear radiating from her body. "He won't hurt you, I promise."

I knew she didn't know me, and my promise meant little to her now, but hopefully by keeping true to my word, we would have a building block of trust. We had to start somewhere.

Brianna didn't relax the entire ride there. She sat with her hands folded in her lap, eyes down. It was okay, I had to keep reminding myself. One step at a time.

When I pulled up at his office, I saw Richard had left a light on for us. He'd agreed to see Brianna, but that didn't mean all was right between us. It hadn't been for the last six months. I took a deep breath and prepared myself.

After parking the car, I walked around and retrieved her from the vehicle. She followed behind me dutifully and remained by my side as I walked through the lobby and back to the offices to find my uncle.

In typical Richard fashion, he was behind his desk reading. When he saw me at the door, he dropped the book and came over to give me an awkward hug. "Stephan. It's good to see you." He paused, glancing at Brianna then back to me. "How have you been?"

He was polite, but I could hear the edge of unease behind it. I answered in the same courteous tone. "I'm good. Things have been busy."

Richard looked past me at Brianna. This time his eyes stayed on her. "Yes, I see that. You must be Brianna. I'm Dr. Cooper," he said to her, offering his hand.

She just nodded without looking up. He frowned.

I handed over Brianna's paperwork, and he instructed us to follow him down the hall.

The room we entered held an X-ray machine and a long metal table. "If you could hop up here, Brianna." She moved without delay and sat on the table waiting for further instructions.

Richard had her lie on the table, and then proceeded to take a multitude of images from her neck down, adjusting her clothing as needed. I stood behind the glass in the adjoining room, watching her rigid form. There seemed to be no life to her.

My uncle had inquired when we'd spoken earlier if I wanted X-rays, and I'd told him yes. I'd thought they were only going to be of certain areas, not almost her entire body. This alternative was perfectly acceptable with me. I just wanted to make sure she wasn't injured.

After the X-rays were put into the machine for developing, the three of us walked back down the same hallway. But before reaching his office, he turned to his right into a room marked Exam Room One. I felt Brianna hesitate.

Wrapping my fingers lightly around her arm, I leaned in and whispered in her ear, "Trust me."

Her eyes flickered up to mine and then went quickly back down, but my heart lifted when she moved of her own free will into the room.

Richard took a seat on a rolling stool and had her sit on a

padded table. I stood a few feet away, trying to remain close but not be in the way.

As he looked over what was now her chart, I wondered if I should have given him greater detail about her situation. I'd been more than vague on the phone, only telling him that I was trying to help someone who was in a bad situation, and I needed a doctor I trusted and that she could trust to give her a physical.

It was a testament to our relationship that he'd agreed with so little information. Especially given how rocky it was of late. The truth of the matter was I didn't want to get him involved. I had no idea how this thing with Brianna was going to play out. If it all went wrong, I didn't want him suffering for my decisions. No matter what was or wasn't between us now, he was still family.

My uncle looked up from the chart and smiled at Brianna. She wasn't looking at him, however. Her eyes were focused on a spot between her feet. He turned to me and frowned again.

He set her chart down and began his examination. I could tell she was nervous, but I didn't know if it was because of Richard or if she was afraid to disappoint me. The thought that maybe I should step out crossed my mind, but then I remembered that when I'd asked her to trust me just a few minutes ago, she did. I remained where I was.

Richard came to stand in front of her, placing his stethoscope against her chest. "How are you feeling?"

"I'm fine, Sir," she whispered, still without looking at him.

He spoke in a gentler voice as he moved around to her back and asked, "Are you hurting anywhere?"

"No, Sir."

I saw his brow furrow. He wasn't happy with her responses, but seemed to understand pushing her would not produce results so he moved on, finishing his examination.

"Brianna, it says here you are on birth control but you don't know what kind?"

"No, Sir," she said so softly that I barely heard it.

He looked up at me, and I knew what was going to happen. He would need to examine her. Although I hated to do this to her, I knew it had to be done. I nodded, and he sighed. "I'm going to need to check it, Brianna. Is that okay?"

I saw her swallow, but she nodded in resignation.

"Okay then. We're going to leave the room for a few minutes, and I want you to put this on," he said, handing her what looked like a paper hospital gown. "We will be just outside if you need us."

Richard didn't wait for her to answer before grabbing my arm and pulling me out the door. Once outside, he didn't stop moving. Instead, he dragged me down to the other end of the hall and back to the X-ray room. We could still see the door to the exam room but it was several doors down. He let go of me just outside the room, and went to retrieve the developed film.

When he returned to where he'd left me in the hall, he turned on an X-ray light box and began examining the pictures. I noticed his displeasure increasing the more he looked at the films.

Taking two sheets he'd looked at previously and putting them back up, he turned to face me. It was a look I'd seen often as a teenager when I'd come home from a place I shouldn't have been. "What is going on, Stephan? You said this girl was in a bad situation, and I'll give you that, but something more is going on here. Are you involved in something?"

I brought my hand up to rub my temples. "You don't want to know, Richard. Trust me."

"Trust you?" he said indignantly. "Trust you? That girl in there is scared to death."

"I know." Since I wasn't willing to reveal her story to him, it was all I could say.

He was waiting for me to continue, but I didn't. "Look, Stephan. I know about . . . your lifestyle . . . choices," he said through gritted teeth. He made it clear, several times over, that he didn't approve of my choice to be a Dominant. "But I won't sit by and ignore signs of abuse."

"And I don't expect you to." I ran my hands through my hair. This situation was beyond frustrating on so many levels. For years I'd gone to Richard for advice and looked up to him. Now there was this rift between us that I didn't know how to fix. I wouldn't be something I wasn't, and he couldn't accept who and what I was.

His voice pulled me out of my thoughts. "Did you go too far, Stephan? Did you hurt her?"

My head shot up. "No! Richard, how could you even think that?" I began pacing. "What I told you on the phone was true. She was in a bad situation." At this, I paused and my eyes met his. "A *very bad* situation." I took a deep breath. "She's hurt, and not just physically. But I need to know what I'm dealing with before I can really try to help her. So, please, can you just trust me on this?"

He looked at me for several minutes and then nodded. "You've never been good at lying to me."

I smirked. "True."

Richard's attention went back to the X-rays. I felt the air around us become somber again. "This girl has been hurt. A lot."

He proceeded to explain to me just how much. His fingers glided over the picture of bones that meant nothing to me but told him stories I needed to know. Her ribs had been broken and then refractured before they could heal properly. There was also evidence of a broken arm. All the injuries appeared to have happened within the last six to twelve months.

"I didn't exam her chest too closely. She seemed very protective of that area," he said as he removed the X-rays and placed them in a large yellow folder.

"I know. I noticed that, too."

He raised his eyebrow in question.

"You don't want to know." The truth was I didn't want to tell him. I was still trying hard to forget my "inspection" of Brianna last week.

I thought for a moment that he was going to push for an answer, but instead he tucked the folder under his arm and strolled back down the hall. It had been at least ten minutes since we'd left Brianna.

Before he could go in, I reached out my hand to stop him. He turned back, looking at me curiously. "There are deep bruises on the inside of her thighs. I put something on them but . . ."

He nodded and knocked on the door lightly before entering. This time I remained outside.

Brianna

When the door closed, I changed my clothes as fast as I could, making sure to stack my things neatly in the corner on the floor. Master said the doctor would be nice to me and so far he had been, much nicer than the other one. But then again, so far I had been clothed.

That was about to change. I knew what was coming. And even though Ian had passed me around to his friends whenever they asked and sometimes when they didn't, I still felt the panic building inside me.

Would my new Master watch? Ian liked to.

I lay back on the table and tried to keep myself calm with steady deep breaths. It would hurt less. At least that's what I had to keep telling myself.

When the door opened again, only the doctor entered. So my new Master wasn't going to watch.

Dr. Cooper smiled at me, and I hoped that meant he wouldn't be too rough.

He walked over to the counter and put on two latex gloves. *No!* I felt all the panic I'd been trying to get a hold of rip through me. *Oh please, please no.* Gripping the side of the padded table, I tried to calm down, but it was useless. I hated anal sex. It hurt so much. Ian said if I'd relax it wouldn't hurt, but I could never manage it through my fear.

That's when I realized I'd begun to feel safe or safer in my new home, at least. Why had I been so stupid? It wasn't a home. I'd never have a home again.

I felt his hand on my leg helping me to slide forward to the edge of the table. I pinched my eyes shut trying to block it out, trying to prepare myself for what I knew was coming. Each of my legs was lifted, spread, and placed back down, leaving me completely exposed.

His hand fell away, and I began counting the seconds before he took me. Would he use lubrication or take me raw? One of Ian's friends had done that once, and I'd bled. I squeezed my eyes tighter, not wanting to relive that memory.

Then someone was prying my hand from the table. I opened my eyes just as my Master's hand came to rest on the other side of my face. "Shh, Brianna."

It was then I felt the tears. I was crying. He must be so disappointed in me. Even though he didn't sound angry, I knew he must be.

What if he took me back? What if he gave me back to Ian, or

worse, sold me to someone else?

I felt the panic rising again. "I'm sorry, Master. Please, forgive me. I'll do anything you want. I'm sorry. Please, please don't send me back."

His hand was caressing my face now, and it was then I noticed his eyes. They were the most striking color I'd ever seen; green, but with just a hint of brown. "Shh. I'm not sending you anywhere, okay?" Then he leaned down and placed a soft kiss on my lips.

I opened my eyes, and he was still there. No one had ever kissed me like that before, and although I knew I should look away, I couldn't. The look in his eyes wasn't sexual at all. It was . . . comforting.

Then I felt Dr. Cooper between my legs again and felt my body stiffen. "Shh," said my Master. "No one is going to hurt you, Brianna."

There were two options. I could try to struggle, which I already knew from experience would do no good, or I could try to relax and just live through this as I had before.

I chose the second option but to my surprise, Dr. Cooper didn't do anything remotely sexual. There was an odd feeling as he pushed something inside me but that was it and whatever it was disappeared after a few minutes.

Then he was gone.

"You may sit up, Brianna." I did so and found him minus the gloves and standing across the room by the counter. "You appear to have an IUD called Mirena inserted. Do you know when you had it put in?"

I looked up at my Master to see if it was okay to answer, but he wasn't looking at me. After considering for a moment, I decided it would be okay to speak since I was being asked a direct question. "About ten months ago, I think, Sir."

Dr. Cooper glanced up at my Master, and they seemed to share a silent conversation. Then he turned back to me. "Well then, you should be protected for another four years at least. We'll want to check it each year when you come in for your annual checkup, of course, but everything looks good for now." He stood and walked to stand directly in front of me. "Do you have any questions for me?" I shook my head. "Very well. We'll just wait outside while you get dressed."

I watched them walk out the door while I remained seated. Was I really done? He wasn't going to do anything to me?

As I began to dress, my thoughts drifted to my new Master. He'd been so nice to me. I hadn't seen him lose his temper yet, and truth be told I didn't want to see it. It was then I made the decision that I would do everything I could to make him happy with me.

If there was one thing Ian taught me, it was what made men happy. I could do that. I would do that for my new Master. I would show him I was worth the price he paid.

Chapter Six

Stephan

I followed Richard out of the room, closing the door behind me. When he'd opened the door, asking me to come into the room to try and calm her, I wasn't expecting to find her in the midst of a full-on panic attack. As I looked into those beautiful blue eyes of hers, I saw so much fear. However, she had calmed with my guidance, and Richard was able to finish his examination.

My uncle was silent as I followed him into his office. He put her chart down on the desk and turned to face me. His look was guarded, and I knew he was holding back what he truly wanted to say.

Leaning back against the filing cabinets lining the wall, I let out a sigh. "You can say it, Richard."

"Obviously, I don't need to since you already seem to know what I'm thinking."

Frustrated, I ran my hand through my hair. "Tell me she's okay."

He looked at me pointedly, but I didn't cave under his glare. Finally he spoke. "Other than the bruising you've already seen and a few places where there appear to be burn marks in various stages of healing, she's basically healthy for an eighteen-year-old." I nodded. "I want to order some blood work. She'll need to get to the lab within the next week," he said handing me a registration sheet with the business hours and contact details.

"I'll take care of it."

Then he leaned back against his desk, crossing both his arms and legs. "Stephan, you're like a son to me, you know this. But are you sure this girl isn't better off with her family?"

I considered what I should tell him but figured this part of her history would make little difference. "I'm not sure she has one, or at least one that she wants to return to. If I thought that was an option, if I knew she'd be safe there, I'd use all my resources to find them."

"Do you think they've done this to her?" His tone was controlled, professional. I could tell he was trying his best to stay detached emotionally so that he could do his job, but I could hear the undercurrent of suppressed anger.

I shook my head. "I don't know. And I won't take that chance with her."

My father figure tilted his head to the side and looked at me with a queer expression on his face. "You care about what happens to her."

"Of course I do," I said pushing myself upright to my full height. "I wouldn't have brought her here if I didn't."

With that, I left Richard in his office and walked back to the exam room to see if Brianna was ready. I saw her jump a little when I entered the room, and as soon as she saw who it was, her head went down. She was fully dressed again. "Are you ready, Brianna?"

She nodded and followed me out into the hallway. Richard met us by the door. "It was nice to meet you, Brianna."

Without speaking, she nodded. My uncle shot another glare at me but softened it when he noticed Brianna had angled her body closer to mine.

I didn't miss her movement either. It was a sure sign of trust, the third of the night.

Reaching for her elbow, I guided her to the car, and we drove home.

It was after nine when we finally walked into my condo, and all I wanted to do was get some sleep. I let Brianna know she was free to go to her room for the evening if she wished. Within seconds she was gone.

I unbuttoned my collar and loosened my tie as I walked into the kitchen to get a glass of water. This last week had been exhausting, and with Brianna under my care twenty-four hours a day, it wasn't likely to get better anytime soon.

I made my way into my bedroom to finish getting undressed then climbed into bed. Although I was tired, sleep didn't immediately come. Instead my mind raced with what to do next with the woman in the other room. I couldn't imagine what had been going through her head tonight to make her so scared.

Going slow was a given, but where to start? I wasn't sure if telling her she was free to come and go as she pleased was a good idea at this point. If she left, where would she go? There was no guarantee she wouldn't end up back in the hands of Ian or someone just like him.

These thoughts plagued me as I considered and tossed away several options including just collaring her already to at least give her familiarity, and deal with specifics later. That didn't sit well with me, though. She needed to know she had a choice and that I wouldn't harm her.

It was a long while before I finally fell asleep, still undecided as to what I was going to do.

Tuesday morning I noticed Brianna watching me more than she had been. It was still covert. She never openly stared or looked directly at me. Her glances were always concealed under heavy lashes.

I did try to talk with her once on Wednesday over dinner, but that didn't end well. All it seemed to do was increase her anxiety, so I ended the questioning entirely.

By Thursday, I still didn't have any answers.

After my frustrating attempt at conversation with her, I decided that maybe it was time to stop avoiding my best friend. He'd called twice this week, and each time I'd refused to answer my phone. Logan and I had been through a lot together, but I wasn't sure how he'd feel about me buying someone. Lily was obviously okay with it now that she'd met Brianna, and although that helped my case with Logan, it didn't mean he'd be so accepting.

Logan waited for me to fully explain before he began questioning me. He wanted to know everything about her. I could tell he was concerned. The potential backlash from something like this could destroy me.

We were on the phone for nearly two hours before he finally let me go. I knew he still wasn't happy with the situation, but he would support me as he always had. Logan had been by my side for some of my stupidest mistakes. He wouldn't back out now, even if this turned out to be my biggest one yet.

Thursday night I contemplated some of the things Logan had told me about Ian, things I hadn't known. He liked to share. He was also a voyeur. It put Brianna's reaction to Richard's exam in a whole new light. My desire to care for her was increasing. Falling asleep that night, I knew that I needed to figure out what I was going to do with her, and fast.

As my mind drifted into the first threads of consciousness, I was lost in a wonderful dream. Warm lips enveloped me. From between my legs, wide blue eyes looked up at me, full of passion instead of fear; her brown hair cascaded around her shoulders as she licked and teased. Every muscle in my body was screaming for the thing that would satisfy. The pull toward my release was impossible to resist with so great a temptation. Reaching down to finish the job my dream had started, my hand was met instead with silky hair.

It took me a moment to register what was going on, but it was a moment too late. As my eyes flew open, my body released with a force unknown to me directly into her mouth.

As I started to regain my senses, I felt her tongue still licking my now very sensitive flesh. This had to stop! Why was she doing this?

Maybe if I hadn't still been in a sex-induced haze I'd have handled the situation better. At the moment, however, all I could think was to get her out of here as quickly as possible before I did something I'd regret. She wasn't ready for us to have sex, and that was exactly what was going to happen if she stayed.

I spoke before I could stop myself. "Leave my room." Her mouth released me but she was still on my bed and that just couldn't be. "Now!" I ordered.

Never before had I seen a person move so fast. She was out the door in less than five seconds.

Bringing my hands up to rub across my face, I sat up to look down at my naked self still at half-mast and groaned. This changed things. We needed to talk. Today.

I reached for the phone beside my bed and dialed Jamie, letting her know I would not be in today, before I headed to the bathroom for a very cold shower.

Brianna

Huddled in the corner of my room I couldn't stop the mantra playing in my head. *Stupid. Stupid. Stupid.*

I thought it would make him happy. Why hadn't it made him happy? It didn't matter. Look what I'd done!

What would he do? He was obviously upset with me. How would he punish me?

No, that didn't matter either. I'd messed up. Brought this on myself. Whatever it was I'd deal with it, try not to cry no matter how painful.

But what if he wanted me to cry? Ian hated crying. He'd always add ten lashes if I cried during my punishments. Stephan wasn't like Ian, though. What would he want? Why did this have to be so confusing?

I felt the tears streaking down my cheeks and tried to wipe them quickly away when I heard the door opening. He didn't come in, just stood there looking at me. "Get dressed and come to the living room, please."

And then he was gone. I was more confused than ever. He wanted me to get dressed and come to the living room?

Then I got it. *He was getting rid of me!*

Traitor tears fell down my face as I did as he told me and got dressed. There was no way out of this. I knew that. Racking my brain, I tried to find some way to convince him to keep me.

As I pulled my shirt over my head to complete my outfit, I was determined to beg if I had to. It was much better here than at Ian's, and I wanted to stay. I wanted to be here with him, my new Master. I would do anything. This was what I wanted. He was what I wanted, the one I wanted to serve.

Walking out of the room, I kept my head down. He was sitting on the couch facing away from me. Using the opportunity and learning from my previous mistake, I knelt down before him, head bowed. I waited for him to say something, anything, but he didn't.

Finally I spoke. "I'm sorry, Master. Please punish me as you see fit."

And then I waited.

He didn't speak for the longest time, but when he did, it wasn't in the tone I'd expected. "Get up, Brianna." I stood. "Have a seat," he said motioning beside him.

Was this where he told me he was taking me back to Ian?

"Look at me, please," he said.

I wasn't about to disobey him again. And then he smiled. My Master smiled at me. There was no hint of anger in his eyes.

His voice was harsher when he spoke again, and the suddenness of it made me jump. "You are not to come into my bedroom again without permission. Do you understand?"

I lowered my head. "Yes, Master."

"No," he said, grabbing my chin in his hand. "Don't turn away from me."

I met his eyes again, fearing what I'd see. What I saw startled me. There was confusion in them and . . . worry? But why would my Master be worried?

Dropping his hand back in his lap, he said, "We need to talk."

This was it. I knew it. He was taking me back or sending me away. "Please, Master. I'll do better, I promise."

"Stop." His tone was firm and brooked no argument. I stopped talking.

I watched as he rubbed his temple with his right hand before sighing. He was clearly frustrated, and it was my fault.

Another apology was on my tongue again when he asked, "Brianna, why did you come into my room this morning?"

Starting to look down, I changed my mind when I saw the scowl forming on his face. "I'm—"

"And do not say you're sorry, Brianna. Just tell me what you were thinking."

"I wanted to make you happy," I whispered. "You've been very nice to me, Master, and I wanted to say thank you." I had to curb the impulse to lower my head. It would only make him angry.

His left hand came up to run through his hair. "You did it to say thank you?" He shook his head, clearly not liking my answer.

"I'm so—"

"Brianna," he snapped. "If you say you're sorry one more time, I *will* punish you, do you understand?"

I knew better than to answer. Instead, I just nodded.

He stood and walked to the other side of the room. Looking out at the Minneapolis skyline, he had his back to me. "You could have just said thank you. That would have been sufficient."

A slight sound left my lips before I caught it. He turned to look at me, waiting for me to slip up and say *I'm sorry*. I pressed my lips together instead, willing myself not to speak.

He seemed satisfied I wasn't going to say anything, because the side of his mouth pulled up in a small smile. I suddenly felt shy, which made no sense to me.

And then my Master did something totally unexpected. He walked to me and knelt down to bring himself to my eye level. "Is it what you wanted, Brianna?"

The confusion was back. "I don't understand, Master."

He sighed, and his shoulders slumped in defeat. Once again, I had to press my lips tightly together and not to utter an apology.

My Master sat back on his heels and brushed the hair away from my face. His touch felt good, comforting. "I want you to feel safe here. This is your home."

I nodded, but even I knew it was weak. What he was saying didn't make sense to me. I didn't have a home, just a place.

His voice brought me back to the present. "Would you like to spend the day with me, Brianna?"

He was asking, not commanding, I could tell. But could I really refuse him? I didn't know the answer to that. And even if I could say no, did I want to?

No. No, I didn't want to refuse him. It would clearly make him happy to spend the day with me, and that had been my goal this morning, right? So I answered the only way I could. "Yes, Master"

Chapter Seven

Stephan

Brianna was a total enigma to me. I didn't understand her. And in order to be able to help her like I wanted, I needed to.

My original plan had been to spend the day at home, talking. But after our brief conversation, I knew that wouldn't work. I would spend the entire day dragging sentences out of her, all the while wondering if she was answering truthfully or just telling me what she thought I wanted to hear.

The new plan involved us going out. It was a risk, yes. I had no idea how she would react to being around people, although Lily said she'd had no major problems. With me, it was different; I knew that. She viewed me as her owner with her sole job to please me no matter what her wishes were.

So today, my goal was to learn about her.

It didn't take me long to come up with a place to take her. I needed somewhere she could open up, let her guard down. Nothing accomplished that better than animals.

Before heading out, we both went into our rooms and changed into jeans. I grabbed my favorite pair, the ones I wore to family barbecues over at Richard and Diane's house. Excitement hummed through me as I got dressed for the second time today.

Walking back out into my living room, I waited for her. Brianna stepped from her room wearing a fitted pair of jeans and a dark blue long-sleeved shirt. Her hair was pulled back in a sleek ponytail, pulling it just slightly off her neck but still allowing it to tumble down across her shoulders. A brief flash from this morning crossed my mind of long brown hair brushing against my thighs, and I had to turn away abruptly before I did something stupid.

I took a deep breath to calm myself. "Are you ready?"

"Yes, Master," she said to my back.

Opening the door, I motioned for her to go first. She did, all the while keeping her gaze downcast.

Our drive was a silent one. She kept her eyes down for the most part, but occasionally I would catch her looking out the passenger window. Then it was like she'd catch herself and look back down at her lap. "You may look out the window if you'd like," I said giving her a smile she didn't see.

She did hear me, though, and brought her head up to look out the window once again. We were getting close to our destination, and I wondered what she'd think of my choice of activity.

I knew exactly when she figured out where we were going. Her eyes opened wide, and she shifted in her seat. "Is there something wrong?" I asked.

"No, Master," she quickly assured me.

I watched as she pressed her lips together. "But?" I prompted.

She glanced down at her hands and blushed. We pulled up to the parking attendant, and she waited until we moved on to find a place to park before speaking. "Why are you taking me to the zoo, Master?"

"Do you not like the zoo?"

"No," she said quickly. "I mean, yes. I do like it. It's just, I don't understand."

And it was clear from her tone that she didn't. It was also clear that those simple words were difficult for her to say. After pulling into a parking spot not far from the entrance, I turned the car off, got out, and walked around to open her door. She exited the vehicle, and I shut the door behind her before taking her hand in mine. Turning her toward me, I brought my free hand up to cup her face, making her look at me. "I thought you might enjoy the animals," I said, rubbing my thumb against her cheek. "If you'd rather we did something else . . ."

The guarded look behind her eyes softened just a little, and she shook her head. "No," she whispered. "I like this very much." She paused a moment, shifting her weight from her left foot then back to her right. Her eyes lowered again, and although the next words were quieter than the rest, they were still unmistakable. "Thank you."

Brianna

I couldn't believe we were here at the zoo of all places. The first thing to cross my mind when I'd realized where we were was that this was somehow going to be my punishment for this morning. When he'd asked me if something was wrong, I'd quickly told him no. After all, if that was what we were here for, I'd brought it on myself by acting so stupidly.

But then he'd asked me why and . . . well, I couldn't bring myself to ask him again if he was going to punish me for this morning. If that wasn't what this was, then I wasn't going to put the idea in his head.

Then he'd surprised me yet again by telling me he'd brought me here because he thought I'd like the animals. I loved animals. Mom had let me get a dog when I was seven. He got me through everything when my world started falling apart.

I followed my new Master up to the ticket counter, and he paid for two as I hung back. When he was done, we walked through a little gate, and a man stamped each of our hands with the outline of a green elephant.

It was still early. The zoo had just opened, according to the sign, and there weren't many people yet. My Master took my hand and led me to a huge map directly across the plaza. Coming to a stop in front of it, he glanced down at me, but I didn't look up. "What animal is your favorite?"

A quick war waged inside my head as I debated how to answer. Was this a test?

"Brianna?" I raised my head a little but didn't meet his eyes. His free hand lifted my chin. "You have to have a favorite," he said giving me that same crooked smile he did this morning.

"The lions," I whispered and hoped it was the right answer.

Apparently it was. He dropped his hand from my chin and looked up at the big map. "Lions . . ." he mused to himself. "Ah. Here they are." I felt a slight tug on my arm. "Let's go."

The lions were all the way on the other side of the zoo. We passed hippos, gorillas, and even a reptile house on our way to our destination. I really hoped he wouldn't want to go into the reptile house. I didn't think I could handle it; I hated snakes. Just the thought of them sent shivers down my spine.

He noticed. "Are you cold?"

I shook my head. He was very observant, of course; so was Ian.

Thankfully, our arrival at the lions' cage cut off my trip down memory lane. There was a bridge running across the top of a platform. On one side was a male with a full mane and on the other three females. They were beautiful.

The first time my mom brought me to the zoo, I'd been drawn to them. Each step was confident, predatory, and yet elegant, especially the male. The movement was like a dance but with music only they could hear.

Quickly moving to the other side of the bridge, I focused on the three females. Two were lounging underneath a tree while the other one was clearly surveying her territory. She was beautiful; I was in awe.

Lost in my memory and my observations, I completely forgot about who I was with until I felt his hand come up to press against the small of my back. "You really do like them, don't you?"

There was a hint of amusement in his voice, but I answered him honestly. "Yes." I sighed.

After a few more minutes, he shifted his weight beside me. "Would you like to stay here a little longer or go see something else?"

I thought about it for a few moments. The zoo was a treat; I knew that. Why he was giving this to me, I had no idea, but I wanted to take advantage of it and see as much as he would allow. It felt odd to speak the words. "I'd like to see something else."

Out of the corner of my eye, I saw movement and figured he must be nodding since he began to guide me back down the ramp. There really was so much to see. I hadn't realized we'd also passed an aquarium full of fish tanks three times my height.

The room was dark, but there were lights inside the tanks. Fish of every shape and color swam by in different patterns. Some of them even came right up to the glass and bumped it, causing me to jump. My reaction made my Master chuckle.

We moved on from the fish to the gorillas. There was a mother gorilla and her new baby sitting in a corner of the enclosure. It was very cute. I felt a pang of longing. Being eighteen, I wasn't in a big hurry for children, but I had hoped to have some one day. And even though I knew that would never be possible now, I still couldn't help the sudden sadness that filled me.

Needing to get away from there, I took the chance and just walked off. After only a few seconds' delay, he was beside me again, his warm hand on my lower back guiding me as I willed the tears to go away.

It was for that reason I didn't realize where we were going until it was too late. I remembered him opening a door and a blast of warm air hitting me.

And then everything else ceased to exist outside the mind-numbing fear that gripped me.

Chapter Eight

Stephan

Coming to the zoo had been a good idea. I knew it the minute we got to the lions. For the first time since I'd known her, I saw the lines of Brianna's face relax.

I was quite pleased with my choice of activity as we walked into the reptile house, my hand on her lower back guiding her. She was even moving around a little without me having to give her instructions to do so.

A gust of warm air hit us as we stepped inside the temperature-controlled building. I was quite neutral when it came to snakes. They weren't my favorite creatures by any means, but I did find them interesting to look at from behind a glass wall.

Two steps inside and I felt Brianna's muscles stiffen beneath my hand. I looked down and noticed she'd lost all color in her face. Moving to stand in front of her, I tried to get her to look at me, to focus but she wouldn't. Instead she crossed her arms, tightly hugging her torso, while her breathing became increasingly shallow.

An older couple walked around us with stares of obvious curiosity at the scene. I couldn't care less. All I knew was that we needed to leave this place. I had no idea what was going on exactly, but something changed the minute we'd entered this building. My only hope was that leaving would correct the problem.

Putting my arm firmly around her waist and pulling her to my side, I practically carried her back out the door. I looked around, spotted a bench across the way, and headed for it.

Thankfully, it was still early enough in the season that there weren't crowds of people. That didn't mean we weren't attracting attention. Several people, including one zoo worker, paused in their progress to assess the situation. I couldn't spare them much attention, however.

As we both sat down on the bench, she continued to curl into herself and was now engaged in a sort of rocking motion. She was mumbling, but I couldn't make out the words.

Wherever she was, it wasn't here. I needed her to calm down and focus.

Drawing on the little experience I had with her so far and what had worked before, I reached out and tried to get her to look at me. My efforts, however, didn't glean me the desired effect. Instead, her head stayed down but was now buried in my chest. The only advantage I gained was that I could understand what she was saying.

"Please. Please, Master, please."

I glanced over at the building we'd just left, closed my eyes, and wrapped my arms around her. It was the first time she'd called me 'Master' since we'd entered the zoo. Obviously, the reptile house had triggered a memory or something for her. What in the world had this beautiful creature gone through?

She needed to know she was now safe, but I had no idea how to accomplish that, given that a simple trip to the zoo could do this to her. All I knew was that I couldn't take her anywhere like this. Even making it to the parking lot would be a challenge.

So we sat, my arms around her and her head against me. Occasionally I'd hear another "please, Master" leave her lips, and I would respond with a quiet "Shh, Brianna."

It took a while, but finally her breathing became normal again, and her muscles began to relax.

When I thought it was safe, I put some space between us and brought her chin up, forcing her to look at me. Her eyes were bloodshot and her face covered with salty streaks left by her many tears.

Bringing my other hand up, I used my thumbs to wipe away the physical evidence of her breakdown. Suddenly her eyes got huge, and I could tell she was once again frightened. Her eyes shot downward quickly, and I saw her lips begin to part. With no doubt as to what was coming and not wanting to hear her insane apologies, my thumb moved to cover her mouth, and her lips instantly closed.

"My instruction from earlier has not changed, Brianna. You are not to utter those words for the remainder of the day, do you understand?"

She nodded.

"Good."

Taking a look around, I noticed we were pretty much alone. I released her face and watched as her head once again bowed. She'd retreated into herself again. It was like one step forward and two steps back.

Sighing, I looked down at my watch and noticed it was almost noon. "Are you hungry?" I asked her.

I noticed her pressing her lips together, a sure sign she was nervous. I assumed she was trying to guess again what I wanted her answer to be. Like I said, one step forward, two steps back. "This is not a test, Brianna. It is a simple question. Are you hungry? Yes or no?" She nodded but didn't ease the pressure on her lips.

Standing, I held out my hand. I wanted to see if she would take it freely. After only a moment's hesitation, she put her hand in mine and stood up beside me. I gently squeezed her fingers in reassurance and approval, both of which I knew she needed from me.

Walking to the food court, I could only imagine what passersby were thinking, especially if they'd been privy to her meltdown. Her head was lowered with her eyes to the ground for our entire walk to the center of the zoo. I thought about stopping and trying to get her to focus on something but reconsidered. My assertion had been to go get food, and more than anything, I needed to be consistent with her; so food it was.

The small food court held four options: burgers, hotdogs, pizza, or chicken. There was also a selection of french fries, nachos, pretzels, and ice cream.

Switching the hand that was holding hers, I moved behind her, placing my mouth at her ear. "What would you like?"

She stiffened for just a second and then relaxed again before raising her head. I watched as she scanned the small menu. Then she was pressing her lips together again. Did she really think there was a wrong answer here?

I moved around to stand in front of her, and her gaze immediately shot downward. I suppressed a sigh. But just as I was getting ready to ask my question again while keeping the frustration out of my voice, she answered, "A hamburger, please." She paused and then added, "Master," in a low whisper so that no one could hear around us.

That had been the reason she'd been pressing her lips together. Although that was still a subject we needed to address, this was not the place. I was just happy she seemed to be making choices faster, easier. Reaching down, I linked our hands once again, and we walked up to place our order.

Brianna

I was . . . confused. That was the best word I could come up with. My new Master didn't make any sense to me. Or his actions didn't.

Once I'd calmed down and realized where we were and whom I was with, I was embarrassed. And a little scared. I was sure I'd drawn attention to us, embarrassed him, but when I'd looked up, his eyes had only held concern. For me.

And then I'd quickly averted my eyes, remembering my place and still unsure how he'd react to my very obvious tears; and as was habit to me now, I started to beg forgiveness. He'd surprised me yet again, though, by stopping my apology, reminding me of his earlier words, and adding that he did not want me to say *I'm sorry* for the rest of the day.

I . . . just . . . didn't . . . understand.

He was so different from Ian, in a good way. I'd been with him for over a week now, and so far, he'd given me my own bed, clothes, and had even taken me to the zoo. My new Master had been kind and gentle to me, only reprimanding me this morning after my stupid mistake.

I kept waiting for reality to set in, for the nightmare I'd lived in for the last ten months to come back. It had to come back, right? This man had bought me, just like Ian had. He was handsome and clearly wealthy. There was no reason he couldn't have any woman he wanted, so why buy a slave unless you wanted to do things no normal woman would allow?

It was stupid for me to think of those things. This was my life. This was what I was and nothing would ever change that. I already knew my new Master could be much nicer to me than Ian ever was, and I would make him happy as much as I was able.

Briefly I wondered what he would have in store for me later; surely today would have a price. But that didn't matter. I didn't think there was much he could do to me that Ian hadn't already done. Just the way he touched me made me think he'd be much gentler than my former Master was. All I had to do was endure it.

I kept my head down as I ate, but I knew he was watching me; he watched me all the time. The old Brianna wanted to ask him why, but I'd learned that lesson the hard way a long time ago, so I remained silent. When we were both done, he took our trays and threw our trash away.

Next, we walked to see the giraffes. There was a raised platform, and we watched as a line of kids held out food to feed the long-necked giants. It was a sight to see, and I felt myself start to relax again. I would enjoy this. He was not Ian, and come what may, I would deal with it. I'd survived before. I'd survive again.

As the giraffes got their fill and ambled away, so did we. There were ducks by the pond, and a house filled with exotic birds. It had been so long since I'd visited a zoo, I'd forgotten how much there was to see and just how enjoyable it could be.

I could tell we were almost done and heading back toward the zoo entrance when I saw a small fenced-in area holding barnyard animals. It was silly, I know, but he'd indulged me so far, so I walked closer.

There were cows, geese, sheep, and goats all roaming together in the small pen. Children were mingled in alongside their parents with food cupped in their hands. I watched as a little girl who looked to be about five desperately attempted to hold onto her stash as a goat tried to find a way through her defenses. She jumped back and squealed when his nose touched her hand.

Suddenly, I heard the weirdest sound. It took me a moment to recognize what it was, but finally I did. It was me. Laughing. I laughed.

It had only lasted a few seconds, maybe not even that, but I laughed. When was the last time I had laughed? I didn't know. I couldn't remember the last time.

The little girl giggled again, regaining my attention. Her mom stood behind her watching, so proud of her little girl for her small accomplishment. I remembered that. I'd been that little girl.

Then I felt my Master's hand on me, and I jumped, startled out of my reverie. My automatic response was to apologize, and I'd almost slipped, allowing the beginnings to cross my lips. He didn't seem to be concentrating on my words, though, as I once again felt his fingertips brush the tears I hadn't known I'd shed away from my cheeks.

"Are you ready to go, Brianna?"

I nodded, and we left.

As he drove us out of the parking lot, I started looking out the window again at the passing scenery. My eyes were on the buildings and trees, but my mind was on what had happened today and my concern for what would happen tonight.

An electronic ringing filled the car. He reached for his pocket and pulled out his cell phone. "Hello?"

For about a minute he was quiet, listening to whoever was on the other line. After a moment, I felt his eyes on me, and I couldn't help but stiffen a little.

"Okay," he said. "I'll be there in about fifteen minutes if you can have everything ready." There was another short pause, and then he closed the phone.

Calmly he placed it back into his jeans pocket and returned his hand to the steering wheel. I was curious as to the conversation, but I knew better than to ask. It wasn't my place. Obviously we were going somewhere.

Ten minutes passed before he spoke. "I need to stop at my office for a few minutes. I won't be long, but I was wondering if you'd like to see Lily while I take care of this?"

Another question. He was giving me an option. Did I want to see Lily again? *Yes.* "Yes, Master." Nothing else was said for the remaining drive.

He parked his car near a set of elevators on the first floor of a parking garage in the middle of downtown. I knew he wanted me to follow him, so I did this time without him asking, hoping this would please him.

We got into the elevator, and he pressed the button for the tenth floor. The ride up went quickly with no stops in between. I could see his reflection in the metal doors. His face was tense as if he was preparing himself mentally for something he really didn't want to do.

My guess was he hadn't wanted to bring me with him. I was sure the part of his life that included me was not something he wanted those he worked with to know about. Just having me here with him could cause him problems. And then what? What would happen to me? Would he get rid of me or . . .

Stop it, Brianna! You won't let that happen. You won't cause problems for him. Make him happy with you.

And so here I was walking down a long hallway beside my Master with one major difference, I didn't have my head down. With my eyes facing forward, I followed him until we turned a corner and walked into a brightly lit office the size of his living room.

"Hello, Megan," Stephan said, smiling.

"Mr. Coleman." She smiled back. I realized immediately that she was flirting with him. It was obvious Megan didn't know.

"Is Lily in?" he asked.

Megan nodded and she leaned forward. Her actions were clearly deliberate, made to flaunt her generous assets. A shudder started to go through me as I thought of the obvious innocence of this woman. She had no idea who she was flirting with, or what the possible consequences of her actions could be. I did, which was why I just stood there in silence.

"Would you like me to get her for you, Mr. Coleman?" Her voice dropped an octave, trying for that sultry sound you always heard in movies.

It was strange. Some of the girls in my high school used to do that with the boys they liked. From what I remembered, most of the boys receiving the attention used to flirt back in response. My Master didn't. Instead, he began to walk again, this time around Megan's desk. "That's okay. I'll get her myself," he said with a polite but dismissive smile.

Following him, we walked around what looked to be a thin paperlike wall similar to something in a Japanese restaurant before going down another hallway. This one was shorter, but we took it to the end where it opened up to another large room. Leaning over a big table filled with piles of large books was Lily.

She heard us enter and looked up. A huge smile broke out on her face. "Stephan." Then she saw me, and before I knew it, her arms were wrapped around me, giving me a tight hug. "Brianna!" she squealed. I didn't know what to do, but I didn't want to offend my Master's friend so I lightly hugged her back.

Lily did eventually let go of me, but she stayed by my side as she turned back to face Stephan. When I looked up for a second to see his face, he looked . . . happy. I breathed a sigh of relief. I'd done something right.

"Lily, do you think Brianna can stay with you for a half hour or so while I run upstairs?"

Her eyes fell to the clock and mine followed. It was four fifteen. "Sure," she said. I wondered if she had somewhere to be tonight.

"Thank you," he replied, already moving toward the door. "I'll make sure you're not late, Lily." He winked at her before leaving. Obviously, my original assumption was right. Lily had some place she needed to be.

I didn't get a chance to dwell on that, however, as Lily pulled me farther into the room and started talking. "Come see what I'm working on."

She dragged me to the table she'd been leaning over when we'd walked in the door. The books I'd noticed were full of fabrics, and there were pictures of large round tables and what looked to be some type of seating chart.

Lily noticed my staring and answered my unspoken question. "For the ball. I'm trying to find just the right fabric for the table dressing." She picked up three samples on the other side of the table and placed them in front of me. "I'm down to these three. What do you think?"

Me? She was asking me? "Um. I . . . I don't know."

She smiled encouragingly at me. "Sure you do."

I pressed my lips together in concentration. All three pieces of material were beautiful, elegant. Whatever ball this was for, I'm sure it would be beautiful.

Fabrics and fashion were never things I'd taken much interest in and for ten months, none at all. However, my eyes kept falling to the square of soft gold. Before I could stop myself, I pointed to it.

"Ooooh. I like that one, too. Good choice," Lily said, beaming.

Then she looked at me, and her expression changed. It was pensive. "You'd look good in this color, I think. But then again, you look great in that blue you have on. Hmm. I wonder . . . oh well, I'll just have to think about it a little more. Not like we don't have time." She smiled.

Time? What was she talking about? "Lily?" I asked quietly. "Time for what?"

She waved her hand dismissively. "Time for the ball, silly."

The ball? What ball? I looked down at the pictures again showing the large round tables with fake guests sketched in. At the top of the paper it said, 18th Annual Coleman Foundation Charity Ball.

Coleman. Stephan Coleman. This was my Master's company.

He owns this place. Just like he owns me.

I felt myself start to panic. He was more powerful than I imagined. My new Master could do anything he wanted. To anyone he wanted, and it wouldn't matter.

The next thing I knew, I was sitting down, and Lily was handing me a glass of water. I felt her hand rubbing along my back, trying to soothe me. It was hard but I tried to calm down. Nothing had changed. Not really. The plan was still the same. Survive. Make him happy with me.

"Are you all right?" she asked, her hand on my arm in a comforting gesture.

"Yes," I managed to choke out. "Thank you."

"Do you want to tell me what happened?"

Should I? I wasn't sure. But then again, I hadn't been sure of anything since last Wednesday night. So I spoke. "He owns this."

Lily pulled back a little before answering. "You mean Stephan?" I nodded. "Yes, he's the president and CEO here." Then she cocked her head and squinted marginally like she was trying to get something into focus.

She didn't get to say anything else as a knock sounded at her door a second before a man walked uninvited into her office. "Have you gotten . . ." His gaze fell on me. "Well, well. I didn't realize you had company." He walked toward me, and instantly I knew I didn't like him.

This man had a predatory walk. He reminded me of Ian, and I

felt a shiver run from my head to my feet.

Lily stepped in front of me to block his progress, and I could see his frown. "What can I do for you, Karl?"

"Aren't you going to introduce me to your friend first?"

"Karl, Brianna. Brianna, Karl."

"Brianna. Mmm. Pretty name. Are you . . ."

"I'm assuming you came here for a reason?" Lily asked, pointedly cutting him off.

He sneered at her but answered. "Yes. I wanted to know if you had the new figures for me. My girls need to get the new number projections together."

Crossing her arms, Lily faced him with a presence of someone twice her size. "No. I'm not done yet. I told you I'd send you the numbers as soon as I had them. You didn't have to make a special trip down here."

This Karl person just shrugged. "I was in the neighborhood so I thought I'd stop by. And I'm very glad I did," he said, brushing past Lily to get to me. I cringed back as far as I could into the couch.

He wasn't deterred, though, and reached out to brush a stray hair away from my face, his fingers lingering on my cheek. The first strains of panic began to rise. It was Ian all over again. And just like then, there was nothing I could do to stop him.

"Maybe we could go get a drink? Or something?" His voice dripped with innuendo.

"She's busy." I recognized the firm voice coming from the doorway. My Master.

Chapter Nine

Stephan

She had laughed. It was brief, yes, but she had laughed. Another step forward. This was good. I liked seeing her happy.

The car ride home was solitary, as I expected it would be. Brianna wouldn't speak unless I initiated the conversation.

She once again looked out the window, watching our surroundings. I had the impression Brianna had not gotten out much in the last ten months. This was another area of excitement for me. So many things would be available to her now, and I couldn't wait to help her take advantage of them. All I had to do was get through that thick shell she'd put up to protect herself.

My phone rang, breaking my thought process. It was Jamie. One of our biggest contributors was reconsidering the amount of his donation due to the tough economy and needed my immediate attention; this wasn't something that could wait until Monday. Looking over at Brianna, I told my assistant to have everything together for me by the time I arrived.

From the corner of my eye, I saw Brianna shift in her seat. She knew we were no longer going home and, truth be told, I was a little nervous about bringing her to my place of business. It wasn't that I was nervous about her, but more that I was nervous for her. Brianna had done well today, with the exception of the reptile house, and I didn't want the pure magnitude of my office to overwhelm her.

That gave me the idea to leave her with Lily—someone she knew—and I was confident it would be a better alternative than coming with me. When I asked her if she'd like to see Lily while I took care of things, she answered with her normal *yes, Master*.

For once, she followed me out of the car, into the elevators, and along the hallway without me prompting her. I couldn't help the small smile that tugged at my lips for a brief second, but then I remembered why I had to come into the office at four o'clock on a Friday.

Ross Builders. They were one of the largest construction companies in the area and had been supporting The Coleman Foundation since its inception eighteen years ago. Things were changing within their company because of Neil's son, Cal. He didn't have the same view on supporting local charities as his father. I had no doubt this latest development was all Cal.

By the time we reached the tenth floor, all I could think about was how I was going to talk to Cal Ross without losing my temper. Didn't he know how many people would be denied medical help they needed if his company withdrew or reduced their commitment? And that was what really burned me. The commitment of donation had been made in January. It was April, and he was just now changing his mind.

I vaguely recalled asking Megan, the floor receptionist, if Lily was in and then walking back down the short hall to find her hard at work on the fall fundraiser. She'd been more than happy to have Brianna stay with her, and I quickly left them alone. I wanted to go upstairs and get this over with.

Jamie was a miracle worker. She had everything ready for me, including donation history, usage, and future projections. So with my weapons in hand, I sat down to call Mr. Ross.

Cal was arrogant and cocky, but one thing he wasn't was stupid. He was playing with me, and I did not enjoy being played with. I was the one who enjoyed doing the playing.

After going over every piece of information I had in front of me, he finally relented and recommitted to his original donation. He'd come home from college last summer to take over the family business. It seemed he wanted to flex his muscles a little and prove just who was in charge now. I wanted to growl in frustration as I hung up the phone knowing it wasn't just money he was playing with, but lives.

Shutting everything off in my office, I walked out to say good night to Jamie only to find she had a message for me from Diane. "Your aunt said to tell you she is expecting you and Brianna for Sunday dinner." She paused, and then smiled as she said the last part, "I was also told to tell you that *no* would not be accepted."

Great. Just what had Richard told her?

Obviously, that didn't matter at this point. Once my aunt got something in her head, there was no changing her mind. I knew even if I called her and told her I had other plans, she'd guilt-trip me into coming.

I thanked Jamie for the message and went back down to the tenth floor. It was already a quarter till five, and I'd promised Lily I wouldn't make her late. But nothing had prepared me for what I saw when I arrived back in her office.

Karl Walker was leaning over Brianna. *My* Brianna. His body language clearly spoke his intentions even before I heard the words come out of his mouth. He didn't even jump when I spoke, but she did.

She'd already cringed away from Karl, obviously not wanting his attentions. He, on the other hand, seemed to be utterly clueless. "Busy, is she?" Karl turned his attention back to a wide-eyed Brianna. "Well, maybe next time." With that, he stood back to his full height and walked by me. "Have fun, Stephan. She looks like she'd be quite the tiger. I'm sure you'll have fun." At his parting comment, he laughed. I could hear him chuckling all the way down the hall, and I clenched my fist in response.

"Can't you just fire him?" Lily asked, exasperated.

Uncrossing my arms, I walked into the room. "No. Unfortunately. I have no doubt he'd try and sue us if I did, so unless you have something solid I can get him on, I'm afraid we're stuck with him for now."

Even though I was answering Lily, my focus was on Brianna. Karl had frightened her. Her head was down, her shoulders hunched over as if she were trying to make herself smaller, and her eyes were unfocused.

Taking another step forward, I stood in front of her just to the side. "Brianna." My voice was firm, but not unkind. And just like a switch had been flipped, her posture straightened. Her head remained lowered, but I knew she was now listening to me. "I'm finished. Are you ready to leave?"

Instead of answering vocally, she nodded and stood. I turned to Lily. "Thank you." My hand found its way to Brianna's lower back, and I felt some of the tension go out of her body at my touch, although she still held herself in the same position. I caught Lily's eyes just before we left the room. They were worried and clearly asking me to take care of the woman before me.

We managed to make it home without further incident, but she was quiet. Not like she'd been for most of the day, but as quiet as she had been those first few days. I knew she'd retreated into herself, something she had to have learned to survive, but it was still frustrating. She and I needed to talk, but I had no idea now if that was going to be able to happen tonight, and it was all because of Karl.

Karl! Right now, I wanted to take my favorite whip to him and not hold back. Unfortunately, logic and reason told me I couldn't do that.

We needed dinner, and I was in no mood to cook. I walked into the kitchen and opened the drawer containing the stack of menus a little too forcefully, causing some of them to fall to the floor. Picking them up, I shoved all but the one I wanted back into the space from which they came.

There was a Chinese restaurant one block over, and they would deliver with the right incentive. I knew what I wanted, so I handed the paper to her. Reluctantly she took it. "Select what you would like for dinner, Brianna."

I knew my voice was harsher than it should be. I needed to calm down, so I took the opportunity while she was reading the menu to walk into my bedroom. She wouldn't follow me, I knew, because I hadn't given her permission.

Once in my bathroom, I turned on the cold water and splashed it on my face. Looking up in the mirror, I was pleased to see that the anger burning in my eyes had dimmed. I felt more in control, which was good. The last thing Brianna needed was to fear me even more than she already did.

My hand was reaching for the doorknob when I felt my phone vibrate. I pulled it from my pocket and looked at the caller ID.

Sighing, I figured I might as well get this over with. "Hello."

"Stephan," my aunt said, her voice resonating through the phone. "And how is my favorite nephew?"

Releasing the doorknob, I leaned back against the sink. "I'm fine. You?"

"Well . . . I was doing fine until I heard you have a new girlfriend that I haven't even heard about."

Closing my eyes, my left hand came up to pinch the bridge of my nose. Girlfriend. Not exactly.

Richard knew of my lifestyle. Diane did not. And even if I wanted her to know, this was not the time to tell her. "I didn't mean to keep anything from you. It's just . . ." What did I say? I had no idea, so I settled on "new."

"Then I guess I won't be too upset with you. Now I know Jamie gave you my message so I expect to see you and Brianna on my doorstep no later than one o'clock on Sunday. Is that understood, young man?" she said in her best matriarchal voice.

That got a chuckle out of me. "Yes, ma'am."

"Good," she said, and I could hear her smile through the phone. "I can't wait to meet her, Stephan."

"We'll see you on Sunday."

And with that, I hung up. I still had no idea how Brianna would react to my aunt. She was very affectionate and I loved her dearly, but the young woman in the other room was shy and reserved. Her family situation was still a mystery to me, but obviously it wasn't good or normal or whatever term you wanted to put on it. I would just have to deal with whatever it was and however she reacted to my aunt. Pushing myself away from the sink, I put my phone back in my pocket and walked back out to Brianna.

Brianna

He was upset, more upset than I'd ever seen him. Obviously, I'd angered him with that Karl man, but I'd had no idea what to do. They didn't appear to be friends, and Master seemed to be upset that Karl had touched me. But I knew what was coming. Knew that it was not Karl who would pay for what had happened; I would.

It didn't matter. I had to keep telling myself that. There was more in my life now than I ever thought I'd have again. Whatever he wanted, I would do, no matter how unpleasant.

Before I knew it, he was walking back out into the room. His shoulders seemed a little more relaxed and the scowl was missing. As he walked closer, I quickly lowered my eyes, not wanting to anger him again.

"Did you decide?" he asked.

I nodded. "Sweet and sour chicken, please, Master."

He didn't say anything but instead went to the phone. His voice was calm as he spoke to the person on the other end of the line. It was good to hear him calm again, even though I doubted it would last.

Ian had always been good at putting on a show for others outside his group. If you were to meet him on the street, you would have no idea what he liked to do in what he called his "playroom." I hated it in there, more than the dungeon even. At least in the dungeon, I would be alone. I was never alone in the playroom. He was always there, too.

My Master's voice pulled me back from my memory, and for that I was grateful. "The food will be here shortly. Would you like to watch a movie while we eat?"

A movie? Really? He wanted to watch a movie with me?

I couldn't help the excitement that flowed through me at the thought. I hadn't seen a movie in so long. When I'd lived with my father, John, the nearest theater was over an hour away; and even though my friends would make the drive every once in a while, I was never allowed to go. The last time I'd seen a movie was in Dallas.

"Yes, Master," I answered softly, still careful not to push things. He seemed to be back to normal now, but I knew better than to be complacent.

"There are movies in the cabinet beside the television. Pick what you'd like to watch," he said and then walked back into the kitchen and began opening drawers.

Slowly I walked over beside the television. I couldn't believe this was happening, that I was getting to pick out a movie for us. And what made this even better was that I knew he was really letting me choose. I was going to take advantage of it until he took it away. Which I knew he would, eventually.

When I opened the cabinet doors I was in awe; the number of

movies to choose from was staggering. The DVDs went from floor to ceiling and were arranged in alphabetical order.

As my eyes ran over the titles, I realized there was a little bit of everything here. The movies ranged from action/adventure to girlie romantic comedies. Of course, there were way more of the former than the latter, but I was still surprised to find them at all.

I used to like those types of girlie movies. *Before.*

Now I didn't know if I could stand seeing the quirky girl and the gorgeous guy fall madly in love and live happily ever after. That girl wasn't me. Could never be me. Not anymore.

So moving on, I concentrated on the more masculine titles. That was when I found it: *No Country for Old Men.* It was based on a book I'd wanted to read before but hadn't gotten a chance. The movie had won an Oscar for Best Picture so it had to be good, right?

Deciding it didn't matter whether it was good or not, at least it wouldn't be all mushy and romantic, I took it down from the shelf and turned, coming face to face with my Master's chest.

Not sure if I should look up or not, I decided to keep my head down. Better to be safe than sorry. "Did you make a selection?" he asked.

"Yes, Master."

He took the movie from my hands. "*No Country for Old Men,*" he said, stepping around me and inserting it into the DVD player. I remained where I was. "I've been meaning to watch this but haven't had the time."

My Master was talking to me. Really talking to me. Again, I was left feeling utterly confused.

Confusion seemed to be a constant for me for the rest of the night. He'd asked me to join him on the couch, which in and of itself wasn't overly odd, but then he really did sit there and watch the movie with me while we ate the food that arrived about twenty minutes into the film.

My Master didn't try to touch me at all.

And when the movie ended, things got even weirder. He'd asked me what I thought about the movie. My mind immediately screamed *TEST,* but then I calmed myself down and remembered this was my new Master, not my old one, and I answered him.

He sat and listened while I told him it hadn't been what I expected, but that I'd liked the twists and turns in the storyline. To my amazement, he'd agreed with me about the twists and turns and said it was very much like the book. And at the mention of the book, my mouth opened before I could stop it. "You've read the book?"

As soon as I'd realized what I'd done, my hand flew to cover my mouth in horror. How stupid could I be? It wasn't my place to ask questions!

But instead of yelling or backhanding me for my slip, he was silent. When he did speak he answered my question and then added one of his own. "Yes. I own it. Would you like to read it?"

What do I say? How do I answer him? The truth, a little voice said. And so I told him the truth. "Yes, Master."

He got up and walked into his bedroom, leaving me where I was. When he returned, he was holding a book that looked as if it had been read and handed it to me.

Flipping it over, I could see the faces of some of the actors staring back at me.

Apparently, this was printed after the movie was released. Without thinking, I opened the book and began skimming the first few pages. For the first time in so long, I felt that growing excitement I always felt when starting a new book. I was so lost in the sensation flowing through my body that I almost missed his words. "You like to read, Brianna?"

My head came up before I knew what I was doing. But as soon as my eyes met his, I remembered my place and lowered them again. "Yes, Master."

"What do you like to read?"

He was asking me questions again. Why? Ian had never asked me anything he really wanted my opinion on; all he wanted from me was, *yes, Master* or *no, Master* and even the latter was rare. My new Master . . . he . . . *cared?* I wasn't sure that was the right word.

Still. "I . . . I like anything really. But . . . I used to love the classics. Mostly. Master."

Then I felt his hand on my chin forcing my head up to look at him. "First, Brianna, you do not need to end all of your sentences with *Master*. As long as you speak to me with respect, I am fine with you just answering my questions."

I was . . . speechless. Ian had required . . . I shook that thought aside. Stephan was not Ian. I had to remember that. What Ian wanted, required, or demanded no longer mattered. I belonged to someone else now.

"Second, would you like to see my library?"

Was he serious? "Yes," I answered, barely able to contain my excitement.

And then I saw something I'd never seen from Ian. A smile. A real, genuine, happy smile.

Releasing his hold on my chin, he stood. "Come with me."

I did.

He walked past the kitchen into a hallway I'd never noticed before. It was small and led to a flight of stairs. We went up one level to a small landing, and before we even cleared the stairs, I saw them. Books. Hundreds and hundreds of books.

As soon as we reached the landing, he stepped to the side and motioned for me to go ahead. I didn't hesitate for once. I hadn't seen this many books in nearly a year, and I was in heaven.

It was like before with the DVDs only better. These were books, beautiful, glorious books. My hands reached out to touch the spines of a few of my favorites, my hand stopping on a hardcover of *Jane Eyre*. I moved to pull it down and then stopped myself. He'd not given me permission for that.

"You may remove the book if you'd like."

I did.

The book felt wonderful in my hands. It was heavier than my copy had been due to its hard cover, and this one didn't look like it had ever been read.

"Would you like to take it with you to your room?" he asked.

"Yes, please."

We went back downstairs. He picked up his dishes and carried them into the kitchen, and I did the same. I followed his lead, and he seemed satisfied as I put my things in the dishwasher with his.

After adding detergent, he closed the door and turned the machine on, filling the space with a quiet hum. I didn't move. My head was down, and there was this weird feeling in the air. He took a step toward me, raising his hand, and then stopped, dropping it once again.

"You may go to bed, Brianna." His voice was clipped again, harsh.

I didn't pause before hurrying to my room. It was only after I'd closed the door that I remembered I'd forgotten my books.

Chapter Ten

Stephan

I was beginning to wonder if I'd ever experience a full night's sleep again. It was now six in the morning on a Saturday, and I found myself upstairs in my gym. Before Brianna or even the thought of her entered my existence, my life had been easy, predictable. Now I found myself in situations where I was unsure of my own responses.

Last night was a perfect example.

After we put our plates and silverware into the dishwasher, I still wasn't sure what had happened, or why. It was almost as if an electrical charge was floating through the air, like the area was magnetized. As I watched her stand there, her head down, completely submitting herself to me, I felt more drawn to her than any other woman I'd ever encountered. Without thinking, I had reached out, eager to touch her.

Frustrated, I let the weights I'd been lifting fall back into place. I had no idea where this weird compulsion had come from, but thankfully, I'd caught myself in time to stop it. She needed to feel safe with me, to trust me. Somehow, I didn't think crushing my mouth to hers and branding the memory of her lips to mine was going to accomplish that.

And I was making some progress. She was beginning to trust

me. At least I thought she was.

Bringing her up here to my library was eye-opening. Her pure happiness when she saw the books warmed my heart. I'd always enjoyed making my submissives happy but with her, it was just . . . different. Better.

For the next hour, I continued with my workout and tried my best to clear my mind, to push back the feelings she was invoking. I needed to concentrate on *her* needs, not mine.

Doing some final stretches, I thought back to the paperwork she filled out for Richard. Her birthday was June 18, and she was still seventeen when she came to be with Ian Pierce, which increased my belief that she'd been forced into this.

The more I thought about it, the more I was certain she'd not graduated high school, if she'd gone at all. It was just one more thing we needed to discuss.

After grabbing a towel and giving a quick swipe across my face and neck, I went back downstairs to shower.

When I rounded the corner into the kitchen, I nearly tripped over Brianna. Taking in the scene before me, I tried to make sense of it. She was once again kneeling on the hard marble floor of my kitchen only a foot away from the soft cushioning of the carpet. The sentiment was not lost on me. I'd snapped at her last night. Brianna thought I was upset with her, and she was providing penance.

"Stand." She rushed to comply but kept her head lowered.

I looked her over, taking in each angle and curve. There was no denying I wanted this woman. The memory of how she'd woken me yesterday was still fresh in my mind.

But those thoughts were of little use to me now. Instead, I held my ground. "How are you this morning?"

"I am well," she answered in a very timid voice.

"Good," I said. "I'm going to my room to shower." Moving to go around her, I noticed her pressing her lips together. I paused. "Did you have something you wished to ask, Brianna?"

She nodded but didn't speak. I was not going to play this game, so I just waited for her to spit it out. It didn't take nearly as long as I'd thought it would before she asked, "May I make breakfast for you this morning, Master?"

Shock crossed my face, although with her eyes still on the floor she didn't see it. But then it also struck me that this was the first real thing she had asked for without prompting. She wanted to serve me. I knew it was her way of apologizing for whatever wrong she thought she did last night to upset me, but this was an improvement over her last attempt at *thank you*. "Yes, that sounds lovely." I was about to walk away again when I saw her lips clamp together a second time. "Was there something else?"

"Do you have a waffle iron?"

I glanced up at my cabinets. Diane had been the one to stock my kitchen with what she saw as the essentials. Racking my brain, I tried to recall if a waffle iron had been included. There really was no telling. I hadn't used half of what she'd installed or shelved. "I don't know, but you are more than welcome to check. My kitchen is at your disposal."

"Thank you, Master," she whispered.

Watching her for only a moment longer to see if there was anything else, I was surprised to see a hint of a smile. She was happy she'd pleased me.

Since I was no longer needed in the kitchen, I made my way to my bedroom. Today would be a casual day. I had some e-mails to catch up on since I'd taken yesterday off, but nothing that would take me more than an hour. I grabbed a pair of jeans and a T-shirt, and lay them neatly on the bed.

The shower was my refuge, my sanctuary. I let the water fall over me and wash the tension from my body. In here, there was no Brianna, no broken woman whose life and well-being were solely in my hands. Just me.

After drying off and getting dressed, I stepped out into the main room. As soon as I opened my door, the most wonderful smell hit my senses. Waffles.

Looking into the kitchen, I was struck by the sight of Brianna standing with her back to me pouring batter into a waffle iron. Apparently, I owned one. Her moves were flawless, almost like a dance as she reached for the things she desired. She was obviously at home in the kitchen, and from the smell of things, could cook wonderfully.

I walked toward her and managed to make it over halfway before she noticed me. Her reaction was such that she almost dropped the plate full of waffles she held. She met my eyes only briefly before her gaze lowered to the floor.

Continuing to close the distance between us, I walked to the refrigerator. She remained where she was, holding the food. I figured instead of telling her to take the food over to the table I'd go with a less direct approach. I opened the refrigerator door and reached inside for the milk. "Would you prefer milk or juice?"

There was only the slightest pause before she answered. "Milk, please."

Having closed the door and tucked the milk under one arm, I went around her to grab some glasses. By the time I turned back around, she was at the table sitting with her hands in her lap. I smiled.

Breakfast was absolutely divine. The waffles were perfect, and she'd even made syrup from scratch. Saying she could cook was an understatement.

After four waffles, I laid my fork down. I just couldn't eat any more. "Those were delicious, Brianna. Thank you."

I saw her eyes widen in surprise at my praise, then heard a soft, "You're welcome, Master."

Watching her as she continued to eat, I asked, "Do you enjoy cooking?" She nodded. "Would you like to be in charge of our evening meals, then?"

Her eyes widened further, but she pressed her lips together again and nodded. She was keeping something from me. "What is it?"

She remained silent.

"Brianna," I said with a hint of my impatience.

Brianna began to raise her head and then stopped. "Does that mean . . . you're going to keep me?"

Keep her? What was she . . .

She thought I was going to give her back. I wasn't sure why I didn't get it right away. It wasn't the first time she'd thought I would send her back. At that moment, I noticed her hand cupping her neck as though she was missing something. Her collar. That was the reason she kept thinking I wasn't sure I wanted to keep her; I hadn't collared her.

I had no doubt Ian had put that symbol of possession on her within the first hour, probably the first five minutes she was given to him. Here I had been agonizing over how to handle her emotional well-being, how to make her feel safe, when the one thing I could give her, I had not.

I pushed away from the table and went to stand behind her. Leaning in, I put my mouth to her ear. She held herself rigid. Waiting. "Yes," I whispered.

A shiver ran through her body, but for once I wasn't sure it was out of pure fear.

Reaching over her shoulder, I picked up my plate and stood again to my full height. "I'm going out for a while," I said as I walked into the kitchen. "Don't worry about lunch, I'll bring something back."

She was still at the table when I walked out the door. I had a few qualms about what I was about to do, but if this would give her security, I would do it.

I took my car and drove across town, still pondering what might lie ahead. Brianna was nothing like the two submissives I'd collared previously, but she needed me like neither of them ever had. This was a huge step, one that meant more, at least to me, than the act of buying her. Before, I had felt an obligation to care for her because of her situation. Once she wore my collar, it wouldn't be a mere obligation anymore. I would willingly and completely be responsible for her.

My family had used the same jeweler for the last fifty years. There was no doubt in my mind that Beth and Roger would have exactly what I wanted.

As I walked through the door, a bell sounded announcing my entrance. A minute later Beth's head peeked through a black curtain. The instant she saw me her face lit up. "Stephan! Roger, Stephan's here," she said, all the while walking toward me.

Her arms wrapped around me for a hug. "Beth. How are you?"

She pulled back a little to look at me. "Oh, how formal we are," she said, slapping me playfully on the shoulder. I laughed.

Then her husband, Roger, made his appearance. The only difference between his greeting and his wife's was that his combined a handshake and a hug at the same time.

When he pulled back, he gave my shoulder a firm pat. "How have you been, Stephan?"

"I've been good. Keeping busy, you know. Are you both coming to the fundraiser this year?"

Beth waved her hand nonchalantly in front of her face. "You know we wouldn't miss it." She stepped back behind the counter. "I am assuming this isn't a purely social visit?" she asked.

I shook my head in awe. She knew me too well. "No, it's not. I need a choker necklace. I would prefer it to be white gold or platinum and it needs to be simple, nothing over the top."

"Hmm," she said, tapping her finger to her chin. "Let me see . . ." Moving to the necklace trays, she scanned their contents. "Any charms?"

I shook my head. "No. Not right now anyway. But I want that to be an option."

She glanced up at me and smiled. I'd come in here once before to buy a choker for a submissive. Any submissive of mine had to have a versatile collar to wear out in public. Since removing it was not an option, it needed to be able to adapt to both casual and elegant settings.

Beth reached under the counter and retracted a simple circle. There was nothing fancy about it but a charm or jewel could easily be slipped onto it to dangle from Brianna's neck.

"Is this what you wanted?" she asked with a smirk, already knowing my answer.

"Yes, I do believe it is," I answered, running my fingers along the metal, imagining it on Brianna. It would look perfect around her beautiful neck.

After saying my goodbyes to Beth and Roger, I made my way to the locksmith. Brianna would need a key to my condo. She was not my prisoner, and if I was going to go so far as to collar her this early, the least I could do was make sure she knew she was allowed to come and go.

With key in hand, I had one more stop to make before picking us up a light lunch and heading back to my place. The University of Minnesota had some great programs, although being an alumnus myself, I was a little biased.

I pulled into the admissions office and went inside to find Karen. Luckily, she was free and more than happy to see me. I knew she had a bit of a crush on me. Unfortunately for her, it wasn't mutual. I, however, was not above exploiting that fact in order to get what I needed.

It took almost an hour and the dodging of at least two dozen indecent proposals, but I got what I was looking for. I wanted Brianna to finish school, and UM had a program that could get her there. So many doors were closed to her right now, and I wanted to correct that. She needed to be able to stand on her own two feet and feel confident again. Getting her high school diploma would help.

The next block of classes didn't start until fall, so we had some time. Karen provided all the registration papers Brianna would need. I'd just have to get her transcripts from her previous school, but I didn't see that as too big a problem. We'd figure it out. She deserved this.

Chapter Eleven

Stephan

I'd picked up some sandwiches at one of my favorite delis. Honestly, I wasn't that hungry after Brianna's breakfast, but she might be. I had also told her I would be bringing something home, and I needed to be consistent above all else.

The closer I got to home, however, the more my eyes kept drifting to the black box on the seat next to me. Was this really the right thing? What if it was pushing her too far, too fast? There were so many things she didn't understand, so many things I didn't feel I could tell her yet. Was collaring her now the best thing to do?

That was the thing, I didn't know. Sitting there watching her this morning, the decision had been clear. Now, the doubts started to creep in again.

Before I could even think it through, I picked up my cell and dialed Logan. After four rings, he answered, slightly out of breath. "Hello?"

"Logan. Sorry to bother you. I didn't mean to interrupt something," I said apologetically. Logan had been out of town on business for the last few weeks. I knew he and Lily had had plans, and I knew without a doubt that I was interrupting them.

"Don't worry about it. It was nothing that won't wait." I heard a door shut in the background and knew Lily was cursing me right about now. After a few more seconds of silence had passed, Logan asked, "So what's up?"

"I'm assuming Lily told you about her time with Brianna?"

His voice turned serious. "She did."

I let out a sigh of relief. Although I'd been positive Lily would share, I didn't want to assume; every relationship was different. "Good. Well, something happened this morning." I took a deep breath and plunged into the story including a mention that this wasn't the first time she'd implied that I'd "give her back" or "send her away." After finishing the story, I said, "I'm going to collar her."

My entire body clenched waiting for his reprimand; I was sure he'd start screaming at me any second. But he didn't. Instead, I was met with silence.

I waited, but still nothing. "Logan?"

"I'm here, Stephan. You're obviously concerned about it or else you wouldn't have called me. What has you worried?"

"I'm just afraid I'm doing the wrong thing . . . that it's too soon."

"Why do you want to collar her?"

My answer came out before I could even think about it. "It's what she wants." I paused. "I mean, she doesn't feel like I'll keep her without it, I guess. And I want her to feel safe, to relax with me and not think every time she turns around that I'll send her back to Ian Pierce or worse."

"What does your gut tell you?"

I sighed. "Collar her."

The smile in his voice came through the line. "There you go."

"Thanks," I said sincerely. Logan had always been my voice of reason.

"That's what I'm here for," he said. "Oh, and I expect to meet her soon. I feel a little left out."

"I'm not sure, Logan." I hesitated. "I mean, she's very skittish."

"That's what Lily said, too. Hopefully this will help, though, her wearing your collar."

"Maybe," I said, the doubt still clear in my voice.

"Call me if you need me. Or us. That girl of yours may need a friend of the non-male variety, and if she does Lily is available."

"Logan, I couldn't—"

"Stephan, we want to help."

"Thank you. I . . ."

"Not a problem, but I really should get back to Lily. She's a little tied up at the moment."

I couldn't help but laugh at his joke. "Tell her I said hi."

With that, we disconnected. I was still nervous but felt better about what I was about to do. It was just in time, too, since thirty seconds later I turned into my parking garage. Brianna was upstairs waiting for me.

Brianna

The second he left, I'd jumped up out of my seat, a huge smile on my face. He wanted to keep me! Even after I'd messed up yesterday morning and the whole thing at the zoo . . . Master wanted me.

Looking over his home, I was still in awe. I was really going to live here. Stay here with my Master.

It was then I realized that somewhere there had been a change in how I thought of him in my mind. I wanted to belong to Stephan. I wanted him to be my Master. I wanted him to *want* me to be his.

My gaze settled on the mess that was still in the kitchen. I would clean. Not just the kitchen, but the whole house. Well except for his bedroom and bathroom, which were off-limits. He wouldn't be back for a few hours at least, since he said he'd bring lunch with him. That would be plenty of time if I worked quickly.

It wasn't hard to find most of the cleaning supplies. What I didn't find under the sink was in a small closet in the pantry.

I dusted, cleaned mirrors, and vacuumed the downstairs before heading up to the library. I wasn't sure I'd have time to take all the books off the shelf and put them back so, instead, I just dusted the tops and fronts, wherever I could reach. It wasn't until I'd finished that I noticed a small little stairway, only three steps, in the back corner.

Up the steps were two doors. I tried the first, but it was locked. The second opened easily and was filled with gym equipment. This must have been where Master was this morning. I could tell he'd been working out. His breathing was heavier than normal, and he was wearing loose-fitting shorts, like the ones he'd given me to wear last week. I didn't notice what type of shirt he was wearing other than the color since I'd kept my head down.

The room had a distinct male scent and was clearly well used. I stood there for far too long lost in my thoughts. It looked so normal.

When I was finally able to pull myself back to reality, I got to work using the cleaner to wipe over all the exercise equipment. There were mirrors along the back wall, so I sprayed them down and made sure there were no streaks.

Finishing, I took a deep breath. The room smelled clean now, but there was still a hint of him that lingered. It just seemed to fit. I also realized that it almost smelled . . . good.

I quickly closed the door and went back down the stairs to put everything away. Going into the room he'd given me, I removed my clothes and headed into the bathroom to shower.

As I washed, my hand lingered over my empty neck. I didn't understand why. If he wanted to keep me, why wasn't I wearing his collar? The first thing Ian did when I'd met him was force me to my knees with the help of two others and put his leather collar around my neck. I'd hated it. And I'd fought him. Them. Of course, the only thing my effort had gotten me was a black eye, a sore jaw, and lots of bruises. A shiver ran through me.

Stepping into the water, I tried to forget my memories. Stephan. Stephan. Stephan. My new Master was all that mattered. I couldn't see him being so mean, even though a part of me knew he must be. Sometimes at least.

I got out of the shower, dried off, and went into the bedroom to dress. Even if Stephan beat me within an inch of my life or shared me with dozens of his friends, I would do it, and I would try to please him. All those things I'd suffered before, and I'd survived. At least now I had more than I'd ever thought I'd have again.

I didn't want to go back to Ian. If I never saw him again it would be too soon. While I was with him, I was nothing, and I was reminded of it every day. My new Master was different. To say I wasn't scared of Stephan would be a lie, but so far he'd been kinder to me than anyone had in a long time. And he didn't have to be. He owned me and could do whatever he wished.

Looking around, I once again took in all I'd been given since he'd brought me here only three days ago: a bed, clothes, hot water, and food that tasted good. Most people take those things for granted, but I knew better.

A bed was not needed nor deserved for a slave, according to Ian. Clothes beyond the . . . well, uniform Alex and I wore were nothing but items that got in the way of what was his. Hot water was a luxury and not to be granted to slaves unless as a reward. I'd never managed to please Ian enough to earn that. He viewed food almost the same as water. Twice a day we were given a bowl of either plain oatmeal or rice along with some sort of vegetable drink. It provided the nutrients we needed but did nothing for our taste buds, or at least mine. But again, Ian didn't see tasty food as a requirement for a slave.

Stephan, my new Master, had given me all those things along with so much more. I didn't know what I'd done to be offered this, but I would not make him sorry for his choice. If he ever did decide to put a collar on me, I would not fight him as I'd done Ian. I would take it willingly and let the chips fall where they may.

After I finished dressing, I looked at the clock. It was almost noon, and I figured he would be back soon, so I walked into the living area, taking with me the book he'd left outside my bedroom door last night. Curling up on the couch, I read until I heard the key turn in the lock.

I dropped the book quickly onto the coffee table, rounded the corner, and dropped to my knees just as he was opening the door. It was strange, but I knew the minute he saw me.

I heard him shut the door and then his heavy footfalls coming closer. He stopped in front of me, his shoes almost touching my knees. Suddenly, I felt his hand on my hair. It was soft and caressing, but soon it was gone.

He walked around me to the table we'd eaten breakfast at only hours before. "Join me, Brianna."

As fast as I could manage, I stood and walked to him. He was sitting in the seat he'd been in earlier, so I did the same.

The first thing I noticed was a square black box. It looked like a jewelry box, a nice jewelry box. I wanted to ask what it was, but I didn't dare.

Master pushed a sandwich in front of me, pulling my attention away from the box. "I got us each a club. If there is something on it you don't like, you may remove it." I nodded and took the sandwich.

When I opened the wrapping, I realized how huge it was. The meat was piled high between two thick slices of bread. I noticed there were both onions and peppers so I removed them and put them on the side of the paper before taking a small bite. It was really good. I hadn't been terribly hungry, but this had to be the best sandwich I'd ever eaten.

Before I knew it, I was finished. I glanced up enough to see that Master was, too. He'd been waiting for me.

He stood and removed the papers and napkins, taking them into the kitchen. He was in there for longer than it took to throw the things away, and I started to get nervous. But then I heard him walking back toward me and a glass of water appeared. "Drink," he said. His voice was not unkind, but it was not a suggestion either.

I finished the entire glass of water while he watched me. A year ago it would have bothered me to be watched so closely. Now, it didn't faze me, especially when it was him. I wasn't sure why that was exactly since Ian's gaze always made me nervous.

When I set the glass back down on the table, he moved it out of the way before reaching for the black box I'd noticed earlier. Master opened it to reveal a metal circle. It was silver in color, plain but pretty.

His voice brought me out of my haze. "Do you know what this is, Brianna?"

I shook my head. "No, Master."

He reached out and brought my chin up until my eyes met his. "This is for you. It will mean you belong to me."

My collar? I was confused again. This was a necklace, not a collar. Would he really give me something so beautiful to show his ownership?

As if he could somehow read my mind, he continued. "I am giving you a choice, Brianna, and it is an important one. If you choose to wear this, you will be mine. Your needs, your wants, your well-being will belong to me. And you should know something else. I do not share. You will belong to me and only me for as long as you wear this."

Then he was silent, and my mind raced through everything he'd just said.

When he spoke again, his voice was softer. "What do you choose?"

I didn't have to think about it. Not really. I'd already made my choice. He was my new Master, and as long as he wanted me, I would be his. But instead of answering verbally, I showed him my desire. Sliding somewhat less than gracefully from my chair, I knelt before him with my hands in my lap and my head bowed.

There was no movement from him at first, but I could feel his eyes on me. And then he stood. I felt him move behind me. "Lift your hair," he requested, his voice soft but firm. I did, and soon felt the coolness of the metal brush against my skin. A soft click sounded in my ears as he closed the clasp. I was his.

Chapter Twelve

Stephan

It was done.

I'd collared her.

The process had gone much easier than I'd expected. There had been no hesitation on her part, and for a moment, I'd wondered if she really knew what she was getting herself into. But of course she did. Brianna understood more than any eighteen-year-old should.

As I closed the clasp on her neck, a surge of possessiveness rushed through me. She was mine. My hands ran up the span of her neck and into her hair, moving it back into place. Beautiful.

"Stand up."

She rose slowly, and I saw her fingers come up to touch her new adornment. I could tell she liked it, and her happiness brought a smile to my lips.

Moving so that I was once again in front of her, I placed my hands on either side of her face and angled it up, silently asking her to look at me. Her eyes locked with mine. They were bright, like a burden had been lifted from her shoulders. I would take care of her, I vowed, for as long as she would allow me.

And to seal that promise, I lowered my lips to hers, softly pressing against her mouth. I kept it chaste with my lips firmly closed, even though I wanted so much more. She did not kiss me back exactly, but she didn't resist either. Her mouth relaxed and gave, following my lead.

I pulled back, but her eyes remained closed for several seconds. When they finally opened, they found mine again. "Do you like your new collar, Brianna?"

She smiled and said, "Yes, Master. Thank you."

Looking down, my fingers skimmed along the surface of her collar before meeting her eyes once more. "It's metal so you will not need to take it off to bathe. It is to remain around your neck at all times unless I say otherwise."

"Yes, Master."

This was the longest she'd ever held my gaze, and I realized that as much as I loved her bowed before me with her head lowered, willing to serve, I also loved staring into those beautiful blue eyes of hers. My hand came up to stroke her cheek. "We have some things to discuss, Brianna," I said, motioning to the chair she'd recently vacated.

Once we were both seated again, I instructed her to raise her head as I wanted her to look at me. "I want to go over a few things with you, and I want you to feel free to ask me any questions you may have about what my expectations are. In return, I expect you to answer any questions I have for you with complete honesty. Will you do this?"

I saw her swallow and knew she was nervous. "Yes, Master."

"Good," I said. "First, I want to discuss your schooling." The look of surprise on her face was almost comical, but I suppressed my reaction and went on. "From what I've learned so far, I'm assuming you did not finish high school. Am I correct?"

"Yes. I mean no, I didn't graduate."

She looked sad, which was a good thing. Hopefully she would be happy with my first command. "I thought so." I grabbed the folder I'd laid down earlier, and placed it in front of her. "You will look through these papers and fill them out in their entirety. The University of Minnesota has evening classes for individuals who, for whatever reason, were not able to graduate high school. The course is twelve weeks long, and at the end, you will take a test for your GED."

Brianna didn't move at first. She was watching me and then

looked almost blankly at the folder containing all the necessary paperwork. Her right hand came up from her lap and caressed the university picture gracing the front. "Why?" she asked almost reverently.

She wasn't upset, and I knew what she was asking. Brianna wanted to know why I would do something like this for her. "You are my submissive, and your needs are my responsibility. It is also my desire for you to finish high school, and when you complete this course successfully, we can discuss college if you'd like."

Her eyes lit up, and I could see moisture there. "Thank you, Master."

I smiled back at her, letting her know I was pleased with her response. "You're welcome. You should know that it will not be an easy course, and you will be required to do a lot of studying. I do expect you to apply yourself one hundred percent, Brianna."

She nodded. "I will, Master, I promise."

"Good." I watched as she started to open the folder and then close it again only to reopen it once more. "You'll have plenty of time to look over the information later, and you will need to complete all the forms this weekend so that we can finish your enrollment."

With that, she closed the folder and put it softly to the side but kept her right hand lying on it as if it might disappear.

Next, I removed the new key from my pocket along with a small key ring. For now, the only key on it was for my penthouse, but soon it would hold a car key as well, as she would need transportation. I held my hand out to her, silently asking her to take it.

It took a few seconds but she removed it from my hand and looked at it skeptically. "It is a key to my home. You will use it whenever you need to. As you've agreed to be responsible for our evening meals, you will need to do the grocery shopping and will be required to get in and out of the house. There will also be school. I expect you to do all of your errands with the exception of school while I am at work during the week. You will be home by the time I am." I paused. "Any questions so far?"

"No," she whispered.

Her answer was soft, but I knew she'd heard me for her eyes had not left my face since I'd started talking again. I imagined this was a lot to take in, but it needed to be done. "We will not have time to get you a vehicle this weekend so unfortunately that will have to wait. Until then, I will see about a rental." And then I thought of something very important. "Do you have a driver's license?"

"I . . . I used to. I mean I . . . well, I don't have anything from . . . before."

"That shouldn't be a problem then, just a matter of tracking down some records."

Brianna

Who was he? First, he was sending me to school, then he gives me a key to his home, and now he's talking about a car? And he was serious. This wasn't a joke. He was really giving this to me.

I wasn't stupid, though. I still knew what I was and that he could take all these things away from me anytime he wished. First and foremost, he was my Master; he owned me along with anything he gave to me.

But for now, I would enjoy them. He was happy with me, and I would continue to try to make him happy.

I was so lost in my musings that I almost missed what he said next. "Tomorrow you will be accompanying me to my aunt and uncle's house for dinner. While we are there, you will not address me as Master. I would rather you touch my arm or shoulder to get my attention should you need it, however I will be paying close attention to you so you shouldn't." He looked at me very intently as he said his next words. "I will be very displeased should you slip tomorrow, Brianna. Do you understand?"

"Yes, Master. I will not displease you or embarrass you."

"Very good." He smiled. I really liked it when he smiled, and not just because it meant he wasn't upset. It lightened up his face, and his eyes almost glowed.

"There is one other thing I wish to discuss with you, Brianna, but I wanted to ask you again if you have any questions?"

There was something I wanted to ask, but I couldn't. Wouldn't. It was another one of those things where if he hadn't thought of it, I didn't want to put it into this head. So instead of voicing it, I just shook my head.

"All right," he said skeptically, as if he knew I was holding something back. "As my submissive, you are free to use my home as you wish while I am at the office. This includes the library upstairs. I will clear off a space for you there where you may study. You will also utilize the gym at least three days a week. On Monday, I will set up a time for my personal trainer to come and work with you on an exercise routine."

He paused and raised an eyebrow at me. I remained quiet, though, not really sure what to say. The study space kind of made sense given he was sending me to school, but the gym? Why would that matter?

His voice cut off my thoughts once more. Again, it was almost like he was reading my mind. "Brianna, I will have you do things at times that you will not understand and may, on occasion, not like. I do, however, expect you to comply with my wishes whether you understand my motivations or not."

I nodded and lowered my head. This was it. The kiss earlier had been almost nice, but I knew it wouldn't end there. He hadn't had sex with me yet, but I knew it was coming. I was wearing his collar now. He was keeping me. It was what I wanted, I reminded myself.

Taking a deep breath, I squared my shoulders and slowly raised my eyes. He hadn't said a word since I'd lowered them, and I knew he was waiting. As soon as I was looking at him again, he continued, "Everything I do, Brianna, will be with you in mind. I will always do what I think is best."

I knew what he meant. He would do what was best for him, but I'd liked the first part. The part where he said he would do everything with me in mind. I wasn't sure what that meant, but it was something. I hoped it meant that he wouldn't hurt me too badly. I really hoped that.

Then he reached out and placed a hand on my cheek. His thumb rubbed along the bone just below my left eye. "You belong to me, Brianna. You are safe."

My Master's words continued to run through my mind long after he left me to go upstairs, but I couldn't wrap my mind around them. I'd felt the possessiveness in his touch when he'd kissed me and again when he'd touched my cheek earlier. It was so contradictory—as so much was with my new Master—in that both were equally as gentle.

I tried to look over the forms for school, but I couldn't focus on anything other than our conversation and its implications. He'd given me so much, and I knew the price would be high. I didn't know why he hadn't used me yet, but he would.

Then his last words echoed in my ears. *You are safe.* I thought about that and realized I was, at the very least, safer. For some reason he seemed to want my trust, and even though it scared me beyond reason, I knew on some level I did trust him, a little.

I needed to stop worrying about what was going to happen. There was no way to stop it either way. Stephan would come back downstairs soon, and I wanted to have this paperwork filled out by the time he did. So I forced myself to concentrate.

Amazingly, the forms were simple, at least until they'd asked my reason for leaving school. How did a person in my position answer that question? In the end I decided to ask Master. It would not do for me to anger him by putting down the wrong answer.

He was still upstairs by the time I'd finished filling out the paperwork, so I took my time going through the rest of the packet of information. There were some brief overviews of some of the undergrad programs they offered, nothing detailed of course, but enough to make me want it. I'd always dreamed of going to college and maybe even teaching someday. The teaching might not be a possibility now, but maybe, if what he'd said were true, college was.

I was so lost in my daydreams of college that I didn't hear him come down the stairs. I didn't even notice him until he was standing a few feet away from me, calling my name. My reaction was immediate. Dropping the papers, I fell to the carpet and lowered my head to the floor. I knew he didn't like me to say I was sorry, so I bit my tongue and allowed my actions to speak for me.

Master stood without moving for several long heartbeats then he bent to pick up the papers I'd dropped. I heard shuffling and knew he was looking them over. He took his time and must have read every word both typed and written. While he read, he did not address me or give me permission to get up. And so I stayed where I was.

I felt movement and then his feet disappeared from my view. The sound of fabric giving a few feet away told me he'd sat down. "Come to me." Again, his voice was firm, but he didn't seem upset. I noted he had not told me to get up or rise, but to come, so I only raised my upper body and used both my hands and knees to bring myself to his feet once again.

Once I was sitting at his feet, he reached his hand out and raised my chin. "You were not paying attention, were you, Brianna? What was so important that you neglected to pay attention to your surroundings?"

I swallowed. Would he take this away from me if I told him the truth?

"I see that mind of yours working; however, I expect you to tell me the truth. There is no greater insult or displeasure you will cause me than to lie to me."

My eyes began to lower, and I felt his hand on my chin tighten in warning. Immediately I brought my eyes back up to his. "College, Master." His brow rose again in question. "I . . . I used to dream of going to college and . . ."

My words drifted off, and he finished them for me. ". . . and you realized that now it may be a possibility. That is understandable, Brianna, but it is still not acceptable for you not to notice what is around you. You must be aware of where you are and who you are with at all times, whether that be inside or outside of this house, is that understood?"

"Yes, Master," I whispered.

He watched me for a long time and then said, "I will let this incident go without a consequence, but do not let it happen again."

"I won't, Master."

He released my chin and picked the papers back up. When he spoke again, it wasn't what I'd expected. "Come sit in my lap, Brianna."

My heart started pounding. This was it. I swallowed down my fear, stood slowly, and did as he requested as gently as possible. The arm not holding the paperwork wrapped around my waist. I kept waiting for it to move up or down, but it didn't. It just lay innocently on my stomach.

As we went over what I'd filled out, I had to concentrate hard on what he was saying. I didn't want to get caught again not paying attention, but it was difficult.

Somehow I managed, and we were able to fill in that empty space I'd been so unsure of with "personal conflicts." Master didn't think they'd want a more specific answer because it was only for record-keeping purposes.

Amazingly, I'd gradually started to relax the longer we sat and talked. The bliss of the moment was cut short as he set the papers down and said, "Kiss me."

I hesitated and began to see the furrowing of his brow showing his disappointment. I didn't want that. I'd promised myself that I would do whatever he asked, and now that he was asking something of me, look at my reaction. It was a kiss, just a kiss. So I leaned in, closed my eyes, and tried to stay calm.

He relaxed under me the moment my lips touched his, but he didn't move other than to kiss me back. It felt odd. I'd never kissed anyone before. I mean, I'd been kissed, but I'd never been the one doing the kissing. Maybe that shouldn't make a difference but somehow it did.

When I finally pulled my lips from his, I opened my eyes to find his staring back at me. Then the knuckles of his left hand came up and brushed my cheek. "Very nice, Brianna. But next time do not hesitate."

Chapter Thirteen

Brianna

I was in a deep sleep when I heard an annoying beeping sound by my ear. And as much as I willed it to go away, it wouldn't stop. Finally, I opened my eyes and located the sound. The alarm.

Reaching out, I hit the snooze button, desperate for it to stop. But as soon as my eyes opened enough to take in my surroundings, I remembered where I was. It had been so long since that had happened.

When I lifted my hand to my neck, my fingers grazed the tiny circle of metal there. My collar. Stephan.

Thinking of him set my mind in motion, and I realized that I'd not set my alarm last night. My eyes flashed over to the source of my wakefulness and rested on the folded note taped over the numbers. I had no doubt as to who had left the note or who had set my alarm. After pulling the tape loose, I opened the note and read it.

> *Dress and meet me in the gym.*
> *Clothes are on the bench at the end of the bed.*
> *I'll be waiting.*

Although I was not a morning person, I'd gotten used to having to wake at a moment's notice and made myself get out of bed. I did not want to anger him this morning. Last night had been so very nice, and I wanted it again.

I dressed quickly in the tank top and shorts he'd laid out for me and headed up the stairs. Just as he'd said, he was waiting for me.

When I entered the room he was facing away from me, but that soon changed. It seemed as if he could tell I was there because not more than five seconds passed before he turned around. I immediately dropped my eyes.

He walked toward me slowly, deliberately. My body went on alert as he got closer. I had no idea what he was going to do to me here.

My Master stopped directly in front of me. "Good morning, Brianna. Did you sleep well?"

"Yes, Master. Thank you."

His hand came up to lift my chin. I knew by now that he wanted me to look at him. My eyes found his and waited. He didn't make me wait long. "I'm glad to hear that. I was going to introduce you to my gym this morning, but it seems you've already become acquainted."

I swallowed. Was he upset that I'd cleaned in here? *Please don't let him be upset.* All I wanted to do was make him happy with me. Why couldn't I make him happy?

The hand that had been under my chin came up and brushed the side of my cheek. "Calm, Brianna," he whispered. "I'm not displeased with you."

I let out the breath I'd been holding. I hadn't messed up again.

"Since you have already been around my gym, I will forgo the tour. I do want you to get used to some of the machines you'll be using with Brad." I assumed Brad was the personal trainer he'd mentioned, but he didn't give me time to contemplate that. He took a step back and held out his hand, clearly wanting me to take it. Bringing my arm up, I put my hand in his, and he quickly wrapped his fingers around mine.

I followed him over to a treadmill. "You will walk today for five miles or until you are unable to continue, whichever comes first. However," he said, his voice taking on that commanding tone, "if you stop before the five miles, and I do not feel you have truly reached your limit, we will be back in here later today to try again.

Do you understand this, Brianna?"

He wanted me to walk? For five miles? I didn't know if I could do that. I'd only been on a treadmill once in my life, and I'd fallen flat on my face, giving myself a bloody nose. But I couldn't tell him no. I had to at least try. "Yes, Master."

"Good," he said. And then he stepped forward again and took my face in his hands. "You will do fine. I will not be far."

He helped me onto the machine and showed me how to start it, stop it, and where it would show me the miles I'd walked. I nodded and hoped with everything I had that I could do this.

Before I knew it, he was stepping back a few feet to watch me, waiting for me to start. With a deep breath, I hit the button and felt the belt begin to move under me.

I was okay at first. The belt was moving slowly, and I kept a tight grip on the handlebar. But then it started to pick up speed, and my legs just would not do what I wanted them to do. I felt my ankle begin to twist and my knees buckle. My last thought as I closed my eyes was to hope that he wouldn't be too mad I couldn't do what he'd wanted.

Surprisingly I didn't hit the floor or the machine. Instead, I felt two arms circle my waist. I knew who had caught me, and I froze, waiting.

My Master's breath was hot against my ear as he spoke. "Perhaps something besides the treadmill to start, hmm?"

His hands moved to my waist and stayed there until I was standing on my own two feet again. I wanted to beg for his forgiveness, to tell him I was sorry, but I kept my mouth shut and just lowered my head.

I felt him take a step back before he turned me to face him. "Let's try the bike instead, shall we?"

He didn't wait for me to answer before taking my arm and leading me several yards away to a stationary bicycle. "This will expend a little more effort than the walking, so we will reduce it from five miles to three."

Master adjusted the machine and then stood, waiting for me to climb up. I'd never been on one of these before, but I knew how to ride a bicycle so I wasn't too worried. It was the three miles I was a little concerned with.

I couldn't say that, though, so I moved myself into position and started peddling while he watched. The numbers began moving, showing my progress, and after a while Master must have been satisfied I wouldn't fall off and walked away. He didn't go far, just on the other side of the room where he picked up some weights and began lifting.

The weights he used weren't overly large, not like the ones you see the bodybuilders use on television, but they were still enough to show the strain of his muscles through his T-shirt. A shiver ran through me at the strength he must have and what he could do with it. What he could do to me with it if he chose.

I felt the fear start to bubble up inside me again as I watched him shift the weights into a different position. Clenching my eyes shut, I tried to will it away. It didn't matter. None of it mattered.

Vaguely, I heard the sound of a timer, but I was so lost in my head that I didn't register what it was. Then I felt his hand on my arm and jumped.

This was not happening to me! He'd caught me not paying attention again after he'd just warned me last night. I knew what was coming. I knew, and yet I still wanted to beg for it not to happen.

"Look at me, Brianna."

I'd been expecting that tone, but it still had me trembling. It was so hard to look at him. His face was rigid, his jaw clenched. "What did I tell you last night about not paying attention?" He didn't wait for me to answer. "I thought you would have learned the importance of that lesson after our talk, but obviously you haven't. I told you there would be consequences next time, and so, as much as I do not wish it, you've made your choice. Go get your books and bring them to me."

My books? What was he going to do with my books? When he noticed my hesitation, he raised his eyebrow slightly, and I knew if I didn't get moving quickly, whatever he had planned would get much worse.

I made it down the stairs as fast as I could, my legs not quite so steady after the three-mile bicycle ride. The books were lying where I'd left them last night on the nightstand. My heart clenched when I thought about what he was going to do with them. As I made my way back up the stairs to the gym where he was waiting, I almost wished he'd do anything but take away my books.

When I entered the room, he was standing right where I'd left him and didn't move as I approached. Standing before him, the books in my right hand, I watched in dread as his hand came out asking for them.

A small whine left my lips as I placed them in his grasp. He heard it, of course, and made a *tsk* sound with his tongue before tucking the books under his arm. "These will remain in my possession for one week. As long as I feel you've learned your lesson, you will get them back next Sunday morning. Until then, the library is off-limits to you as well."

He was taking my books. I didn't know why, but that felt worse than if he'd have hit me. It had been so long since I'd been able to read, to lose myself in a novel, and he was taking them away.

There had been no doubt in my mind that eventually I'd displease him, but I'd never thought he'd choose my books of all things to take away from me.

Stupid. He can take everything away, remember? You are nothing. You have nothing.

His voice brought me back to him again. "I expect you to pay attention to your surroundings at all times, Brianna." Master's voice changed slightly before he spoke his next words. "Now, as for your hesitation in complying with my request . . ." This is it. What will he do to me? "We are finished here for today. You will go shower and dress for dinner with my aunt and uncle. Pick out a skirt and blouse from what Lily got you. If you need help, come find me; I will be in my room getting dressed as well." Then he took a step toward me and lifted my chin. "I want to make sure you are paying attention today, Brianna. Only cold water for your shower."

And with that, he walked away.

Two hours later, we were in his car. It had been less than two weeks since I'd started taking warm showers again, but it was enough time to make me forget how much I hated cold ones. Because of the workout, I'd had to wash my hair. By the time I'd stepped out of the shower, I was freezing.

I had to do better. It couldn't be that hard to stay focused and pay attention. Daydreaming was something I'd always had a habit of doing. When I was younger, my teachers had given me more than one lecture on paying attention.

We drove for almost an hour before he pulled over along the side of the road. There was countryside all around us, but I saw no house nearby so I wasn't sure why he'd stopped. I kept myself still but focused my complete attention on him.

He shifted in his seat to look at me. There was silence in the car for several minutes as I waited. Finally the words came. "While we're here, you will keep your head up. If someone asks you a question, it is up to you whether or not you answer it; however, I do expect you to be polite."

"Yes, Master," I whispered obediently.

He brushed his fingers against my cheek and then ran them though my hair down to my shoulder. "You will do fine, Brianna. I will not leave you alone. Remember, you are safe."

I was safe. He kept saying that.

Master pulled his hand away, turned back around in his seat, and put the car in drive. Less than a mile later, we turned down a long driveway, and I could see a huge house in the distance.

We were here.

The house was massive, at least from what I could see. It had to be just as big as Ian's, but where his was creepy and intimidating, this one was elegant and regal.

We walked to the door, his arm at my lower back. I felt calmer knowing he was there, which was strange. I couldn't explain this weird mixture of fear and trust I had.

The fear I understood. He owned me. It was the trust that boggled my mind. I had no reason to trust him except for the fact that he had yet to lie to me. Even down to the consequences this morning, he'd been truthful. I cringed at the reminder that I had no books to occupy my days or evenings for the next week.

My Master didn't knock when we reached the door, but instead walked in as if he owned the place. He guided me through a foyer bigger than my room and down a long hallway that opened up into a kitchen. There stood a woman with long brown hair very similar in color to Stephan's.

Seeming to have the same sixth sense as Master did, she turned moments after we entered the room. "Stephan!" she screamed, dropping what she'd been holding in her hand and wrapping him in an exuberant hug.

She pulled back and looked at him as if assessing. "You are not allowed to stay away for that long again," she said, playfully slapping his arm. "Do you hear me?"

He chuckled. "Yes, ma'am."

Then her eyes fell on me. "Aren't you going to introduce me to your girlfriend?"

Girlfriend?

She didn't know what I was. It hit me like a ton of bricks. I wasn't a slave to her. I was just a person.

A person she thought was Stephan's girlfriend. Is that what he'd told her? I was beginning to wonder if I'd ever be able to figure my new Master out.

"Diane, this is Brianna. Brianna, this is my aunt, Diane."

He'd said to be polite so I was going to say *nice to meet you*, but before the words could leave my mouth, two arms surrounded me. Her arms were holding onto me like vise grips, and I started to panic.

The next thing I knew, I felt his hand in mine. I didn't know why, but it calmed me enough to endure the affection I'd received.

Stephan

I'd wondered how Brianna would react to my aunt's exuberance. She could be a lot to take at times, and it seemed that my concern was warranted. I saw the panic cross Brianna's face moments after Diane started to hug her. It didn't matter that my aunt meant her no harm. Brianna was scared, and I needed to give her what comfort I could, so I reached out and took her hand.

It worked. I watched as the tension in her body eased a little and before too long, my aunt was stepping back to look at her as she did me. Fearing the scrutiny would cause her more discomfort, I moved in, closing the small distance between us. My arm slid around Brianna's waist, and I pulled her against my side.

This action on my part did two things. First, it did accomplish my goal of relaxing Brianna, but it also drew Diane's attention. A sly smile crossed her face, and I had to suppress rolling my eyes at her. She and Richard could never have children of their own, so when I came to live with them at fourteen, she quickly did everything she could to make me feel as much love as possible.

Diane was as much of a mother to me as my own had been. She'd seen me through my grieving teenage years no matter how much trouble I'd gotten into and supported me through college. I loved her very much, but her eagerness for me to settle down made me uncomfortable. She saw the woman at my side and saw a happy future for me, complete with the white picket fence.

It was useless to try and convince her otherwise, so instead I went with distraction. "Is Richard around?" Diane's focus changed from Brianna to me, and I felt the woman under my fingers relax just a little more.

My aunt sighed, but then said, "He's in his study working on something, as usual. I have a few more things to finish here and then it will be time to eat. Maybe you can go get him for me?"

I noticed my aunt's eyes shifting to Brianna again and knew what was coming. She wanted to get to know "my girlfriend" and grill her about our relationship. My aunt meant well, I knew, but I would not break my promise to Brianna and leave her alone. So I told her *sure* and maneuvered us both back down the hallway.

Leaving my aunt like that had been rude, but I didn't know what else to do. I knew how hard this had to be for Brianna, and I wanted to make it as easy as I could. She was trying and so would I.

Richard must have heard us coming down the hall because his eyes were focused on the door when we entered. "Hello, Stephan. Brianna." He nodded.

She'd stiffened up again, and I rubbed my fingers along her hip, trying to offer some comfort. It seemed to work as I felt the muscles beneath my fingers give a little more.

Turning, I addressed the man who'd been my father since the day my own passed away. "Richard." I smiled. "Diane said dinner is almost ready and sent us to get you."

"Ah," he said. "Very good." He rose from his high-backed leather chair and walked over to us. His eyes discreetly roamed Brianna's body as he made his way over to where we were standing. I knew that look. He was checking to see if she'd suffered any further damage, and I felt the anger bubble up inside me. Did he really think I'd harm her?

His eyes met mine then, and he seemed to notice my shift in demeanor. The look in his eyes turned apologetic, but it wasn't enough. I couldn't believe he'd think me capable of such a thing. Turning us both, I lead Brianna toward the dining room.

Halfway there, I felt his firm hand on my arm, which caused me to release my hold on Brianna. She kept walking at the same pace for a few more steps before slowing. I whipped around to face Richard, not waiting for him to speak. "Whatever it is you want to say will have to wait," I said, keeping my voice low so that only he would be able to hear me. "I promised her I would not leave her alone today, and I will not have her thinking my word means nothing."

I wrenched my arm away from him and closed the distance between us. She was almost at the door when I reached her, and her posture was once again stiff. I stopped her before we went in, not caring if Richard saw us or not. With one hand once again around her waist, I turned her toward me and placed the other on her face. "You are doing great," I said and leaned in to give her a soft peck on the lips.

When her eyes came open again, she looked calm, or at least calmer, so I guided us both into the dining room to take our seats. It was getting harder and harder for me not to kiss her every time I felt the impulse. Last night was a perfect example. Just having her on my lap had been a distraction. I hadn't thought much of it until she was sitting there pressed up against me.

Asking her to kiss me had been purely a last minute decision. I wanted to feel her lips again, and I justified it by telling myself it would give her a little sense of control while also preparing her for her role the following day at dinner. But all my justifications were just lies. Seeing her happy about school had triggered something in me. She had triggered something in me. And even now, sitting beside her, across from my aunt and uncle, the only thing I could think of was when I'd be able to touch her again.

Chapter Fourteen

Stephan

Having dinner with my family was something I used to do often, even after I'd left home. It wasn't until Tami, my last collared sub, had laid bare my lifestyle on a silver platter for my uncle that I'd made my visits less frequent.

I'm not sure which word best described Richard's reaction to the information: disappointed, embarrassed, angry, or all of the above. He'd called me at the office one afternoon and asked if I could stop by the house on my way home.

The request he made wasn't all that unusual, even though it didn't happen often. When I got there, however, I found Richard in his office with a strange look on his face. He had an exaggerated calm about him that reminded me of the time Logan and I'd snuck out of the house to meet up with two older women we'd met in town earlier that day.

It had taken me the better part of an hour just to calm him down once he'd gotten started, and another two hours after that to try and explain the way I lived. We'd ended the conversation in a stalemate of sorts. I knew he still didn't like my choices, but there was nothing I could do to change his mind.

This dinner reminded me of that night all over again. Diane

carried most of the conversation. She asked Brianna all the usual questions: how old she was, where she grew up, and how long she'd been in Minneapolis. All the while, Richard just sat watching. His eyes were mostly on Brianna but would occasionally fall to me, a clear look of concern in them.

My aunt didn't seem to notice the silence of her husband, or chose not to acknowledge it, as she continued with her motherly questioning. However, her inquiries came to an abrupt halt when Diane asked Brianna about her parents. I felt all the tension return to her body and listened to her breathing stagger before she finally whispered that her mom had died of cancer three years ago.

Thankfully, my aunt realized she was uncomfortable and started directing questions to me regarding the foundation. I answered all of them, keeping the conversation flowing but also keeping my eyes and my thoughts on the woman beside me. Although I was sad that Diane's line of questioning had upset Brianna, I had learned two valuable pieces of information: her mother was dead and she hadn't mentioned her father. Maybe the latter was an oversight due to the gravity her mother's death still held for her, but I didn't think so.

I was afraid Diane would try to approach Brianna again about her mother, so I made excuses to leave as soon as possible. After helping Brianna into the car, I turned to find Richard standing in the driveway only a few yards away. Sighing, I closed the distance between us knowing he would have his say one way or the other. He did not disappoint. "Is that necklace what I think it is?"

"Yes," I said, keeping my answer simple.

This time there was no question as to the emotion behind his eyes; he was disappointed in me. His next words put voice to that fact. "Stephan, that girl is obviously in need of help. I don't know what's happened to her, but what you're doing to her can't be helping. You have to know that."

My temper broke at that moment, and I did not restrain my words. "You have no idea what she's been through, not the slightest clue." I saw him start to speak and cut him off. "Just because you examined her does not mean you know anything about her. You haven't lived with her for the last two weeks. I have. So don't go trying to tell me what she does and doesn't need."

"Stephan, she needs help. I have people . . ."

"You don't have *people*. Your *people* would corner her and make her talk about what happened to her. You've seen her, Richard. She's talked more in the last twenty-four hours than she has in the last ten days. Brianna is making progress, and I will not have you ruin that. Don't try to get in the middle of something you don't understand."

Just then, I saw Diane come through the door. I was hoping she hadn't heard anything I'd said, but my hopes were dashed when I saw her face. Turning to her, I said in the calmest voice I could manage, "Thank you for dinner. It was delicious as always."

Without saying another word to my uncle, I walked to my car and got in.

Brianna sensed my mood and was incredibly still. I waited until I'd settled my emotions before saying, "You did well today, Brianna. I'm very proud of you."

"Thank you, Master," she said, but I noticed her posture had not relaxed in the least.

"What's on your mind?"

"Did I . . ." She paused. "Did I do something to upset him?"

With her question, I felt my anger at my uncle come to the surface once again. She did not need this. "No. He was upset with me. You did nothing wrong." She seemed to relax a little after that, and we finished our drive home in a comfortable silence.

The next morning, I went into the office expecting to find a load of paperwork on my desk, and I was not disappointed. What I hadn't expected to find was Lily. "Good morning, Lily. What brings you to my office first thing on a Monday morning?"

She pushed her small body off my desk with a flair that only she could pull off and turned to continually face me as I rounded my desk and took a seat. "How's Brianna?"

I looked at her closely, trying to find out what she was getting at when I realized that Logan must have told her my plans. "She's fine. And yes, to answer your question."

Lily tilted her head as she considered that. "So did it help?" she asked.

"Yes, I think it did," I answered. "At least, she hasn't woken me up screaming for the past two nights. I'd say that's progress."

She frowned. "I want to help her, Stephan."

Although I had tons of work in front of me, I needed to talk. "I know, and I want you to. I'm just not sure how to accomplish it."

"Bring her over to our place for dinner Thursday night." I looked at her skeptically. Lily was not a very good cook. It was something she was working on, but I wasn't sure if I was as brave as Logan. She must have read the look on my face because she sighed and said, "Logan will cook. I promise I'll stay out of the kitchen."

I pressed my thumb and forefinger to my temples as I considered my options. I knew I couldn't keep Brianna under lock and key the entire time. She needed to get out and socialize, especially since she'd be starting school in the fall. She knew Lily, and both Lily and Logan knew the situation. "Sure," I said with a sigh and turned back to the stack of paper on my desk. "Now, I need to get to work. Somehow I've got to manage to get out of here early."

"Anything I can do? I mean I'm waiting for some quotes to come back so everything is at a standstill for me right now."

A wave of protectiveness surged through me at the thought of someone other than me going with Brianna today, although I knew it was irrational. How had I become so attached to a woman in such a short time? The reality, however, was that if Lily was offering, I needed to take the help. Besides, I told myself, Brianna needed a friend and who better than Lily? "That would be great, Lily. Thank you. Are you free this afternoon?"

Lily's face broke out into a huge smile, and I could see the excitement radiating from her. "What do you need?"

The sight before me was just so funny that I couldn't help but laugh. "I haven't been able to get her a vehicle yet, and she needs to go to the lab near my uncle's office for some blood work."

"No problem," she said.

"She's also in charge of dinner and will need to pick up supplies." I paused before asking, "Are you sure you don't mind? She's still really unsure around people, and I don't know—"

"We'll be fine, Stephan. Don't worry."

I held my tongue, bottled up all the worries floating through my mind, and just said, "Thank you."

As soon as Lily left my office, I asked Jamie to come in. I knew she had work of her own to do, but there were certain things that could not be put off. She took down the list of things I needed done, including getting both my lawyer and Brad on the phone, adding an additional user to my cell phone plan, and getting another phone, along with setting up temporary transportation for Brianna. They were things I'd normally do myself, but I was not used to having a submissive 24/7 either.

By the time the morning was over, I'd given my lawyer all the information I had on Brianna, and he assured me he would have something to me no later than this afternoon. One of the things I loved about Oscar was that he didn't ask more questions than necessary. I arranged for Brad to spend tomorrow morning at my home and gave him detailed instructions of what I wanted. And my last call had been to set up a checking account for Brianna. She'd need money to buy the food and pay for gas.

Jamie came in shortly before lunch to tell me that the car would be delivered this evening and the cell phone was arriving via courier this afternoon. Thankfully, everything was falling into place, except for the fact I'd not gotten much of my own work done. That was what my afternoon was for.

Brianna

I spent my morning cleaning. It wasn't like Master's home needed to be cleaned, but I didn't know what else to do with myself. I missed my books.

There wasn't anything I could do about that, though. I knew where they were. I'd seen him place them on his nightstand when we'd come downstairs yesterday.

But I wasn't stupid enough to go against the punishment he'd handed out. Although I hated not having my books, I knew it could have been much worse. And it wasn't like he hadn't warned me.

By the time noon rolled around, I couldn't find anything else to clean so I sat down to watch some television. I found a local news station and watched them talk about all the horrors happening around the city.

My head whipped around as I heard a key in the front door. I jumped to my feet, rounded the couch, and took my position.

Soft clicks I recognized sounded on the hardwood floor, and I looked up. Lily.

"Hi," she said, her grin nearly splitting her face.

"Hi," I answered back.

I wasn't sure what to do for a second. What was she doing here? Did Master send her?

Lily's smile turned into a smirk as she looked down at me. "You can get up, you know. I'm not Stephan."

Oh, right.

Quickly I stood and decided to go with the fact that she wasn't my Master and asked, "Did he send you here?"

"Yes," she said, walking farther into the room. She picked up the remote, switched off the television, and turned back to me. "And you can call him Stephan." She paused and then whispered, "I won't tell him if you won't."

She giggled at the last part. I wasn't sure if she was laughing at what she'd said or at me. And I didn't know how I felt about calling Master by his given name out loud. Sure, I did it in my head sometimes, but voicing it was different. So instead I told her okay and left it at that.

"Well," Lily said, coming back to stand in front of me, "Stephan said you needed to go get some blood work done today, and that I'm to take you to the grocery store."

Master had mentioned the blood work last night, but he made it sound as if he was going to be the one to take me. It wasn't that I had an aversion to Lily, it was just I'd been expecting him. Careful with my wording I asked, "So you're going to be the one taking me?"

Her face sobered. "Is that okay?"

She looked almost sad. It just didn't seem to fit her. "Yes." I nodded.

Then the smile was back. "Well, okay then. Let's get going, shall we?"

Having my blood drawn wasn't as bad as I'd thought it would be. Lily stayed with me the whole time. And then, at the grocery store, she even held my hand when I started to panic after a man brushed against me.

I liked Lily. She was so nice to me even though she knew what I was. And she talked to me, asked me questions. There were so many things I wanted to ask her, but I didn't know how.

She helped me put the groceries away and stayed while I started dinner. Lily carried most of the conversation as I worked, but I liked having her there and keeping me company.

Just before five, she said goodbye, promising to see me soon, and left me to finish dinner on my own. I decided to make fettuccine alfredo with grilled chicken. The sauce took a little work but other than that, it was pretty straightforward. I just hoped he liked it.

Right on time, I heard the key in the door. With a flick of my wrist, I turned the sauce to simmer and took my place on the floor.

His steps were solid as he walked toward me. And just like Saturday, his hand found its way into my hair. "Good evening, Brianna."

I took a chance and answered, "Good evening, Master."

The fact that I'd answered seemed to please him as the tips of his fingers grazed my scalp before his hand left me. "Stand," he said, his voice warm.

Lifting myself up, I stood, still keeping my eyes on the floor. I saw his right hand twitch slightly and thought he was going to touch me again, but it remained at his side.

"Dinner smells wonderful. Is it ready?"

I nodded. "Yes, Master."

"Very good," he said, taking a step back. "Set everything on the table, and I'll be back in a minute."

As soon as he disappeared into his room, I went into the kitchen and started putting everything in the serving dishes I'd found. He had such a well-stocked kitchen. Everything I needed was there and then some.

By the time he walked back into the main room, I had all the food on the table and was standing close by. Keeping my head lowered, I waited for him to approach me. He came to a stop in front of me and this time he did bring his hand up to touch my face very lightly before sitting down in his chair. "Join me, Brianna."

I took a seat and waited for him to fill his plate before hesitantly reaching to fill my own. We ate in silence for a while, and he seemed to be enjoying what I'd prepared.

Sometimes I found myself watching his hands and remembering how often his touch had calmed me, but then the knowledge of the other things those same hands could do brought me back to reality. It was like he was tearing down my defenses and that scared me more than anything. He would hurt me just like Ian did; it was only a matter of time.

When he was finished, he patiently waited for me. As I lay the fork down on my empty plate, he reached out to lift my chin. Once I was looking at him, he released me. "I've arranged a vehicle for your use this week until we can find you something more permanent. I also spoke with Brad, and he'll be here at eight thirty tomorrow morning. I expect you to give him your full cooperation," he said, looking meaningfully at me. I nodded.

He looked like he was going to say something else, but the phone ringing cut him off.

Master stood, leaving me at the table waiting while he spoke with whoever was on the other line. When he hung up, he didn't come back to the table. Instead, he instructed me to clean up and that he would return in a few minutes.

I waited to get up and do as I was told until after he had walked out the door. It didn't take long to put everything away and get the dishes into the dishwasher. When everything was done, I wasn't sure what to do with myself, but only moments later, he came back through the door.

Instead of walking toward me or addressing me at all, he went to his bedroom and disappeared. He was gone for a couple of minutes and then walked back out as if nothing had happened.

Master walked over to the same plush chair he'd sat in the night we'd talked about my school paperwork. And just like that night, he told me to come to him. I went and he extended his hand indicating that, once again, I was to sit on his lap.

When I sat down, his arm came around me just as it had the other night. I was still nervous, but not as much as before. His touch was different when he was displeased with me; it was firm and almost detached. Right now, his touch was calm and gentle. I had no problems sitting here all night if that was what pleased him.

I kept my head lowered as he began to speak. "I have some things for you."

He reached into his pocket and pulled out a cell phone and a key ring with a remote attached. He held them out for me, waiting for me to take them, so I did.

Looking them both over, I noticed the key was for a BMW. I wondered if it would be similar to the one he drove. The phone was nothing overly fancy, but it wasn't a basic model either. Of course, it could have been just that for all I knew. I'd never owned a cell phone before, but this one fit his personality, if that made sense, and nothing I'd seen of his yet struck me as low end.

After allowing me a few minutes to look them both over, he had me open the cell phone and we went through how to use it. He'd already programmed his numbers into the phone for both cell and work, but he'd also put Lily's in there.

I couldn't help the smile that covered my face and he noticed. His free hand drew light patterns on my arm. "You like Lily? You enjoy spending time with her?"

"Yes, Master. Very much."

"Well, that's good then. She has invited us over for dinner Thursday evening." I smiled at the knowledge that I'd get to see Lily again in a few days.

"I also spoke with my lawyer. He was able to locate copies of your records and is sending them via messenger to my office tomorrow. I was hoping to have them today as well, but apparently he encountered a little trouble."

My brow creased and the smile on my face disappeared. Trouble. Where would he have gone to get the information? Dallas or Two Harbors? I really hoped it was Dallas, but I was putting my money on Two Harbors. Dallas had no reason to give him trouble.

I felt Master shift his weight and suddenly I was flush against him with my head on his shoulder. But for once, I wasn't scared of him. He wasn't the monster I was afraid of.

Chapter Fifteen

Brianna

Over the next two days, a pattern started to form. Although my days varied, my nights were very much the same. When Master came home, I would be waiting by the door for him. After a brief greeting, he'd disappear into his bedroom while I put the food on the table. We'd eat dinner together, mostly in silence, and then we'd retire to the living room and his chair.

Every night when he'd have me sit in his lap, it was the same. First, he'd ask me about my day, what I'd done. Then he'd tell me about his.

I learned a great deal about him. The Coleman Foundation raised money to help those who couldn't afford medical treatment. They used the money to set up funds accessible through local hospitals. Master even told me several stories of how the money from the foundation had saved lives.

It was one more thing about my new Master that didn't add up. I couldn't see how a man who helped people every day could be like Ian. But he wasn't like Ian, except for the fact that I was his property. I was beyond confused.

On Tuesday, he'd asked me about Brad and the fitness routine he'd set up. Wednesday, it was about the veal I'd made. Master always found something to question me about, and he expected me to talk. It always felt strange getting those first few sentences out, but after that it was easier.

And then he'd always end our talks with a kiss. Monday and Tuesday he kissed me. But last night he'd asked for me to kiss him again. I'd still been nervous but not nearly as much as last time. His lips were familiar to me now.

Tonight would be different, though. He'd called me during his lunch, on the cell phone he'd gotten me, to let me know he'd be home around four and to be ready to leave when he arrived. Master didn't give me any details, but I had a feeling we were not only going to Lily's tonight. None of that mattered, however. I would do as he asked and be ready when he came home.

I walked out of the room I'd been given just after four, freshly showered and dressed in a pair of black slacks and a deep purple blouse. It was dressy, but not too fancy since I'd chosen to wear more casual flats. After taking a final look in the mirror, I took my place on the floor and waited.

Less than five minutes later, the lock turned in the door and Master entered. I heard some movement as he set something down on the floor, and then he walked over to me. "You may stand, Brianna."

I stood up and closed my eyes as his hand found my hair as it always did. It was so strange how much I liked this moment when he came home. His fingers came down to lift my chin, and I raised my eyes to meet his. Something seemed to float behind the surface as he looked at me, but soon it was gone.

"Are you ready?" he asked.

"Yes, Master."

"Good," he said, already moving us both toward the doorway. "We have a stop to make first."

I would have never guessed this was where we were going in a thousand years. He maneuvered his car into a front parking spot at the DMV. Master seemed to sense the unspoken question of my thoughts and answered, "You need a license. We will just say that yours was lost and get a new one printed."

He made it all sound so simple, and as it turned out it was. Master walked up to the window with me and handed the woman several pieces of paper. I didn't see what they were until she gave them back: my birth certificate and a copy of my school records complete with photograph. After that, she asked me a few questions covering my height and weight, had me sign a piece of paper, and took my picture. It took until almost five thirty for everything, but in the end I once again had my driver's license.

As we got back in his car, I continued to look at the picture staring back at me on the shiny new license. It was me, but yet it wasn't me.

I knew that didn't make any sense since it was *me*, but I seemed different somehow. The picture on my old license had been of a sixteen–and-a-half-year-old girl who, while so happy to be able to drive, was also still dealing with the loss of her mother. This woman looking back at me now lacked the innocence of the other. She could pretend the world was good and wonderful. I could not.

Glancing over at the man sitting beside me, I once again tried to figure out his motives. He was a contradiction that I couldn't figure out, and I didn't know if I wanted to anymore. If I was supposed to spend the foreseeable future with him, I would not complain or worry. He was my Master, and I was his slave. I was okay with that.

Stephan

Brianna had slowly begun to relax over the last few days. She still had her moments, but they were becoming less frequent. It was so hard to believe that this was the same broken woman from two weeks ago.

But she was. I had to remember that every single second of every day. Mostly, I tried to keep things predictable for her, and it seemed to help.

I wanted her to trust me, and selfishly I needed some form of physical contact with her. As a result, I'd arranged it so that when we'd talk each night, she would sit in my lap. Amazingly, it seemed to be working. My touch had calmed her in the past when we'd been outside my home, but now it seemed to have the same effect inside.

However, feeling her on my lap and not acting on my instincts was difficult. I continued to settle for kissing her at the end of each night when what I truly wanted was to explore that body of hers. I knew it was wrong, which was why I had taken to ending every night this week in my shower. My nightly solo sessions were not enough, but they had to be for now. She was still scared of me, and I would not have any sexual relationship we might have be based on that.

As we pulled up to Logan and Lily's condo, I began to wonder once again how Brianna would react to my best friend. He was usually very good at reading people, so I was hoping he'd find a quick way to make her feel at ease.

I walked to the other side of the vehicle and opened the door for her. She got out slowly, and I knew she was nervous. I lifted her chin to make her look at me, and brushed my lips gently against hers. "These are friends. You do not need to be afraid."

Brianna nodded and whispered, "Yes, Master."

I stepped back and guided us inside the building and into the elevator. I pulled her closer to my side as I pressed the button for the top floor. To anyone on the outside, we would look like a normal couple.

The doors opened, and we walked down a short hallway until we reached a door with two decorative steps in front. I knocked, and in less than a minute the door opened revealing a very excited Lily.

Lily was no longer in work clothes but had donned a little black skirt and frilly tank top. She managed to pull off the dressy casual look well, even with her current bare feet.

Before I knew what was happening, she had pulled us both inside with a squeal and enveloped the woman at my side in a hug. Brianna's reaction was delayed for no more than two seconds before she hugged Lily back, and I released a deep sigh, relaxing just a little more. Maybe tonight would be okay.

We were ushered farther into the apartment, and we found Logan in the kitchen moving expertly from one dish to the other. He looked up. "Hey, Stephan." He smiled at me and then shifted his attention to the woman Lily had her arm wrapped around. "And this must be Brianna." Logan wiped his hands on the towel he had tucked at his waist and came around the island. Extending his hand, he said, "It's good to finally meet you."

She didn't take his hand, but instead looked at me. I nodded, letting her know it was okay. Her hand came up cautiously to shake his.

Logan didn't hold on for long before moving once again to take his place behind the counter.

There was tension in the room that hadn't been there moments before, and once again I was worried. I knew she wasn't good with people, especially new people. It would just take time. But even though I knew this, all I wanted to do was shield her from it.

Lily broke the tension by asking if she could get us something to drink. I told her water would be fine, and she moved behind Logan to get glasses. When she handed our water to us moments later, she asked, "Can I steal Brianna for a while? I want to show her the new dress I bought." I nodded, and she was off with Brianna in tow.

I could hear Lily rambling on until a door shut in the background. And although I knew she was safe with Lily, I still worried anytime she was out of my sight.

Logan cleared his throat, drawing my attention. I raised my eyebrow, silently telling him to go ahead and say what he had to say. He reached into the oven, took out four beautifully cooked steaks, and set them on the counter. Taking a piece of tinfoil, he covered them loosely and then turned back to me. "Lily says she's doing better."

"She is. Much better, actually."

He raised his own eyebrow at this and then shook his head. "If that's really the case, I do hope you know what you're doing. I know you collared her, but do you really think she's ever going to get to the point you need her to be?"

For some reason his words lit a fire in me that I didn't understand. "I will not give up on her, Logan." He jerked at my tone, and realizing what I'd done, I softened my voice. "There's no telling what tomorrow might bring or what she'll want once I tell her she is free should she so choose. Truthfully, that possibility scares me. I know the chances of her wanting to stay with me are not good after what she's been through. And Logan, it was bad. She hasn't talked to me about it yet, but just by her reactions to certain things . . . I don't know if she will ever fully trust me. Or anyone for that matter."

Logan threw a strainer full of asparagus into a pot of boiling water. "She's like this all the time?"

I shrugged. "The first few days were worse. She's a little calmer at home now, more relaxed. But anytime we're out around people, yes, she's like this."

"She drew closer to you when I approached her. And she deferred to you."

"Brianna is very submissive. Too submissive sometimes. Like I said, when she's home it's better, but I think that has a lot to do with the fact that she knows what to expect. I'm trying to keep us in a routine as much as possible."

"Probably a good idea."

"Yes."

"I already know the answer to this, but I'm going to ask it anyway. Are you planning on involving the police?"

Taking a deep breath, I closed my eyes and pinched the bridge of my nose. "No. First, I have no idea how I would explain my involvement without it becoming fodder for the press. And second, I can't see that helping her. What's done is done. It would be her word against Ian's. He would fight, and she would back down."

Just then, Lily and Brianna reentered the room. Lily strolled to Logan's side and asked if there was anything she could do to help. He quickly gave her several plates to take to the table.

Brianna came to stand beside me, but kept her head down. I brought a finger up under her chin. "No looking down tonight." She nodded, and we made our way to our seats.

Dinner was pleasant enough. The food was wonderful, almost as good as Brianna's, and I said as much. I saw her blush at my compliment, but she refrained from commenting. Logan did ask her some questions, and she answered but didn't elaborate. Everything she said was to be polite, nothing more.

It was after nine when we arrived home, but I wasn't ready for bed yet. I wanted to keep our evening ritual and asked her to join me in the chair. She sat down on my lap, folding her hands in front of her as always. I brushed her hair back so that I could see her face. "Did you have a nice time tonight?"

"Yes, Master."

"What did you think of Logan?"

She hesitated before answering. "He seems nice."

"But?"

"Nothing, Master."

"Brianna," I said in a voice that brooked no argument.

"He's your friend," she said. Brianna clamped her lips together but said no more.

"Yes?"

"You said you don't share," she whispered.

Never in my wildest dreams did I think that would be what was on her mind.

"Have I ever lied to you?" She shook her head. "Answer me, Brianna."

"No, Master. You've never lied to me."

"So why do you think I would do so now? Logan is a friend. He is also with Lily. But even if that wasn't the case, I told you I don't share, and I meant it. You are my submissive, Brianna. You serve me, no one else."

My voice was harsh. This was the first time she had truly angered me. I couldn't believe she was thinking this.

"Please forgive me, Master. I didn't mean to make you upset. I just . . ." She paused and then said, "I was scared." She cringed as the words left her mouth.

Suddenly all my anger left me, and I pulled her close, bringing our noses together so she had to look directly into my eyes. She admitted she was scared. This was a huge step.

"You are mine, Brianna. You do not have to fear me or anyone else. Tell me you understand."

"I understand."

"Good," I said. "Now give me a good-night kiss. I have a long day tomorrow, and I need to get to bed."

She didn't hesitate before her mouth covered mine. Her lips moved with more confidence each time as she pressed against me.

When she pulled back, I cupped the back of her head and placed one more soft kiss on her lips before we both got up. I walked her to her bedroom door and pushed her hair back over her shoulders. "Good night, Brianna."

"Good night, Master."

Chapter Sixteen

Brianna

Before Master left for work Friday morning, he told me not to worry about dinner that night. He said that he would order a pizza and told me to select a movie for us to watch.

The morning seemed to drag after breakfast. I went upstairs to work out as instructed, and I managed to go through his DVD collection and pick out a movie for later. I drew out making the selection just to have something to do. I'd never been a big television person, and that hadn't changed. In the end I'd settled on an action film from a few years ago.

At noon, I made myself some lunch in Master's kitchen. I loved it in there.

After eating, I had nothing left to do with myself, so I sat down and turned on the television. I flipped through the one hundred and two channels, but came up empty. You'd think after ten months of not being allowed to watch television at all that I'd be able to find something that would hold my interest, but that just wasn't the case. All I wanted was my books. The one thing I couldn't have.

Sighing, I started again from the beginning, hoping that this time something would catch my eye. But less than halfway through, my cell phone rang. I'd left it on the counter earlier, so I rushed over to answer it, thinking it might be Master. It had already rung four times before I picked it up. "Hello?"

"Hey, Brianna," Lily said in an excited voice.

"Hi, Lily." My voice was much more subdued.

"Are you busy?"

"No." I walked back into the living room.

"Great!" she nearly screamed through the phone. "I wanted to ask you what you thought of Logan."

I felt my nerves beginning to take over, and I tried to stay calm. Did I do something wrong last night? Did Master say something to her? Or did she say something to him?

He seemed all right last night. Well, except for my stupid question. And in a way, it had been stupid. Master was right; he'd never lied to me.

Obviously I'd been quiet for too long, because Lily's voice came through the line again. "Did you not like him?"

"No," I said quickly. I pressed my lips together as I considered what to say. Finally I decided to stay consistent. "He was nice."

"He is nice," she declared adamantly. "He's wonderful." She sighed and then went in a totally different direction. "Stephan said you were going to go back to school."

"Yeah," I said, sheepishly. I hadn't been a big talker before, and now . . .

"So tell me, when do you start?"

She sounded so excited, and it was rubbing off on me a little. "This fall. September."

"Are you excited? The first two years of college for me were kind of boring, but once I got into the classes for my major it was so much fun."

"Yes, I'm excited."

Then she sighed. "You can talk to me, you know. I know things are strange for you right now, but you can trust me, and you can trust Stephan."

When she said Stephan's name, my entire body reacted with a weird mixture of fear and something else I really couldn't name.

"I . . ." I didn't know what to say. There was no way I could tell her what I was feeling and why. She knew my Master. Worked for him, even. No. I couldn't share those things with her. I trusted her, but I didn't trust her, if that made sense. And there I was again, in the state that I seemed to constantly live in: confusion.

Finally, I heard her sigh on the other end. "Okay. I won't push. Stephan would have my head if I did. But will you promise to call me if you want to talk?"

I heard the pleading in her voice and couldn't say no. "Yes."

"Good." She paused. "Okay, well I'd better get back to work. I'll see you later, Brianna."

Lily didn't wait for me to say goodbye; she just ended the call. I was really glad she hadn't pushed me. I didn't think I could say no to her indefinitely, but I didn't want to either lie to her or anger Master.

I spent the rest of my afternoon watching some home improvement shows. They really held no interest for me, but at least it was neat to see the before and after.

Usually I'd start dinner around four or four thirty, depending on what I was cooking, but tonight I just remained where I was. Master would be home soon. At least once he was here I'd have something to do.

At five twenty-five, I took my position on the floor. Less than five minutes later, Master walked through the door. I waited with my head down for him to approach me and took a deep breath when his fingers found my hair.

His hand fell away, and he reached out, helping me to stand. "Good evening, Brianna."

It was the same greeting every evening, and I answered with the same response. "Good evening, Master."

He stepped back from me and slipped off his suit jacket. "What would you like on your pizza?"

I knew from experience that giving him a whatever-you-wish-Master was not what he wanted. If he asked me a specific question, he expected a specific answer. "Anything but peppers and onions."

"Very good." The smile in his voice was clear, although I was not looking at him. It made me happy that my answer pleased him, and a small smile tugged on my own lips.

He walked away from me then, leaving me standing where I was. I heard his voice behind me ordering our pizza. It was soft and calming tonight; he was in a good mood.

Master didn't acknowledge me as he hung up the phone, and walked across the room and into his bedroom. I stood in my spot, not sure what to do but knowing he wouldn't leave me here for long, or at least hoping he wouldn't. I wasn't too worried, though, given his mood. He'd give me instructions soon. So I relaxed and waited.

Several minutes later, I heard him reenter the main room. He didn't come toward me, though. Instead, I heard the sound of him sitting. And somehow I knew what would come next.

"Come here," he instructed. I went to him.

He opened his arms, and I knew he wanted me to sit in his lap. We did this every night, but usually it was after dinner.

I sat demurely with my head down while he wrapped his arms around my waist.

"How are you today, Brianna?" he asked.

"I'm fine, Master."

"What did you do while I was gone?"

And so I cataloged my day for him. He listened intently. When I'd pause, he'd prompt me to continue. These talks of ours were getting easier, but it was still strange to me. Master seemed to want to know my answers, but I didn't know why it would matter to him. This crossed my mind every night, and I'd decided that again it didn't matter. I would give him whatever he wanted from me.

After I was finished, he said, "Lily told me she called you. She also told me you seemed afraid to talk to her."

I clamped my lips together. Was he angry that I hadn't talked to her, or that she could tell I was afraid to?

His next words answered my question. "Brianna, I'm not upset with you," he said, rubbing his right hand up and down my arm. "But I want you to know that you can talk to Lily about anything you wish. I promise that I will not be upset." Master paused. It was obvious that he was expecting an answer from me.

"Yes, Master."

A hand came up to cup my cheek as he lifted my eyes to his. "I'm not like Ian. I hope you know that by now, Brianna."

I did know that. He was so completely different from my former Master. There were times in the last two-and-a-half weeks that I'd actually been happy. That had never happened in the ten months I was with Ian.

Before I could answer him, though, the home phone rang. He patted my leg, indicating he wanted me to get up from his lap. I slid off and onto the floor, kneeling.

He rose from the chair and went to answer the phone. I could hear from the conversation that our pizza had arrived. When he hung up the phone again, he approached me.

Without instructing me to stand, he raised my chin so that I was looking up at him. "Set the table. I'll be back in a few minutes, and we will eat. Then we shall watch the movie you've selected." His fingers brushed my face as he released me, and then he was gone.

Knowing he wouldn't be gone long, I set plates, napkins, glasses, and a pitcher of water on the table. Master rarely drank anything other than water except for the juice or milk he sometimes had for breakfast.

Once everything was in place, I knelt beside the table to wait for him. It took a little longer than I'd thought it would, but eventually he came back through the door, and I could smell the pizza.

I was hungry; my lunch had been hours ago. His heavy steps came toward me along with the delicious scent of cheese and grease. I heard him set the box down on the table, and then he said, "Join me."

Tonight's dinner was not much different than the others we'd had at this table. We ate mostly in silence, concentrating on our meal. He finished first, as usual, and watched me finish.

Afterward, he instructed me to clean up and then join him in the living room. It didn't take long, and soon I was once again sitting in Master's lap, and we were watching the movie.

Stephan

When Lily told me about her conversation with Brianna, I knew I needed to give her permission to speak freely, or she never would. We were making progress, little by little. She rarely hesitated anymore when we were at home and seemed happy when I walked through the door each night. It gave me hope.

Our evening sessions in my chair were making her open up. I hadn't mentioned her time with Ian at all since she'd been with me, but I'd felt that I needed to tonight. The time would come soon for me to begin pushing her again, and she needed to know going into it that I would not act or react as he had.

I knew the trust I had gained from her thus far was fragile, but it was something. Something to build on, something I could use.

She sat on my lap with my arms surrounding her while we watched *Transformers*. It wasn't really my type of movie, but the CGI was pretty good. I'd noticed that both times I had asked her to select something for us to watch, her choices had not been what I'd expected. Brianna's choice of literature made me think she was a romantic, and yet she'd steered clear of the romantic comedies I had in my collection. I would have to explore that later.

It wasn't that I was a big fan of those movies personally, but I did have guests and subs occasionally in my home. I needed to have a variety to meet various needs and tastes.

When the movie was over, I wasn't ready to let her go. Her head was resting back against my shoulder, and she felt so right here with me. I'd always felt a sense of possession with the submissives I'd collared, but this wasn't possessiveness exactly. That was there, too, but it wasn't just that.

I couldn't explain it, so I pushed it aside. What I needed now was focus. "What did you think of the movie?" I asked her, turning her in my lap to face me once again.

She scrunched up her nose as if considering her answer. "There was a lot of action," she finally answered.

"Do you like action movies?"

"Yes," she said hesitantly.

"But?"

"I don't know," she whispered. I was just about to prompt her again a little sterner when she added, "I thought there'd be more story."

I smiled. "I agree. I tend to like my movies with more depth of plot and less over-the-top graphics." The corners of her mouth turned up.

We talked a little more about the movie before I noticed the time. There were things to do tomorrow, and we needed to get to bed. "It's time for bed, Brianna." She nodded and waited. I did not need to tell her what came next; she knew. The only thing she was waiting on was the instruction on who would lead tonight.

The desire to push her overwhelmed my senses, but I resisted. Not tonight. So I brought her chin up, watched as she closed her eyes, and pressed my lips to hers.

Oh, how I wanted to deepen the kiss. I wanted to tilt her head back and push my tongue between her closed lips. She would taste so sweet, and I wanted more.

But instead, I kept my lips together and contented myself with the gentle gliding and sucking motion we shared. Over the last few nights, she'd gathered confidence in our nighttime kisses and was no longer impassive. Brianna met me movement for movement.

When I pulled back, I kept a hold of her face so that when she opened her eyes, she was looking directly into mine. Her lovely blue eyes held the trust I so desperately wanted from her. I smiled, and she smiled back before we both got up and walked to our respective bedrooms.

I stripped before walking into the bathroom and turning on the shower. Stepping in, I walked into the spray. The warm water pounded my shoulders, which were begging for relief from the tension they were holding, but I knew the only thing that would do that. Without further pause, I reached down and grasped my already hard shaft in my hand. If my life for the last five years hadn't been about control, I don't think I could have managed the last four hours. By thinking of anything but how her body felt against mine, I'd been able to keep my erection to a minimal state while she sat in my lap.

As I increased my rhythm, I let all those feelings go. This woman was doing things to me, and she wasn't even aware of it. She wasn't even trying! Her hair, her lips . . . I bit the side of my cheek to stifle the moan that broke through my throat as I exploded all over the wall of my shower.

Letting my head fall forward out of the spray, I waited until my breathing was back to normal before quickly rinsing and shutting off the water. Turning, I let my back hit the wall. I hadn't jacked off this much since before I left for college. I had no idea what was wrong with me, what it was about her that did this to me.

The next morning, I let her sleep in while I went upstairs to check my e-mail. There was one from Lily, reminding me of the annual dinner coming up in three weeks for North Memorial Hospital that I was to attend. She wanted to know if I'd be bringing Brianna.

It was a question I didn't have the answer to. I was very proud of the progress she'd made, but she was still very unpredictable around strangers. What if it would be too much for her?

But the fact that she would be starting school this fall made me reconsider. She wouldn't have me there with her at school if something happened, which I hoped it didn't, but she would have to interact with people she'd never met before.

Maybe coming with me would not be a bad thing. At least at the dinner, I would be with her. I could intercede if necessary. With my mind made up, I replied to Lily letting her know Brianna would need a dress.

Shortly after I hit send, I heard movement downstairs that let me know that Brianna was awake. I closed down the computer and made my way down the steps.

Hearing me coming, she was waiting, in position, on the floor. Brianna was wearing jeans and a fitted red T-shirt. Her hair was pulled up off her neck in a simple ponytail.

She looked absolutely beautiful as always, and I felt those all-too-familiar stirrings. I pushed them down and walked into the kitchen.

"Good morning, Brianna. You may stand."

She stood but remained where she was. I decided I wanted some interaction this morning. We would be going out today, and she needed to relax. I knew cooking would do that for her. "Would you like to help me with breakfast?"

"Yes, Master," she answered and moved quickly to my side.

"I was thinking maybe pancakes. Do you think we can manage that?"

She smiled. "Yes."

I smiled back, although it went unseen by my companion. "Lead the way, Brianna. Just tell me what you need me to do."

It was the first time I'd given her clear instructions to take the lead other than the times I'd told her to kiss me. She hesitated for a few seconds, but then began to move.

Brianna disappeared into the pantry and came out with her arms full. She laid her items on the counter, pressed her lips together for over a minute, and then very quietly asked, "I need . . . could you get one egg and the milk, please, Master?"

I wanted to laugh, but I didn't because in a way it was more sad than funny. I'd told her to tell me what she needed, and even with that, she was still nervous about asserting herself. I got what she'd requested out of the refrigerator and laid them down beside the items she'd gotten.

Without hesitating, she reached into a lower cabinet and retrieved a mixing bowl I'd never seen before. She also turned on the flat surface of my stovetop and sprayed it with Pam. I watched as she flawlessly put exact amounts of each ingredient into the bowl before stirring.

Once everything was all mixed together, she took a ladle and placed three near-perfect circles onto the sizzling hot surface. Watching her never got old.

While the batter was cooking, she retrieved three plates from an upper cabinet. She laid one plate down on the counter but continued to hold the other two. This was where she stopped.

I realized she was waiting on me to tell her it was okay to leave the kitchen to set the table. Instead, I decided to make things easier. Taking the plates from her, I said, "How about I set the table, while you make sure our breakfast doesn't burn?"

As soon as I turned my back, I felt her move. I knew she was flipping the pancakes and even half done, they smelled wonderful.

It didn't take me long to set everything out, but when I returned to the kitchen, Brianna had a stack of finished pancakes on a plate and was stirring a smaller pan full of syrup. She stiffened just slightly when I approached but didn't stop what she was doing. I stepped up behind her and reached around to take the now full plate. The urge to kiss her neck was strong, but I resisted and quickly took the new items to the table along with glasses and milk for the both of us.

After breakfast, we headed to the university. I'd gotten a list from Karen of the books Brianna would require, and we also needed to get her photo taken for her student ID. I knew it was early, but given what she'd been through, I wanted to give her plenty of time to prepare and get used to the idea. On the way there, I'd told her where we were going and why.

As we got closer to campus and began seeing signs indicating various UM landmarks, her excitement seemed to get the better of her. I was excited for her, too, but she needed to keep her focus. She knew better than anyone how dangerous this world could be. I needed her to do her part to stay safe.

I kept an eye on her as we walked into the campus bookstore. We passed a group of guys on the way in, and they each paused to look her over briefly. I didn't need to read their thoughts to know what they were thinking. And with that knowledge came that feeling of wanting to mark what was mine.

It was stupid, considering the situation. I tried to shake it off. Putting a hand on her back, I guided her the rest of the way.

Brianna stayed by my side the entire time. I could tell she was very aware of her surroundings, which was good. She needed to be.

We walked out of the bookstore with more books than I thought possible for a twelve-week course. Brianna was holding onto her bounty with zeal. I loved seeing her this happy.

Next, I took her into the admissions building, where they took the student ID photos. An upperclassman sat behind the desk doing some paperwork when we came in.

He greeted us pleasantly enough. After telling him what we were there for, he ushered Brianna into a small room that had been set up for pictures. She went with him, but I could tell she was reluctant to leave my side.

I could see them both through the open doorway. The student worker took his position behind the camera. "All right. Just look right up here," he said, smiling at her.

I watched her clamp her lips together, and then she surprised me by reaching up to touch her collar.

Then, with a deep breath, she relaxed, looked up at the camera, and gave a small smile. If I'd ever had doubts about collaring her, they were now gone.

"Okay, all done," the student said, walking back to his desk. "It usually takes about ten days for the ID to be ready," he said, "so you can come back to pick it up anytime after that." He handed her a paper to sign. She did so and handed it back to him.

He looked it over quickly, then set it down on the desk, looked back up at her, and smiled. "Welcome to the University of Minnesota, Brianna."

I felt her move closer to me. "Thank you for your help," I answered for her and hurried us back out the door.

Once we were outside, she seemed to relax again. She hadn't reacted this way with the woman in the bookstore, so that told me it was the fact that it was a man. That wasn't surprising, but it could become problematic, as I had no idea if her teacher would be male or female.

We got into the car, and I navigated back out of the campus

area, heading straight to my favorite BMW dealer. The car was already purchased. It was just a matter of signing some paperwork.

I didn't tell her where we were going, so when I pulled into the dealership her eyes widened in surprise. She didn't question me, but I knew she wanted to.

After getting out, I went to her door and opened it for her. She followed me silently into the dealership where Joel greeted us. "Mr. Coleman, you're right on time. I have everything you need over here."

As we sat down, I asked, "How's your mom doing, Joel? Is she still undergoing treatment?"

"No, Mr. Coleman. She got the all clear from the doc six months ago."

"That's great." I smiled as I took the papers from him. "I'm glad she's doing better."

Reading over the paperwork took a while, but Brianna sat stoically by my side. Once everything was signed, Joel made copies and handed me the packet of ownership information I'd need. "The car arrived this morning. Would you like to see it?" Joel asked.

"Yes. I think Brianna would like to see her new vehicle."

It took her a minute, but then she managed to say, "Yes. Thank you."

We walked to the back of the parking lot until we came to the 7-Series I'd ordered for Brianna. It was exactly the same as mine, except hers was blue, where I had classic black.

The woman in question stayed close to me but remained silent as I made my way around the car. I went to the driver's side and opened the door. New car smell hit me full in the face.

After giving the inside a cursory look, I turned to Brianna. "Would you like to have a seat in your new car?" She was pressing her lips together again, but after a brief pause she nodded.

Brianna slid into the car. She sat motionless for a few minutes. I debated whether or not to prompt her but decided to wait her out. Finally her hands came up and touched first the steering wheel and then the center console and dash. Her fingers were reverent as they explored, and I had a sudden flash of what it would feel like to have her touch me like that.

This was getting ridiculous. I wasn't a teenager anymore.

It was Joel who broke me out of my lusting thoughts. "What do you think, miss?"

She jumped a little at his interruption, but answered him. "It's very nice." Short, simple, polite, that was all Brianna gave when out in public. I could get more out of her in my chair but sometimes even that took work.

After she got out of the vehicle, she moved as close to my side as possible without touching me. I finished up with Joel, and before we took our leave, I confirmed that the car would be delivered later today. As soon as we were both inside my car, I placed my hand over hers, waiting to feel her relax.

It happened almost instantly. I smiled, removed my hand, and set the car in motion to take us home.

Chapter Seventeen

Stephan

Brianna was quiet the entire ride home, and I wondered what she was thinking. I caught her clamping her lips together a few times, which told me she wasn't just passively watching the buildings go by.

When we arrived back at the condo, I went upstairs and let her know she was free to do as she wished until it was time to make dinner. As I logged onto my e-mail, I could hear her moving around downstairs and wondered what she was doing with her time. My mind seemed to be on little else but her these days.

Never had one woman dominated my thoughts as she did. I had no idea what it meant, but I had to know everything I could about her. As the search engine appeared on the screen in front of me, I typed in the name *Brianna Reeves*.

After only a second, a list of options popped up. Many of them were irrelevant, but I did find the obituary for her mother, Carrie. I clicked on the link and read through the article. There was no mention of a husband. What piqued my interest, however, was that Carrie and Brianna did not share the same last name.

I reached in my drawer for the stack of papers I'd taken with us to the DMV and began reading.

Brianna Lynn Reeves
Transferred
Sophomore
Emergency Contact: Jonathan Reeves – Father

Brianna said she grew up in Dallas, however the school records I held in my hand were from Two Harbors, Minnesota. She was a transfer into her sophomore year, which would place it just after her mother's death. It made sense. She'd obviously moved in with her father after her mother's passing. But why hadn't she mentioned him? Every time her family had been brought up in conversation, she'd shut down. The next name I typed into the search engine was *Jonathan Reeves*.

When the list of links popped up on my screen, I was more than surprised. If this was the same *Jonathan Reeves*, and from the location I would have to assume that it was, he was the county sheriff. My gaze drifted to the stairs that would lead me to the broken woman who had recently entered my life. Was she scared of what he'd think of her now? Was that why she hadn't mentioned him? Didn't want to go home? Or was there something more?

Just the thought that her father could have had something to do with her ending up with Ian made my blood boil. How could anyone do that to one's own flesh and blood?

The sound of plastic cracking brought me back to my senses. Looking down, I saw I had split the side of my keyboard. It didn't look like any keys were damaged, thankfully, but I would most likely need to buy a replacement.

After shutting everything down, I sat back in my chair and closed my eyes. I'd known this was a conversation we needed to have, but I'd been waiting. The last thing I wanted was to send her back into herself. Maybe starting with something else would be better.

Deciding I wasn't ready to go back down to her yet, I reached up and removed the key I had hidden on an upper shelf of my desk. I stood, walked up the three small stairs, and turned to the locked door I hadn't opened in a month.

The key fit snug in the lock, and I twisted the handle in my palm. As I pushed the door open, I could smell the polished leather that filled my playroom.

The chances of Brianna coming upstairs to find me were slim, but I closed the door behind me just to be sure. This room would open up an entirely new dynamic to our relationship that she wasn't ready for and might never be.

Walking across the room, my fingers trailed across first the whipping bench and then the restraints close by. I could see her here, spread out naked before me, with me standing over her. Her eyes were filled with trust and longing. For me.

It was then that I realized just how much I wanted this, her, here. I wanted her to want me. All of me.

Brianna

As I put dinner on the table, I was still trying to wrap my mind around the fact that he'd bought me a car. A new car. An *expensive* new car.

Okay, it wasn't really my car, it was his, but he'd bought it for *me* to use. I felt a smile on my lips.

"You're in a good mood, Brianna," he said as he entered the room.

"Yes, Master," I answered while finishing my task, still smiling.

He took a seat at the table. "It looks wonderful as always."

"Thank you."

When I'd gotten everything set up he invited me, as he always did, to eat with him. I ate faster than I normally did and with an excitement I hadn't known since I was little.

After dinner, we would go sit in his chair, and I wanted to thank him for the car. He noticed my excitement, of course.

"Are you hungry tonight, Brianna?" he said with amusement.

"Yes, Master," I answered back, still smiling.

Master didn't say any more as he finished his food, but I could tell he was in a good mood, which made me even happier. Once he was finished, he walked over to his chair while I cleaned up.

As soon as I was done, I came to him, and he opened his arms to me. I sat down and relaxed as Master's arms wrapped around me.

"What's on your mind tonight, Brianna?" he asked.

"Thank you for the car," I said shyly.

My head was lowered so my hair was slightly obscuring my

face. His hand rose to brush it out of the way. I liked it when he touched me like this.

"You're welcome. You'll need the car for school and to go shopping."

At his mention of shopping, I stiffened a little. He noticed and brought my chin up so that I was looking at him. Master didn't say anything. I could see everything I needed to know in his eyes. "I forgot about . . . shopping," I whispered.

He didn't say anything for a minute but released my chin once he was sure I wouldn't look away again. "You're nervous about going alone." It was a statement, not a question.

"Yes."

Nodding, he tightened his hold on me a little. "I know being out alone is hard for you, but I want you to try." Then he brought his fingers up to trace the front of my collar. "You have a part of me with you at all times."

I pressed my lips together, but finally I nodded.

"Good," he said.

I felt him take a deep breath before he said his next words. "When we were at the zoo last week, why did you get upset?"

What? I was confused. And then I wasn't. The snakes. He wanted to know about the snakes.

But why?

No. I couldn't tell him. He'd . . . he'd . . .

I couldn't breathe! Why couldn't I breathe?

Slowly I began to register his hands on both sides of my face. I hadn't realized I'd been shaking my head until now. He was murmuring something, but I couldn't make it out at first, and then the words filtered through my brain and started to make sense. They were the same ones he'd said that day to calm me. And just like then, they did.

I had no idea how long it took me to breathe normally again, but I was still on his lap. My head was lying on his shoulder while his hands gently stroked up and down my arm and face.

"Are you better?"

I closed my eyes tight, wishing the last several minutes hadn't happened. But they had, and I knew I'd yet to answer him.

"Yes," I whispered.

"Do you think you can talk to me now?"

"I . . . I don't know," I answered honestly.

"Please try, Brianna. I can't help you if you don't talk to me."

He wanted to help me. It was strange, but I believed him. "Okay," I said weakly.

Master sighed. "Why are you afraid of snakes? Can you tell me?"

His voice was gentle. I knew he was trying not to scare me, and that gave me courage.

"They crawl on you," I whispered, trying to keep the shaking out of my voice.

He tightened his hold around me, and I felt safer than I'd ever felt before. "Why were they crawling on you?"

I swallowed. Could I tell him? Would he be mad at me? But then again, maybe he was the only one I could tell.

"I . . . I did a bad thing and Master Ian—"

He didn't let me finish before asking. "What did you *do*, Brianna?"

I heard the extra inflection he placed on the word *do*, and I wasn't sure why that was.

"I . . . I tried to get away." And then I felt like I needed to apologize. "I know I shouldn't have, but—"

"Don't be ridiculous," he said cutting me off sharply. I flinched, and his voice softened. "So you tried to get away and then what happened?"

"I . . ." I paused, trying to find the right words. "He caught me . . . trying to squeeze through the gate," I said in a hushed voice. "He said that if I was going to slither on the ground like a snake . . ."

And then I shivered as I remembered it. *Ian grabbing a fistful of my hair in his hands and dragging me back to his house. Taking me downstairs.* I felt the tears coming and there was nothing I could do to stop them.

"You're doing fine, Brianna. Remember you are safe. What happened after he caught you?"

"He . . . he took me back. Ch . . . chained me . . . p . . . p . . . poured snakes . . ." I could feel them on me, and I couldn't breathe again.

Suddenly I was moving. And then I was sitting on the floor with Master's face right in front of mine.

"You are safe, Brianna," he chanted. "You are safe."

Finally I began to calm, remembering where I was. I was with Stephan, not Ian. I was okay. I was . . . safe.

Chapter Eighteen

Brianna

I woke up Sunday morning without the sound of my alarm. Looking over at the clock, I saw it was already eight o'clock.

Sitting up, I searched my nightstand and even the floor looking for Master's note, but there wasn't one. I frowned. Did I do something wrong? He'd seemed okay last night when he'd said good night to me. After I'd calmed down, he'd carried me into my bedroom and had lain me down. He'd said he was proud of me.

I sat there in the middle of my bed for more than ten minutes before deciding to get up. Sooner or later I'd have to face him and deal with whatever consequences there might be. Going to my dresser, I selected a set of workout clothes and got dressed.

As I stepped out of my room to go to the living room, I almost tripped over something. Looking down I saw the two books he'd taken away from me last Sunday. On top of them was a note.

Remember the lesson.
I do not wish to take something you so treasure away from you again.

I read it twice. The tone didn't sound angry, but it did hold a promise. He would take them away again if he had to.

Having picked up the books, I cradled them to my chest. There was just something about the feel of books that could not be duplicated.

I walked back into my room and placed the books on my nightstand where they'd been only a week ago. Then I turned and went into the living room and up the stairs to the gym.

Stephan

I'd been up since four this morning when I'd heard Brianna tossing and turning in the next room. I knew I'd pushed her last night by making her relive what was obviously a very traumatic memory, but it had to be done. She needed to deal with the things she'd experienced in order to move past them.

But what she'd said had caused *me* nightmares last night. The knowledge that someone could do that to another human being was unthinkable. I couldn't imagine doing something like that to anyone, let alone living through it.

I picked up the weight in front of me and began my bicep curls. She'd clearly said last night that she'd tried to get away, to leave, and he wouldn't let her; had punished her even—*if you could call it that*—for trying. Who does that?

Did Ian think it was a scene? If that was what it was meant to be, then it was a poor one. A Dom's main responsibility is the welfare of his sub. This was clearly beyond traumatic for her. How could he not see that?

And then there was the consideration that he did know it and didn't care. That he'd blatantly disregarded both her physical and mental well-being. It was a hard thought to swallow.

After setting the weights down, I walked over to the treadmill to begin my run. I needed to continue our progress, but I was unsure if making her relive the last ten months right now was a good thing. She needed to trust me. And although I had many questions for her, they would have to be put on hold.

Throughout the rest of my five-mile run, I went over various ways I could continue to grow that small amount of trust we'd developed so far. I had just settled on a plan when I saw movement out of the corner of my eye.

"Good morning, Brianna."

"Good morning, Master," she answered.

Her voice sounded fairly strong considering the rough night I knew she'd had. "I'm almost finished here," I said. "You may start the routine Brad gave you and then meet me downstairs when you're done." She nodded, walked over to the mats, and began to stretch.

My eyes trailed over her figure as she moved. She was beautiful. As my gaze traveled up over her hips to her lower back and then a little higher, I stopped.

Last time she'd been in the gym with me, I'd laid out a tank top for her. Today, she was wearing only a sports bra and shorts, revealing much more of her back to me. And there on her pale skin were small scars.

I forgot the remainder of my run, as I turned off the machine and stepped toward her. As I got closer, it was obvious who had done this to her. The marks were precise, covering only the section of her back that would have been hidden by the tube top she'd been wearing when I'd first met her. Before I knew what I was doing, I was standing directly behind her, reaching out to the marks on her flesh.

Brianna went rigid at my contact. My eyes rose to meet hers in the mirror in front of her. She began to lower her gaze. "Don't," I said as gently as I could.

Her eyes rose again and held mine as my fingers traced the patterns of raised tissue on her back. I didn't need to ask if Ian had done this to her. I already knew the answer to that. Instead I said, "I would never do this to you, Brianna."

And I wouldn't. I had left bruises before but never scars. I'm not even sure I would do it if a submissive asked me to, and I was absolutely positive that Brianna had never asked to be marked like this.

My declaration was met with nothing but silence, but I knew she'd heard me. Her breathing had become more labored, and her eyes opened just a bit wider as if surprised.

I had no idea how long we stayed there watching each other in the mirror, until I finally stepped back and broke the spell. "Finish, shower, and then meet me in the kitchen. We'll get breakfast, and then I have plans for us."

With that, I turned and left her alone.

Two hours later, we were both dressed and fed. I took her hand and brought her into the living room. Standing in front of her, I asked her to look at me.

"Do you know what a safeword is, Brianna?" I was almost positive I already knew the answer to that question given what little she'd already told me, but I had to know. She confirmed my suspicions when she shook her head.

I nodded. "Has anyone ever asked you to rate something on a scale of one to ten?"

She nodded.

"Good," I said. "Do you trust me, Brianna?"

Immediately I saw her clamping her lips together. She was thinking how to answer, but this was exactly what I wanted. "On a scale of one to ten, with ten being the most and one being the least, how much do you trust me? Answer honestly."

She seemed to consider her answer for a minute and then very softly said, "Five."

Well, that was better than a one or a two, even a three or a four. "Thank you. I am pleased that you at least trust me halfway at this point. I will do my best not to break the trust you have in me."

Her expression was one of utter confusion. I knew what I said couldn't possibly make sense to her now, but hopefully it would soon.

"Periodically I will ask you to tell me your level of comfort at any given moment. Whenever I do, I want you to give me the number between one and ten that best describes your current level of discomfort. Do you understand?"

"I . . . I think so," she answered.

"Okay. Let's try it. How would you rate your level of discomfort last night?" I noticed her breathing quicken, and I reached out to touch her face. Her breath started to calm. "Stay with me," I whispered. "What number?"

"Nine," she whispered.

Interesting. She'd been in a full panic attack and yet she had not said ten. That made me a little nervous. What would she consider a ten?

But instead of commenting, I nodded and moved on. "From now

on, I want you to remember this number system. If you ever get to an eight, I want you to say the word *yellow*. If you get to a ten, I want you to say the word *red*. Can you do that?"

"Yes, Master."

"Good. Now, we are going to do some experimenting today."

I felt her body immediately tense. "What number, Brianna?"

"Six."

"Why?"

"I'm . . . scared."

I stepped toward her and cupped her face with my hands. "What do you fear?"

"I'm afraid you'll hurt me," she whispered, obviously scared that her answer would upset me.

I gave her a half smile to try and ease her anxiety. "Do you remember that five you gave me earlier? What happened to that?"

Her eyes closed. I felt her trying to find that faith again, and I was grateful.

"I need you to place your trust in that," I said softly. "Do you think you can?"

"Yes," she whispered back.

I knew just that little *yes* was difficult for her. She really was placing her trust in me, and I cherished it.

Leaving her standing in the living room, I went into my bedroom and found a black scarf. We might not get to all I had planned, but I wanted to be prepared. After tucking it into my pocket, I grabbed my jacket off the back of my chair and returned to Brianna. She was standing right where I'd left her, not that I'd expected anything else.

"Would you like to take a jacket with you? It might be a bit chilly."

"Yes, Master," she answered.

I could tell she was still nervous by the slight shakiness to her voice, but she quickly disappeared into her room and came out with a spring jacket I'd seen her wear only once prior.

Before I led her out the door, I took her chin in my hands and said, "Today is about trust. Remember that."

Brianna

I tried to be brave as we drove. What was happening didn't make sense. Although truthfully nothing had really made sense since this man had come into my life.

There were times when he could make me forget what I was, even if it was only for a brief second. And then other times, there was no doubt that I belonged to him. But even then it felt different than it had when I was with Ian.

When he'd asked me to rate how much I trusted him on a scale of one to ten, I'd really had to think hard. I knew I shouldn't trust him at all, and yet somehow I did. He'd never been unkind to me. Yes, there were rules, and he expected them to be followed, but at least I knew what they were, and they were things I *could* do.

And when I'd messed up, he'd handed out his punishment and then it was over. He didn't yell at me or continue to make me pay for messing up for days. Of course the no-books rule had lasted for a week, but in that time, he'd never brought it up, never rubbed it in my face. It was for that reason that I'd told him five in the end.

To say I fully trusted him would be a lie, and he would have known that. I still remembered the hard look in his eyes when he'd told me that I could give him no greater insult than to lie to him. It was something I never wanted to know the consequences of.

He came to a stop in the parking lot of what looked to be a mall. We both got out of the car, and I followed him as he walked inside. I felt my anxiety begin to rise a little at the prospect of being so close to all these people in a busy place, but I tried to remember that I was not alone. Master was with me.

Taking my hand, he led me into the mall and the crowds. As we moved, I could feel the air around me shifting as people came close and then moved away. I closed my eyes, trying to calm myself, and then suddenly we stopped.

"Number?"

"Four," I whispered.

"Look at me," he said firmly. I opened my eyes to find him staring intently at my face. Once he had my attention, he said in clear disbelief, "Only four?"

I swallowed. What was I supposed to say?

But before I could answer or reassess, he asked, "What if I

walked to that store over there and left you standing here?"

No! Please no.

There was no doubt he saw the panic in my eyes. "What number, Brianna?"

"Seven." I gasped.

He nodded. "I'm not going to leave you alone today. So take a deep breath and get back to that four. Or better yet, down to a one or a two. I'm not going to let anything happen to you. Remember, Brianna, this is about trust." Again I swallowed and tried to do what he said.

Finally, he seemed satisfied and began walking again. We made our way into a store at the far end of the mall. It was a small boutique, but it had some very beautiful clothing.

A woman greeted us and asked if she could help us find anything, but Master said no. Instead, he pulled me farther into the store and took several items off the racks before ushering me to the dressing rooms. Turning toward me, he put the items in my hands and told me to go try them on one at a time and then come out and show him.

I felt a little awkward, but I rationalized that it really was no different than what I did every day. It wasn't like he was watching me dress or anything. Then the thought crossed my mind that that didn't really matter either. My Master had seen all of me.

Okay, well maybe not all of me, but enough.

Once I was out of my clothes, I selected the first outfit. It was a fitted pair of jeans that sat low on my hips and a rust-colored shirt that dipped a little lower than I would ever pick for myself. It showed my cleavage, but not overly so, and the hem ended about an inch above the waist of my pants. With a look in the mirror at myself and a deep breath, I walked out of the dressing room so that he could see me.

He'd been looking at a magazine when I stepped out, but quickly his eyes rose and skimmed over me. I felt instantly uncomfortable. There was something in his eyes that was almost predatory.

With practiced grace, he stood and walked toward me, only adding to my nerves. Silently, he walked slowly around me like a cat stalking its prey. I felt my panic rising.

Then I felt his breath caress my ear as he whispered, "Number?"

What number? It was hard to get my brain to think, but I tried and settled on a five again.

"Why?"

I closed my eyes and tried to answer honestly. "I'm afraid."

"Of?" he prompted.

The next words were so hard, but I was determined not to lie to him as he'd asked. "You," I squeaked out.

He was still behind me, hovering over my shoulder with his mouth so close to my ear I could feel every breath he took. "Why?"

How could I explain to him my fears when I wasn't sure I understood them myself? Our entire conversation was done in whispers. The shop was empty except for the lady who had welcomed us, and she was on the other side of the store. So I just simply said, "I'm afraid you'll . . . touch me."

His response did not come right away, like he was thinking about how to answer me, but then, "Do you not like it when I touch you?"

I closed my eyes. This was one of the confusing parts because, yes, I did.

My breathing was unsteady, coming in short pants. His hands came up, rubbing up and down the sides of my arms as he spoke the next words. "I will not have sex with you until you ask me to, if that is what has you worried."

What? He wouldn't . . . why?

And before I could stop it, I heard myself utter, "Why?"

Within seconds, he was in front of me. His hand came up to grip the back of my neck more aggressively than he'd ever touched me, angling it until I had no choice but to look at him. "I want you, Brianna, don't doubt that," he said in a voice that made me shiver. "But you will give yourself to me willingly. If I have you, I want all of you."

Suddenly, he released his hold on me and took a step back. His grip had been so strong that I still felt it even after it was gone.

The look in his eyes was full of hunger, and in that moment I had no doubt that he wanted me just as he said he did. That knowledge made me nervous, but for some reason not as much as I thought it would. My heart was pounding hard against my chest as he continued to stare.

Then suddenly, the spell was broken. He turned, retook his seat, and picked up the magazine. Without looking at me again, he said, "I like that one. Go try on another."

As quickly as I could, I fled back to the safety of the dressing room to change.

Chapter Nineteen

Stephan

I sat perfectly still as she turned and almost tripped on her way back into the dressing room. It wasn't until she'd disappeared that I allowed myself to breathe again.

What in the world had I been thinking, declaring myself like that?

When Brianna came out wearing that deceptively innocent outfit, something inside me clicked and took over. Millions of other women her age wore similar clothing every day, but on Brianna it looked like the most provocative outfit I'd ever seen.

The jeans hugged her curves perfectly, leaving my fingers itching to grab a hold of her hips and wrap her legs around my waist. And that top . . . I groaned just thinking about it again. It was chaste, really. Everything that should be covered was, but there was just a hint of cleavage showing, not to mention that narrow strip of skin left visible.

Clenching my eyes shut, I ordered myself to calm down. Sitting here remembering and thinking about what I wanted to do to her was pointless. Her reaction just a few minutes ago proved that. I just hoped my stupid words didn't destroy the trust we'd built.

Everything I'd told her was true. I wouldn't touch her until she asked me to. That didn't mean telling her that in the middle of the local mall had been the most brilliant decision of my life.

I was so distracted by my thoughts, I only vaguely registered that another couple had entered the store. It wasn't until they came close to the dressing room where I was waiting for Brianna that they completely drew my attention.

"Come on, baby. Try it on for me. Please?"

"I don't know if I should," the woman replied back flirtatiously.

"What do I have to do? Do you want me to beg? I will, you know."

I could see them now out of the corner of my eye. They were standing at the entrance to the fitting room, and their volume didn't provide for a private conversation. Either they didn't care or they were totally oblivious to my presence.

"Hmm. Begging sounds good." The woman wrapped her arms around the man's neck with obvious amusement. "Beg me," she said with a little more force.

I was ready to completely dismiss this game they were obviously playing and go back to my magazine when I heard a small noise come from inside the fitting room. I was up and out of my seat before I even thought about it.

I found a row of six doors behind the curtain, but only one of them was closed. The closer I got, the louder the sound I'd originally heard became. I tried the doorknob, but it was locked.

Just as I was considering my options, the saleslady came in waving her arms around, telling me I wasn't allowed back here. Completely ignoring her protests, I easily removed the key ring hanging from her wrist and began looking for the one that would fit the lock and get me through the door.

The woman was still yelling at me and had been joined by the couple that had been standing outside, but I kept my focus on the task in front of me.

Finally, after trying the third key, I felt the lock turn and the door gave. Brianna was naked from the waist up, huddled in the corner on the floor, whimpering. Without a thought to anyone other than her, I crossed the small room, grabbed the nearest shirt, and knelt in front of her. I reached out with the garment in my hand to try and cover her naked torso, but she flinched away from me and her volume increased.

"Brianna?"

"Please." She gasped. "Please don't hurt me. Please."

Tears were running down her cheeks in a steady stream, and she had a blank look on her face. I knew she wasn't here. She didn't know it was me in front of her.

I threw down the shirt and tried once again to touch her, this time going for her face. Again, she flinched but not nearly as much as before. Brianna was still whimpering, but she let me raise her chin.

"Brianna, look at me. It's Stephan. You're here with me and you're safe. You're safe," I said, then repeated myself with more force. "You're safe." Slowly, I saw recognition register in her eyes and felt her pulse begin to slow back down.

"Is she all right?" I heard someone behind me ask.

That was a loaded question. Instead of answering, I kept my focus on Brianna and asked, "Maybe we could get a glass of water?"

The saleswoman quickly disappeared, which left only the couple. They were watching us closely. My hands were still cradling Brianna's face, but she'd lowered her head when my grip had slackened and was now looking at the floor.

Ignoring our audience, I leaned in, placing my mouth an inch above her ear where our observers could not see my lips and asked, "Are you okay, love?" Brianna was the only one who mattered to me at the moment.

She nodded, and I let my lips graze her hair as I pulled her closer to me. "Are you able to put your shirt on for me?" Brianna nodded again, and I pulled back enough to hand her the shirt. She took it without hesitation and only fumbled a little as she put it on.

Just then, the saleslady pushed her way through and handed me a small cup full of water.

"Thank you," I said to her before turning my total attention back to Brianna.

Her hands were resting flat on her thighs. I reached down and one by one placed her hands around the cup. "Drink," I ordered softly.

Obediently she raised the plastic to her lips and began to drink. Satisfied that she wasn't about to fall apart on me for the first time since entering the small room, I turned completely to our audience. "Thank you for your assistance, but if you don't mind we'd like a few minutes alone."

To their credit, the couple seemed a little embarrassed as they pulled themselves away and disappeared from the dressing area.

The store employee hesitated a few seconds, but finally said, "Of course."

I turned back to Brianna and watched as she drained the cup before laying it as an offering at her feet. I picked up the now empty container and put it up on the bench behind me so that it was out of the way. With a slight shift in position, I was kneeling in front of her with our knees almost touching.

Brianna had once more placed her hands in her lap, but I noticed her pressing her lips together, alerting me to her nervousness.

"Tell me what you're thinking."

She remained silent.

"Brianna," I said in a firm voice to let her know that I expected an answer.

"Will you take my books away again, Master?" she whispered.

Take away her books? What was she talking about? "Do you think I should take your books away again?" I asked, wanting to hear her answer.

"Please, anything but my books, Master. Punish me however you want, just . . . just please don't . . ." I heard a choking sob and although I couldn't see her face at the moment, I knew she was crying again.

I reached out to her and pulled her head into my chest. This was not a conversation I wanted to be having in the middle of a store or out in public, for that matter. I gently stroked her hair in the way she liked until I felt her calm.

"Are you able to walk?" I asked.

She nodded and whispered, "Yes, Master."

I pulled back and helped her to stand. Lifting her chin, my eyes met hers. "We will discuss this at home."

She nodded and cast her eyes down.

Walking back out into the store I kept my hand in hers. The saleswoman met us almost immediately, as I'm sure she'd been hovering close by since she'd left us. Giving her my credit card, I instructed her to put the clothes we'd left behind aside for one of my staff to pick up tomorrow. As soon as I had the card back in my hands, I guided Brianna back out into the mall.

This time we didn't linger. To make it easier on her, I positioned us on the edges of the crowd and kept us moving. I just wanted to get her home. She'd had enough for one day and deserved some rest, even though we still needed to talk.

The entire drive home Brianna was tense and looking down at her hands. Usually she liked to watch out the window as I drove, but her entire body radiated anxiety. I wanted to comfort her, but I was unsure how at the moment. She seemed to think she was in trouble, although I didn't understand what she could have done to warrant punishment.

I didn't linger in the parking garage, and we quickly made our way into the elevator and up to the top floor. She was still quiet. Brianna hadn't said a word since we left the store. Although in her defense, she never initiated conversation, and I was still mulling over everything that had transpired in the last hour.

I unlocked the door, stepped through, and threw my keys down on the table. She followed me inside without stopping, and knowing she would continue to follow me, I went directly to her bedroom, and then into her bathroom.

As I walked through the door separating the two rooms, I heard her enter the bedroom behind me. Under the sink I found the bottle of bubble bath I was looking for. It was something I had provided for Tami when she was using the room, so she had not taken it with her, thankfully. After taking it over to the tub, I turned on the tap, regulated the temperature to a comfortable level, and poured in some of the fragrance.

I waited until the water reached the desired level before shutting off the tap. When I turned around, Brianna was kneeling just outside the doorway. When I strolled over to her, I reached down, took her hands, and indicated that I wanted her to stand.

Placing my hand under her chin, I brought her face up so she could look at me. "You are to get into the tub and take a bath, Brianna. You are to stay in there at least thirty minutes. When you're finished, there will be clothing laid out for you on your bed. Put them on and meet me in the kitchen." I didn't wait for her to agree before I dropped her chin and left the room.

Brianna

As soon as he left me, I collapsed on the floor sobbing. Stupid, stupid, stupid. He'd been so happy this morning at breakfast and now . . .

He was acting like everything was okay, but I knew it wasn't. I would be lucky if he only took my books away. It had been insane for me to ask him not to, to ask him for anything but that.

If it were Ian, he would have taken them away just to spite me on top of whatever else he had in mind. But I had no idea what Stephan would do.

Wiping my eyes, I got up off the floor, walked into the bathroom, and removed my clothing one piece at a time. As I stepped into the bath the last of my tears dried up.

The water was warm and inviting. It only added to my confusion. Why did he want me to take a bath? I couldn't think of any type of punishment where I would need to be clean and smelling like . . . coconut?

Taking a deep breath, I decided not to worry about it for the thirty minutes I was alone. I closed my eyes and ordered myself to relax. This was just another example of how nice my Master was. Whatever punishment I had to endure later, he was giving me a chance to collect myself first, and I was grateful. Maybe now I wouldn't embarrass myself again by begging as I had earlier.

I felt the tears returning to my eyes.

"Beg me."

The images started to flood back through my mind.

"And what do we have here?"

"I found her trying to get out the back door again, Master."

"Tsk, tsk, Brianna. You know better than to try and escape."

His cool voice held a level of menace unlike any I'd ever heard in my previous life. Before I knew what was happening, my head was wrenched back hard. I could feel it all the way down to my roots.

"Please," I pleaded.

"Please?" he mocked. *"Please? Please what, Brianna?"* Then *he was in my face, and I could feel every syllable he spoke.* "YOU. ARE. MINE!"

Suddenly, he released my hair. In the next second he grabbed my arm and wrenched it hard behind my back. The force of the movement caused a searing pain through my entire limb and a distinct cracking sound, making me yell out.

"*Please. Please. I'm begging you.*"

"*Oh, Brianna, you are learning aren't you? Now. BEG ME!*"

"AGH!"

My screaming filled the room as my arms flew about me in an effort to make it all go away.

Suddenly, I wasn't in the water anymore. Strong arms were wrapped around me, and the most soothing voice in the world was chanting my name. It was the last sound I heard before my eyes drifted shut and sleep claimed me.

Chapter Twenty

Stephan

I'd just put the finishing touches on our sandwiches when I heard a blood-curdling scream come from Brianna's room. Dropping the knife I had in my hand, I raced toward the sound.

What I found when I entered her bathroom caused my chest to clench painfully. Her arms were flaying about as if they were trying to fight off an unknown attacker, and her body was slowly slipping farther and farther down into the water.

Without thinking about the fact that I was fully clothed or that Brianna was naked, I reached into the tub. Amazingly, she didn't fight me as I scooped her up and pulled her into my arms. She was sobbing, and her body was shaking as I brought her onto my lap.

"Shh, Brianna. You're safe, sweetheart. No one will hurt you here."

I kept repeating my mantra until I felt her calm and slowly begin to relax in my arms.

It wasn't long before I realized that she'd fallen asleep. She'd had a long and trying day today. It was no wonder she was tired.

Carefully, I reached up to pull the towel down from the bar just to my right. Being as gentle as I could, I wiped the remaining water droplets from her bare body before lifting us both off the floor.

I carried her back into the bedroom and over to her bed. It took some maneuvering, but eventually I was able to pull the sheet back and lay her down. Only then did I notice the marks on her breasts. Around her nipples were small round scars the perfect size for cigarettes. I felt a lump develop in my throat as I fought hard to swallow down the mixture of sorrow and outrage I felt. How could someone do this to another human being? How did they sleep at night?

Without thought to what I was doing, I reached out and touched one small circle and traced its pattern. The skin was only slightly raised, but the marks were visible against her pale flesh.

Removing my hand, I decided to take this opportunity to inspect the rest of her.

Slowly, I let my eyes roam down her torso. At the juncture of her legs I could still see the burn marks I'd noticed that first day visible through the new hair growth just starting to show. I didn't find anything that I hadn't seen before, until I reached her feet. On the bottom of her right heel was what looked to be burn marks of some kind.

Again, I couldn't resist the impulse to reach out and run my fingers over it. He'd burned her and left scars that might never fully heal. It wasn't enough that she'd worn his collar; he'd had to permanently mark her as his property. I was beginning to feel sick again.

Feeling the sudden urge to leave the room, I reached to pull the covers over her body when I glanced up at Brianna's face and noticed she was watching me. I tried to give her a reassuring smile. "How are you feeling, Brianna?"

Her gaze held mine for several seconds before she closed her eyes tightly. Seeing movement, I looked down and noticed her hands had clenched into fists. Brianna's chest rose and fell more rapidly as her breathing picked up.

Leaning in, I cupped her face. "Please look at me," I said.

Slowly her eyes fluttered open and I watched her swallow. "Am I acceptable for you, Master?" she whispered.

I blinked. It took me a moment to understand what she meant, but as I continued to look into her eyes I saw the mixture of fear, determination, and something else.

There were so many responses I could give. Yes, she was more than acceptable to me. Brianna was the most beautiful woman I'd ever met, and she became more so every day. But she was talking about the physical only. She was asking if her body was pleasing to me.

Without a doubt I knew I had to handle this situation with care. She'd come a long way, but she was still so fragile. The woman who'd graced my home that first night was still there just beneath the surface.

Raising my right hand, I reached up first to stroke her hair. "You are beautiful, Brianna," I said making sure she was looking at me. Then slowly I let my hand travel down her neck to the marks on her left breast. "All of you."

She took a deep breath and closed her eyes. I could feel her heart pounding under my fingertips, the motion causing her chest to rise and fall beneath my hand.

Without thinking, I brought my mouth to hers. For the first time, I let my emotions come to the surface and allowed her to feel some of the passion she invoked within me.

Brianna gasped but did not fight me. Pulling back only enough to speak, I demanded, "Kiss me."

My lips came back down upon hers. She didn't hesitate and returned my kiss with an equal amount of force. I wrapped my arms around her and pulled her into a sitting position. The feeling of her naked breasts pressed against me was heavenly and incredibly erotic.

I had one hand wrapped securely in her hair and the other around her waist. It wasn't enough. My tongue begged entrance into her mouth. She opened to me, and seconds later I was able to taste the sweetness of the woman in my arms as my tongue rubbed and explored. Brianna tasted even sweeter than I'd imagined her to be.

Reality came crashing back in on me as I realized that I was holding a naked woman in my arms and that it wouldn't take much to discard my clothing and bury myself deep inside her. But I wanted more than just sex with Brianna. If I took what my body desired right now, sex would be all we would ever have. She would never learn to trust me.

So, reluctantly, I pulled back. My breath was coming hard and so was hers. It took everything I had to pull away from her and walk to the other side of the room.

Minutes passed, and the only sound filling the room was our

breathing. "Your clothes are on the end of the bed, Brianna. Since you're awake, you should eat. Get dressed and meet me in the kitchen."

"Master?" she asked softly.

"Do as you're told," I snapped. Then, realizing what I'd done, I took a deep breath to calm myself. Turning back, I saw her big blue eyes staring at me in hurt and confusion.

Carefully I walked back to her, placed my hands around her face, and tilted her head up so that I could look into those glorious eyes of hers. "You need to eat. You can sleep after." I dropped my hands and left her room as quickly as my feet would carry me.

As soon as I entered the main room, I took a deep breath and tried to clear my head. That woman was doing something to my brain.

I went directly to my room to change out of my now soaked clothing and into something dry. After donning a clean pair of jeans and a T-shirt, I returned to the kitchen to pick up where I'd left off with our lunches.

Why was it that I couldn't think logically near her? And what was with my libido going into hyperdrive lately? Yes, she was beautiful, sexy beyond belief. And yes, it had been a while, but that wasn't unusual for me when I wasn't in a relationship.

I tended to be rather picky when it came to my partners. Because of that, and my particular tastes, I didn't invite women into my home often, nor did I go to many parties. It just wasn't my scene. I was a very private person.

Only after a month of begging from Lily and Logan had I gone with them to a party about two months ago. They were hoping someone would strike my interest.

That was where I'd run into Daren.

I was still lost in my thoughts when I felt Brianna enter the room. When my eyes located her, the memory of her naked and in my arms came flooding back to me even though she was now fully dressed in yoga pants and a fitted T-shirt.

Her eyes were focused on the floor as she walked tentatively toward me in the kitchen. Swallowing, I tried to get a hold of myself.

When she reached the island, I placed the sandwich in front of her. "Eat your lunch, Brianna."

Originally I'd planned on sitting beside her at the counter as we'd done many times over the last few weeks, but I was afraid I wouldn't be able to keep my hands to myself if I attempted that at the moment. So instead I ate my sandwich standing up at the counter, keeping several feet between us.

She ate in silence, as did I. We needed to talk about today, about everything, but I just couldn't. I needed my wits about me, and she needed me to be calm. Right now I was anything but.

When she finished, I took her plate along with mine and put them in the dishwasher. Turning back to face her, I saw silent tears flowing down her cheeks. Without a second thought I was moving toward her and wrapping her in my arms. "Why are you crying, love?"

She shook her head. "Please don't be angry with me, Master. I'll do better, I promise."

Instinctively my arms held her tighter. "I'm not angry with you."

"But . . ." she said in a strangled voice.

"Shh," I whispered, taking in the lovely scent of coconut now covering her skin. "Are you tired?" She nodded. Pulling back enough to see her face, I placed a kiss on her forehead and said, "Go take a nap. When you wake up we'll talk about what happened today."

I felt her stiffen, but she dutifully answered, "Yes, Master."

She began to get down from her stool, but I caught her by the chin. "You are not in trouble, Brianna." After nodding she walked toward her bedroom and disappeared.

I stood looking at the door to her room for several minutes before heading upstairs. Looking at the clock, I debated whether or not to call Logan. It was the weekend and I hated to disturb them, but I needed to talk to someone. Before I could stop myself, I picked up the phone and dialed.

Logan picked up on the second ring. "Hello?"

"Logan, it's Stephan."

"Hey, Stephan." Then concern laced his voice. "Everything okay?"

"No."

"Are you at your place? We'll be there in thirty minutes."

"I can't ask you to do that."

He laughed. "You didn't ask. I offered. Besides we're just

finishing up here anyway, and I know Lily would love to see Brianna."

"All right."

I hung up the phone and took a deep cleansing breath. Maybe Logan and Lily would have some idea how to handle this situation. I knew Brianna and I needed to talk about so many things, but maybe having Lily here would help put her mind at ease for a while.

After straightening my desk, I went downstairs to wait for Logan and Lily. Exactly thirty minutes later, I heard a knock on the door.

Before I'd even opened it all the way, Lily was bouncing through the door. She took a quick look around and then turned on me. "Where is she?"

By this time Logan had made his way inside as well.

I shut the door as I answered her. "She's taking a nap. We had a long morning."

"What did you do, Stephan?"

I felt slightly offended, even though I knew she was right. It was my fault. "Why does it have to be something I've done?"

"Because I know you."

I snorted. "Thanks for the vote of confidence." She glared at me.

Logan seemed to think this was a good time to enter the conversation. "You said something was wrong?"

Nodding, I motioned for them to follow me into the living room. Logan and Lily sat on the couch while I took a seat in my chair. Just sitting there made me think of her.

Lily's voice brought me back to the present. "So what happened?"

I sighed and started talking. It wasn't difficult until I got to the part in her bedroom. As I described what happened and my actions, Lily gasped. "Stephan, you didn't?"

There was no doubt in my mind as to what she was asking. "No, Lily. I didn't. But I wanted to. Very much."

"Well, that's good, right?" she said, unsure now.

"Yes. It's good. I just . . ." My head fell to my hands in defeat. "I don't know what's happening to me. I've never been on the edge of control like that before. And then after I pulled away . . . she looked so hurt, and I just had to comfort her, although it just about killed me to be that close."

Neither of my friends commented, and their lack of response had me looking up. Each of them wore knowing grins on their faces.

"What?"

"You love her," Lily declared.

Love her? How in the world could I love her? I barely even knew her. "No. Lily. It's just not possible."

"Sure it is," she said, her voice gaining conviction.

Then Logan joined in. "I have to agree with Lily. Stephan, you've spent every waking hour you're not at work with her. You're obviously attracted to her. You care what happens to her, whether or not she's happy or sad. Why is it so inconceivable to you that you've fallen in love?"

"But I don't even know her!" I threw my hands up in the air. "She barely talks to me. And even then she edits everything she says."

"It doesn't matter," Lily said.

I stood then, unable to sit, and began pacing. "What do you mean it doesn't matter? I don't even know if she wants what I would be able to offer her in the form of a relationship. A relationship that requires . . . demands, communication."

Lily stood and walked to me. She took my hands in hers and looked me in the eye. "Stephan, you are a good Master. I know. Any submissive would be happy to serve you. You're right that she isn't ready, but it's only been three weeks. Give it time."

Hearing movement, Lily dropped my hands and we all turned our heads to see Brianna standing just outside her bedroom door. Her eyes met mine for only a second before lowering to the ground. I reached out my hand and said, "Come. Greet our guests."

She walked immediately to my side and took my offered hand. I saw Lily smirk. "Hello, Lily. Logan."

I saw Logan make a subtle movement toward Lily just before she stepped forward and reached for Brianna's free hand. "Maybe we should leave the boys alone for a little while."

Lily was tugging on her arm, but Brianna didn't move an inch. Instead she turned to look up at me, silently asking for permission. I nodded and let go of her hand.

Immediately I felt the loss. Could Lily and Logan be right? Did I love her?

Brianna

When he sent me back to my room to take a nap I went straight to my bed and got under my blanket. I didn't go right to sleep, though. My mind was still racing over what had happened today.

He said he wasn't upset with me; that I wasn't in trouble. My first instinct was not to believe him, to think this was some mind game.

But then something changed and my brain took over as I reminded myself he did not lie to me. If he said I wasn't in trouble, then I wasn't. I had to believe that.

Then my mind drifted to when I'd found him hovering over me as I lay fully exposed in my bed. I had been frightened by his presence and what I was sure would happen. But something in me wanted him to be pleased with how I looked. I knew there were ugly scars on my body. Ian had enjoyed marking me in many ways.

As I felt his fingers touch my breast and he called me beautiful, I'd almost started crying. He thought I was beautiful. The word was almost reverent as it left his lips.

When his mouth met mine it had been different than the times in the past. It had been harder, more possessive. Then he'd commanded me to kiss him and something inside me rose to the challenge.

I remembered the feel of him as he'd pulled me up and pressed me against his chest. Even though the kiss was more aggressive than any in the past, it was still very different than what I'd received before coming to live with Stephan.

The want to make him happy surged through me as I felt his tongue press against my lips. I knew what he wanted, and I granted it to him without pause.

Then suddenly he'd gone. I didn't know what I'd done wrong even after his soft words took the sting out of his harsh ones.

Finally I'd been able to fall asleep remembering his gentle words to me just before coming to my room. I could still feel his arms surrounding me as I closed my eyes and sleep took me for the second time that day.

The first thing I became aware of when I opened my eyes was that there were voices coming from the main room. I couldn't make out what they were saying, but I knew Master was not alone, and I was unsure what to do.

After about ten minutes of indecision, I figured that it would be better to show myself. Master would not like me hiding in my room.

When I stepped through my door, the first thing I saw was Lily standing there holding my Master's hands. I didn't know why, but I didn't like it. They were friends, but there was something about the way she was doing it that wasn't right.

Just then Master saw me, and Lily stepped back. That was when I noticed the other person in the room was Logan.

My attention didn't linger long as I saw movement and turned my attention back to Master. He'd extended his hand, clearly wanting me to take it, and told me to come to him. I walked quickly to his side and linked my hand with his. Instantly I felt better.

I was slightly disappointed when Lily wanted us to leave the room and looked up to Master hoping he'd say no. Instead he nodded, and I knew there was no getting out of it.

Reluctantly, I released his hand and let Lily pull me back into my bedroom where she headed straight for my closet and began pulling out clothes and holding them up. I only heard about every other word that she said. My thoughts were in the other room with my Master.

Then Lily was in front of me with a strange look on her face. "Are you okay?"

"Yes," I said and nodded.

"Are you sure? 'Cause if you need to talk . . ." She left the sentence hanging as if waiting for me to speak.

I thought for a minute and then decided there was something I wanted to ask her. "How long have you known him?" She'd asked me to call him Stephan with her, but I just couldn't do it.

Her expression changed to one of puzzlement. "We met at a party a little over two years ago."

Two years. That wasn't a long time, and the way she'd touched him . . .

We stood in silence for several long minutes. It was the longest I'd ever heard Lily go without talking, and that made me curious. Reaching down into the depths of my being, I made myself ask the question burning in my brain. "Were you . . . were you his slave?"

A frown crossed Lily's features, and then she took my hands in hers. "No," she said softly. "I was never Stephan's slave and neither are you."

What was she talking about? Of course I was his slave. He bought me.

But before I could ask her to explain there was a knock on my door. Logan's head peeked in, and he smiled at me shyly but didn't enter. "Are you ready, Lily?"

She seemed to hesitate. It wasn't until Master joined Logan at the door that she sighed. Then, after giving me a brief hug, she joined Logan.

I saw her whisper something to Master. His brow furrowed slightly before going back to the smooth features that I was so used to seeing from him. And then with a quick wave she was gone, leaving me standing in my bedroom staring at my Master with even more questions.

Chapter Twenty-One

Brianna

He didn't stare very long before he turned and followed the path of our guests. I stood rooted to my spot until I heard voices again and the door opening. I came out of my room to find Master closing the door. He slowly turned to me, and I dropped my eyes to the floor.

I heard every step he took as he moved closer to where I stood. My mind was racing more with every footfall. If I wasn't his slave, then what was I? What had she whispered to him at my bedroom door? And what about the way she touched him before? Why did that bother me?

All my questioning came to an abrupt halt as Master stopped right in front of me. My head was bowed, and I could feel his breath fanning my hair. He was so close.

We stood not speaking for several long minutes before he finally broke the silence. "Come," he said, in a soft controlled voice before turning on his heel and marching to his chair.

I followed. He sat and opened his arms to me. I sat down on his lap and felt his arms surround me. His warmth wrapped around me, and I instantly felt better, calmer.

All was quiet again for several minutes. Usually his hand would gently rub up and down my arm, but tonight both were still. Finally,

I felt him shift beneath me and say, "We need to talk about today." I nodded.

Minutes passed again before he continued, "Before we start, do you remember the number system I gave you earlier?"

I nodded again, but that wasn't good enough as he commanded me to answer him verbally. "Yes, Master."

"Repeat back to me what I told you."

"Whenever you ask, I am to give you the number between one and ten that tells you how uncomfortable I am at that time."

"Very good." He nodded. "And what are you to say should you reach the number eight?"

"Yellow," I answered obediently.

"And the number ten?" he questioned.

"Red."

He nodded again, and this time he rubbed his hand up and down my arm, letting me know he was pleased with my answers. "I want you to use this system even when I don't ask you, Brianna."

There was silence again, and I realized he was waiting for me to speak. The problem was I didn't understand what he meant.

"I don't understand," I said honestly. The last thing I wanted was to mess up because I didn't know what was required of me.

Master sighed. "It means that I want you to constantly keep that number system in your head and if . . . when you get to an eight, I want you to say the word *yellow*." He pulled my chin up so that I was looking directly into his eyes. "Even if I don't ask you."

He waited, as if letting this information sink in before asking, "Do you understand?"

"Yes."

"Good. Repeat it."

I took a deep breath and repeated almost word for word everything he'd said. At the end, he seemed pleased.

"That goes for *red* as well. If you reach a ten at any time . . ." He paused and gave me a look that left me no doubt as to how seriously he took his next words. "You are to say *red* immediately."

I nodded. "I understand, Master."

"Okay then, let's get started."

I tensed up instantly. There was no doubt in my mind that he felt it, too, but Master didn't comment. Instead, he asked me where I wanted to start. All the questions from before began swirling in my head, but I wanted to think about them more before I brought them up to him. They weren't what he was asking me about anyway.

In the end, I decided to ask what had been the most pressing question on my mind prior to Lily and Logan's arrival. "Are you going to take my books away?"

But instead of answering me, he asked, "Do you feel you should have your books taken away?"

"I . . . I guess," I said, defeated.

"Why?"

"Because I wasn't paying attention," I whispered.

"Hmm," he said, as if considering what I had just said. "To me it looked like you were having a panic attack, Brianna. Am I wrong?"

A panic attack? I had never thought of it like that. Was that what it was?

Obviously I was silent for too long. "Tell me what happened after you went back to the dressing room," he said, softly stroking my hair.

"I took off the clothes," I said softly. If I weren't sitting with my face inches from his, he would not have been able to hear me. "Then I heard voices," I said even lower. "And then . . ." I stopped because after that I really wasn't sure what happened. One second I'd been in the dressing room changing clothes and then the next minute I'd been kneeling in front of Ian.

"Then?" he prompted.

"I wasn't . . ." I gasped. Just remembering was making the panic rise again, and it was then that I knew he was right. I'd had a panic attack.

Through my rising heartbeat and my labored breathing, I heard him tell me to focus, to remember the numbers, to remember I was safe with him in his home. It helped. The fear gripping me slowly ebbed, and I was able to take in my surroundings again.

We sat there in his chair for the next two hours talking about the day, about everything that had happened. He made me tell him about Ian breaking my arm. "Which arm," he asked. When I'd shown him, his response was to pick up said arm and place a soft kiss directly in the middle. It was an unbelievably sweet thing, but one I had started to expect from him.

When we got to the kiss in my bed, he asked me to tell him how

I felt about it. I tried, but my words were weak and feeble. I'd stuttered and stopped several times around words like nice, scared, happy, and confused. Finally, he took hold of my face and said, "I told you the truth today, Brianna."

His eyes left me no doubt that he was talking about his declaration that he wanted me but would not take me until I asked. I wondered again why that was important to him. He said he wanted all of me, but he *had* all of me. I was his slave after all. He owned me. Right?

I sat in his arms pondering what he'd said. He would not have sex with me until I asked. The question that came to my mind, however, was would I *ever* ask?

Stephan

The talk with Brianna had been difficult for both of us. I'd almost lost her twice to panic attacks as she told me about her time with Ian, those experiences were still so real for her.

Dinner was solemn. I could only imagine what was going through her mind as we ate. Mine was focused on what Lily had whispered to me just before she left. Brianna had asked her how long she and I had known each other. I wasn't sure of the significance of this, but Lily seemed to think it was an important piece of information for me to have.

After dinner we settled back into my chair and just watched some television. I'd never spent so much time with a woman before, and I found myself devoting most of it to watching her more than what was on the screen.

At the end of the night, we followed our normal ritual. With what had happened earlier I wanted to give her control of our kiss tonight. She pressed her lips to mine with more pressure than her usual kisses but nothing compared to this afternoon. I moved my mouth with hers, enjoying the only closeness from her that I was able. My hands itched to find purchase in her hair, but this was her kiss, she had the control.

Slowly she pulled away and raised her eyes to meet mine shyly. But before I could say anything, she rose from my lap. She waited for me to get up and walked just behind me until we reached the section of wall separating our two rooms. "Good night, Brianna."

"Good night, Master."

I waited until she disappeared into her room before walking into mine for my nightly shower.

~ * ~

Monday morning started out fairly normal, for which I was eternally grateful. There had been no Karl and no Lily waiting for me when I arrived. Jamie brought a bottle of water in for me just before ten, and I gave her instructions to hold my calls from twelve to one.

It had been over two weeks since I'd done more than a speedy workout in the small executive gym down the hall. I'd had one of the old offices that had previously been used for storage converted into a gym almost immediately upon taking my full-time position. Fitness had not been a high priority for my father, but it was for me. Given my lifestyle choice, I needed to be in excellent shape.

All the executives were invited to use the space, although not many of them did besides Lily. Of course, her reasons for staying in shape were the same as my own.

At twelve o'clock I locked down my computer and changed into my workout clothes before heading down to the gym. Jamie smiled and waved to me as I walked past. It was good to feel some normalcy again.

After some basic stretches, I got on the treadmill and began walking. A mile registered on the machine, and I began picking up the pace. Soon I was running and it felt wonderful.

When the timer went off, I was drenched and feeling good. Moving over to the free weights, I began my regular routine of curls and presses. My muscles were feeling the burn when I heard the door open and Jamie's frantic voice. "He doesn't wish to be disturbed."

When I turned, I saw my uncle standing just inside the door, trailed by a rarely flustered Jamie.

"I'm so sorry, Mr. Coleman."

"It's okay, Jamie."

She hesitated for a moment, giving my uncle one last look, and then left.

Figuring my workout was pretty much over at this point, I replaced the weights and started stretching. I didn't address my uncle's presence. He'd been clear on his position regarding Brianna, and I had no desire to hear more from him.

When he realized I was just going to ignore him, he asked, "Aren't you curious why I drove across town to see you in the middle of the day?"

"Not really, no, but I'm assuming you're going to tell me."

I heard something land on one of the benches. Whatever it was wasn't heavy. "I brought the results of Brianna's lab work. Everything came back clean."

For just a moment my heart softened toward my uncle. He'd driven through traffic on his lunch hour to hand deliver the results.

"Thank you," I said with sincerity.

He didn't respond to my thanks. That put me on alert, and I was not disappointed.

"Stephan, I wish you would reconsider getting her professional help. I have no idea what happened to her, but you have to—"

That was it, the last straw. "I am not discussing this with you," I said, finality in my tone.

This seemed to silence him for a few minutes. I turned to pick up the towel I'd brought in with me and the envelope he'd thrown down on the bench. My workout was over. I needed to get back to my office and shower.

He followed me out into the hall and down to my office. Jamie was still looking wary as we passed, and I tried to send her a reassuring smile.

Continuing to ignore my uncle, I walked straight to my closet, took the suit I'd hung up less than an hour ago, and headed into my bathroom.

The shower felt good. I wanted to linger underneath the spray, but I knew Richard wasn't finished and would be waiting for me.

After drying off and dressing quickly, I exited my bathroom to find my uncle sitting in the chair directly across from my desk and looking deep in thought.

Taking a seat behind my desk, I looked directly at him, my gaze hard and unwavering. When his eyes met mine, they didn't hold the hostility I'd expected. "After last Sunday, your aunt is convinced that I'm the reason you don't come over anymore."

I snorted. "You've made your feelings regarding my choices quite clear."

He sighed and shifted nervously in his seat. "Just tell me you're not having sex with her."

"Brianna? You think I'm having sex with her?"

"Aren't you?" I heard the uncertainty in his voice this time. When I didn't say anything more, he added, "I mean she's living with you and, well . . . with your . . . I mean . . ."

"You can say it, Richard. With my being a Dominant."

"I didn't mean . . ."

"Yes, you did." I pressed my thumb and forefinger to my temple in frustration. This was getting us nowhere fast.

I took a deep breath and cleared my head of everything other than the task at hand. "First, she may be living in my house, but she is staying in the guest room. Second, I have not had sex with her. Of any kind," I clarified. "She is in no mental condition to be making such decisions."

"But at the house you kissed her," he stated as if trying to give evidence to his case, but there was no venom behind it.

I sighed. "Yes, we've kissed. Kissing is all we've done," I said pointedly. "No matter what you think of me, I wouldn't take advantage of her like that."

Silence floated heavy in the air for several minutes before he said, "I'm sorry. I've not been fair to you."

"No, you haven't," I answered calmly and without the sting I still felt at his lack of faith.

"Will you come to dinner Sunday? You and Brianna?" The look on my face must not have been promising when he added, "Diane misses you. Please don't let me be the reason you are staying away."

I sighed and nodded.

He smiled at me and then got up to leave. "I'll tell Diane to expect you around one, then." When he reached the door he paused, looked back at me, and said, "Take care of her, Stephan." Then he was gone.

My plan had been to leave work at three so that I could go shopping with Brianna. Originally I'd hoped she would be able to attempt it on her own, however after what happened yesterday I didn't want to chance it just yet.

But at three, I was only halfway through a report that needed to be finished today, so I picked up the phone and dialed Brianna. She picked up on the second ring. "Hello?"

"Hello, Brianna."

"Hello, Master."

The smile in her voice came through the phone. I remembered the first few times I'd called her from work. Her voice had been full of fear. It was nice to know things were getting better for her.

"I'm going to be later getting home than I planned. Don't worry about dinner tonight. We'll get something out and then go to the store."

"Okay," she said, still sounding relaxed and happy.

"I'll call you when I leave so you can be ready."

"Yes, Master."

Our call disconnected a few seconds later, and I pushed my way through the rest of my work. It was after four by the time I was finished, and as promised I called her when I reached my car to let her know I was on my way.

When I arrived home, she was waiting for me as always just inside the door. Reaching out to her, I did what I'd been longing to do all day and ran my fingers through her hair. A breathy sigh escaped her lips as she leaned into my hand.

"Good evening, Brianna."

"Good evening, Master."

I took a step back and reached out a hand to help her stand. She took it and stood before me with her eyes cast down. "Are you ready to go?"

"Yes," she answered. Taking her by the hand, we got back into the elevator and headed to my car.

I took her to one of my favorite restaurants and asked for a booth in the back. This was going to be another first for her, and I didn't want an audience should something go wrong.

We got a few curious looks from the hostess as she waited for us to take our seats. Brianna was doing well so far. While she had stuck close to me ever since we exited my car, I had not felt her stiffen as she had this weekend. I did have to acknowledge, however, that neither the sidewalk nor the restaurant were as filled with people as the mall had been.

The hostess handed us our menus and left, saying our waiter would be with us shortly. It didn't take me long to decide on what I wanted as I'd been here many times before. When I set my menu down I noticed that Brianna had not even looked at hers. "Do you know what you want?" I asked her.

Brianna's eyes widened slightly at my question, but I just continued to wait. She knew I expected an answer.

First she looked down at her menu and then back up at me. "Am I allowed to choose?" she asked quietly.

"Of course," I said trying to keep the surprise out of my voice.

A small smile tugged at her lips before she picked up her menu and began reading in earnest. I watched every movement she made. The smallest things gave her joy, and I was pleased to be part of giving her that.

I was still watching her when our waiter approached. There was no doubt as to when Brianna noticed him because every muscle in her body went rigid. Reaching for her hand, I linked our fingers and turned my attention to our server.

Roger, our waiter for the evening, set two glasses of water in front of us while introducing himself. After a few pleasantries, I ordered an appetizer and asked for a few more minutes. With a small bow he left us alone once again.

As soon as he was out of sight, I turned to Brianna, moved our linked hands down under the table, and brought my other hand up to turn her face toward me. "Number, Brianna."

"Four," she whispered.

I nodded. Truthfully I had been expecting her to say something higher. However, looking at her closely I could see that her breathing was still fairly steady and her color was good.

I rubbed her cheek gently with my thumb. "He won't hurt you," I said with conviction.

It took her a moment to respond, but when she did I saw her square her shoulders and nod. Her strength constantly amazed me.

I kept my hand in hers as I asked her if she'd made a selection. "The chicken parmesan," she said, but it came out as more of a question.

I gave her a reassuring smile as I squeezed her hand. "That is an excellent choice."

I noticed our waiter across the room at another table and got a sudden burst of inspiration. Angling my face so that I was not looking directly at her but could still see her reaction, I said, "When the waiter comes back to the table you will tell him what you want for dinner."

There was nothing for a long second before I both felt and heard her reaction. Last week I would have jumped in and tried to comfort her right away, but tonight I wanted to see if she could get a hold of herself. She had the number system I'd given her and the safewords. Now I needed to see what, if anything, she would do with them.

I watched her panic continue to rise as our waiter walked to our table. He stood before us and smiled. "Are you ready to order?"

Neither of us responded for a long moment. I was almost ready to speak up since Roger was already eyeing Brianna with slight concern when I suddenly felt her grip on my hand tighten almost painfully and a small voice beside me say, "Chicken parmesan. Please."

"Excellent choice, ma'am. And for you sir?" he asked.

"I'll have the special this evening."

"Very well, sir," he replied, picking up our menus. "Your appetizer will be out shortly."

I barely waited for his back to turn before pulling Brianna into my arms, kissing her solidly, and burying my nose in her hair. It took her a moment to respond to my sudden action, but when she did it was like something deflated inside her. All at once all the tension she'd been holding left her, and I heard her sob.

Placing a kiss on her temple, I pulled back to look into her glistening eyes. I knew right then that without a doubt, Lily had been right. I loved Brianna Reeves.

Chapter Twenty-Two

Brianna

I did it. I really did it.

Master was staring at me with a huge smile on his face, but I could barely see him through the tears pooling in my eyes. His right hand came up and brushed lightly across my cheek. I hadn't realized the tears had started falling until that moment.

His touch was so gentle, and I knew without him saying it that he was proud of me. For some reason he wanted me not to be afraid. And I wanted that, too. For him. Master was so wonderful to me that I wanted to give him something back, and it was the only thing I had to give.

The waiter came to our table and laid down a plate. I knew he was there, and my body stiffened slightly even though I tried to will it not to. It helped that Master didn't release me or move at all. He acted like nothing existed outside of us.

Slowly Master removed his hand from my face. It was almost like he didn't want to but was forcing himself. He turned back to the table, releasing his hold on me altogether, and I immediately wanted it back.

No. I was never his slave. And neither are you.

I watched as Master moved the small pieces of bread, cheese, and basil from the large plate the waiter brought onto the small ones in front of us. His movements were so fluid, so graceful.

What had Lily meant?

He took a small bite of his food and chewed. When he realized I wasn't following his example he glanced over at me and ordered, "Eat."

With a deep breath to steady myself, I reached for the bread and took a bite. It was delicious. The bread must have been made fresh today, and the mozzarella was fresh, too. A leaf of basil created a nice contrast to the other two flavors. It was perfect.

I was so lost in my food and also keeping a covert watch on Master's movements that I didn't see our waiter approaching with our dinners. His voice caused me to jump, and Master's hand fell onto my arm. Nothing could calm me like Master's touch, but my heart was still pounding in my chest until the waiter went away.

We ate our meal in silence. It was just as good as the appetizer had been. Master let me taste a piece of his. I'd never had duck before.

After dinner we went to the grocery store just as he'd said. There were more people there tonight than when I'd come with Lily, and I moved closer to Master. He put his arm around my shoulders and pulled me closer. I felt his breath against my hair.

"You're doing fine, Brianna. Just remember your numbers."

Numbers. Yes. Remember the numbers.

He took a small step away from me and placed his hand in mine. Master didn't move; he just stood there waiting. I realized he was waiting for me. With a deep breath, I took a step forward.

Master walked beside me as I pushed the cart through the store. Occasionally he'd pick up something and put it inside but mostly he just watched me.

At one point, Master walked several feet away to select something he wanted from the shelf. He'd done the same thing a couple of times before, but in that same moment a man holding a basket walked into the aisle about ten feet ahead of us. I felt my body tense and my breathing pick up. He looked directly at me.

I'd never seen this man before, but for some reason the way he was staring at me sent chills up my spine.

Remember your numbers.

Numbers, numbers.

The man walked toward me at a steady pace, and my eyes flashed to Master. His back was to me. I didn't think he'd seen the man. What should I do?

Numbers.

Five.

He came closer.

Six.

The man was only a few feet away. His eyes were now filled with an expression I didn't understand.

Seven.

I felt pain in my chest as the man slid between Master and me. His chest brushed against me as he turned to the side to get through the narrowed space. I could feel his breath against my neck he was so close!

Eight. Eight!

"Yellow," I choked. Oh please, please.

I felt someone pulling at my fingers that were now holding onto the cart in a death grip. No. Please no. No.

"Brianna."

The fingers that had been pulling at my hands were gone now.

Soft hands touched my face. "Brianna, open your eyes," said a firm voice.

When I forced my eyes open, it was Master's face that I found. I knew I shouldn't have, but I needed to be close to him. I released the cart and fell against him. The worst he could do was push me away here in the store. I didn't care what he did to me later.

But he didn't push me away. Instead he wrapped his arms around my shoulders and held me tighter. All the panic I'd felt faded away. I was safe. Master would protect me.

I had no idea how long we stayed like that. Someone asked Master if I was okay, and he answered that I was fine. We were causing a scene. I was causing a scene. But he didn't seem to care.

Tilting my head up just a little so that he and he alone could hear me, I whispered, "Thank you, Master."

He kissed my hair and squeezed me tighter. "Are you all right?" I nodded.

Now that I'd calmed down I realized how silly my reaction had been. Master was right there only a few feet away. I was his. He wouldn't have let anything happen to me.

Then he surprised me by asking, "Do you wish to go home or do you want to continue?"

I glanced over at our groceries, but his hand pulled my chin back so that I was looking at him. "Brianna, I don't care about the food. It can rot here in the middle of the store for all I care. Do *you* want to finish shopping or do *you* wish to go home?"

The thought of leaving all this food to *rot*, as he'd said, didn't feel right, but I knew he meant every word. Master would leave, just as he said he would, if that was what I wanted. He was leaving the option up to me.

"I'd like to finish, please." He nodded and released me.

We finished our shopping, but he never left my side again. His hand touched some part of me at all times.

Stephan

I continued to think about what happened at the store the entire way home. In a way I was glad. At least I'd been there, and she had used her safeword. The downside was that she had panicked and had to use that safeword.

She walked behind me as we entered my condo, both our arms full of groceries. Once we were in the kitchen, I set the bags down and left her to put them away.

In my room, I removed the jacket and tie from work I was still wearing since I'd not taken the time to change before we left. Unbuttoning the top two buttons of my shirt, I looked at myself in the mirror.

I could hear her moving around in the other room. The pull I felt toward her continued to get stronger as did the conviction I'd felt tonight at dinner. Somehow in all this mess I had fallen in love with the woman now gracing my kitchen.

Running a hand through my hair, I took a deep breath. I had no idea what I was going to do, no idea how to deal with these emotions I felt.

Why did the first time I fell in love have to be with a woman who may never be capable of loving me back?

For one moment I let myself imagine what it would be like to have her feel for me what I did for her. To be able to show her how I felt. Just thinking about it made my heart race like never before.

The memory of her spread out naked on her bed flashed in my mind, and I had to force it away. As much as I wanted her, I couldn't have her. I had to face the very real possibility that she would never want me like I wanted her. Never be able to look at me as anything more than the person who bought her.

My head fell into my hands and I groaned. Just the idea caused me pain. I would let her go, though. I loved her enough to let her go.

After spending several minutes pushing my fear of losing her deep inside, I made my way back into the main room to find her sitting on the couch. Glancing in the kitchen, I could see that everything was put away and in its place, not that I'd expected any different. Brianna took her responsibilities very seriously.

She didn't look up when I came in, but I could tell she was aware of me. Good.

Brianna kept her eyes lowered as I made my way over to my chair. I sat down, placed my hands on the armrests, and told her to sit on my lap.

Her progress amazed me. She was gaining confidence every day. Brianna was the strongest woman I had ever met.

She sat on my legs with hands folded loosely. Her posture was alert but relaxed.

With my left hand I brushed her hair back away from her face. "You did very well this evening at the restaurant. I was impressed."

She nodded. "Thank you, Master."

I saw a small smile play at her lips. She was obviously impressed with herself as well.

My hand moved up and down her arm slowly. I needed to touch her in some way, to show her how I felt, even if I couldn't tell her with words. "You started to panic at first. What changed?"

She didn't answer me right away, but I could tell by the look on her face that she was thinking so I waited. We sat for at least ten minutes before she finally said, "I don't know. I was . . . scared," she said and then paused for several seconds. I was sure she was gauging my reaction to her confession.

When I didn't respond in any way, she continued. I saw a light blush color her cheeks as she said, "Then I . . ." She swallowed. "I told myself you wouldn't let anything happen to me."

My heart jumped at her confession. I knew my touch calmed her. I'd seen it firsthand many times before. But for her to admit such a thing, to connect it, and have it help her . . .

I pulled her closer to me and tucked her head beneath my chin. She leaned into me, and I thought I felt her release a small sigh. "I would never let anything happen to you," I confirmed.

We sat for a long time without a sound between us except our breathing. I knew we needed to talk about what had happened at the grocery store, and it was getting late.

Without moving either of us from our current position, I said, "You used your safeword tonight." I felt her stiffen. "Thank you." She needed to know above all else that I wanted her to use her safewords. I didn't want her to be afraid of them.

Brianna relaxed once more in my arms, and again I let a few moments lapse before continuing. "Will you tell me what caused you to reach an eight? Why did you panic?"

She took a deep breath, and I could feel her preparing herself. I rubbed my hand up and down her arm, trying to comfort her. "That man . . ."

I waited for her to continue, but after several minutes she did not. "What about the man?"

"I don't know," she confessed and I believed her.

"I know this will be hard, Brianna, but I want you to close your eyes and think back. What was it about the man that scared you?"

A small motion brought my attention to her hands. They were balled into fists. I hated that this was so difficult for her, but it was necessary if she was ever to attempt a normal life.

"His eyes," she whispered.

"What about his eyes?"

I felt her shake her head against my shoulder and then heard a sob. "I don't know."

Pulling her tighter against me, I placed a soft kiss to her head and held her while she calmed down.

I looked at my watch and knew we needed to be going to bed soon. With my left hand I took her right one and brought it up to her neck. "This," I said, brushing both our fingers along her collar, "is a symbol to show that I am always with you. I would never let someone take you away from me, Brianna."

I gave her a moment to process that information. "Do you

believe me?"

"Yes," she said without hesitation. I nodded and just took a moment to enjoy the feeling of her in my arms.

Long before I wanted to, I repositioned her on my lap so that I could see her face. "I want to talk about this some more, but I would like for you to try and figure out what exactly it was about this man's eyes that bothered you. I don't want you to always be afraid."

"I will try for you, Master."

Bringing my hands up to surround her face, I leaned in and pressed my lips against hers. The feel of her soft mouth against mine was absolutely amazing. She leaned into me, and even though I knew I shouldn't, I took the invitation.

My tongue slipped through my lips and pressed against hers. She opened to me, and I wasted no time diving in and tasting her once again.

Brianna moved her tongue with mine as she had before, but this was so much different than the first time. On her bed it had been aggressive, heated. Here it was softer, and for my part, filled with love rather than lust.

The problem with that, however, was that my body had difficulty telling the difference. Before I wanted to, I had to pull back. She had had a rough day and the last thing she needed was for me to lose control and push our physical boundaries. I shouldn't even be kissing her like I was, but I couldn't find it within myself to be sorry.

Her eyes opened and met mine.

I love you, Brianna.

But instead of saying the words shouting at me in my head, I walked her to her room and said good night.

Chapter Twenty-Three

Stephan

Tuesday morning I said goodbye to Brianna with a little more reluctance than usual. For some reason it was harder to separate myself from her than it had been before, not that before it had been easy. She accepted my soft kiss just before I walked out the door and had a smile on her face when I left her.

The day was uneventful, thankfully. Sure, I'd had to deal with a few everyday problems, but nothing that added too much stress upon my already complicated life.

At five o'clock, I said good night to Jamie and drove home.

My excitement grew as I rode the elevator to my condo. And just like always, she was there on the floor, waiting for me.

Crossing the short distance between the door and where she knelt seemed too far. But it was like a breath of fresh air when my hand made its way into her hair, and I felt her lean into me. "Good evening, Brianna."

"Good evening, Master." Her voice held more confidence each day.

Three weeks. I couldn't believe it had been three weeks.

Raising her chin, I peered into her eyes. They were open, looking directly into mine. So much different than that first night, that first week.

She held my gaze for several moments before I pulled back and helped her to stand. "Prepare the table. I'll be there in a minute." With that I walked away, leaving her standing near the door.

Dinner was uneventful. Although I wanted to ask her questions, I knew it was best to wait until after. Talking seemed to be easier for her when we were touching.

After going through our days, our conversation revisited her experience the previous night. We talked about why the man's eyes had bothered her, and it seemed she viewed them as *aggressive*. Her word, not mine.

"I want to try something. Stand up for me." She nodded and stood, waiting.

I guided her to an open area of the room and took several steps back from her.

Brianna started to lower her head, but I stopped her. "No. I want you to look at me. Look directly into my eyes."

She complied and waited. I didn't make her wait long. I closed my eyes, took a deep breath, and let a part of my nature that I'd been keeping tightly under wraps come to the surface. When I opened my eyes, I saw her reaction immediately.

Her entire body stiffened, and her eyes widened in fear and apprehension. Her breath picked up as my eyes roamed her body, the hunger in them painfully obvious. This was a side of me Brianna had only gotten a glimpse of once before and in a very small dose.

With measured steps I stalked toward her, each step predatory. She was trying very hard not to react to her obvious fear. I saw her legs twitch like she was preparing to run.

Closing the last feet between us, I kept my eyes firmly fixed on hers. "Was this the way his eyes looked, Brianna?"

I saw her swallow, but she didn't answer.

"Answer me!"

"Yes!" she cried as the first tears erupted down her cheeks.

I pulled her into my arms. She held herself stiff, every muscle ready to react.

"Shh. Calm down, love. It's just me. You are safe," I said, kissing her just above her ear.

It took several minutes before I felt the tension begin to leave her body. And when it did, the tears came in endless waves. I held her to my body for a long time before picking her up and carrying her into her bedroom.

I laid her down and tried to pull back, but she held tighter. I wasn't sure what to do, but before I could make a decision her arms fell away.

After standing, I looked down at her lying there. Her eyes were looking down, not meeting mine.

Brianna had a fear of men in general, but especially predatory men, aggressive men. The man in the store had obviously found her attractive and had been expressing that want through his eyes. Sadly he didn't know that his look of hungry appreciation would have the opposite effect with Brianna. It didn't turn her on or make her feel wanted.

I knew Ian could have that predatory look. I'd seen a little of it in his office. But how many other men had Brianna seen that look from?

She'd been so sure that I'd share her with Logan, so I had no doubt in my mind that she'd been shared in the past. The question was, how many men had she been shared with, and just what had they done to her to make her so fearful of being desired?

With that thought, I felt anger growing inside again. All those unknown men touching her against her wishes. I shook it off. Letting what happened in her past get to me would not help her.

Several minutes had passed, but she still wasn't looking at me. I didn't address her right away, though. Instead I walked over to her dresser. I grabbed a pair of shorts and a tank top for her before walking back over to her bed.

I debated whether or not I should proceed. It wasn't like I hadn't seen her naked before, but I still hadn't forgotten how the last time had ended.

But then again, maybe that was exactly why I should continue. She needed to know that I wouldn't do anything she didn't wish me to, even when I could look at her as I had in the other room.

Laying the clothes down on her nightstand, I extended my hand to her. "Sit up."

She took a deep breath and then pushed herself into a sitting position while taking my hand. Her gaze fell to her lap as I twisted her around so that her feet were on the floor.

I released her hand and reached for the hem of her shirt. "Raise your arms above your head."

Her entire body tensed again, but she did as instructed. I pulled her T-shirt up her torso and over her head. She still wasn't looking at me.

I reached behind her, unclasped her bra, and tossed it over to join her shirt at the end of the bed. My movements were unhurried as I took the tank top and placed it over her head. She didn't fight me when I placed her arms through the straps and slid the garment into place.

Then I knelt before her and removed her shoes and socks. My hands gently slid up her ankles and wrapped around them as I looked up at her. She was watching me but she looked away again almost as soon as our eyes met.

I didn't comment, but instead rose again, my hand outstretched. "Stand up," I said softly.

Her body was close to mine as she stood. There was so little separating us, and I didn't stop the impulse I had to kiss her. I took her face in my hands and brushed my lips against hers.

It was such a light touch, but I needed the contact. I hated to see her so scared even though I knew this process would uncover all her fears.

Her eyes fluttered open and met mine as I leaned back. "You never have to be afraid of me, Brianna." She clamped her lips together, and I ran my thumb over them until I felt them relax and soften.

I released her face, brought my hands down to her waist, unbuttoned her jeans, and pushed the zipper down before sliding them down her legs. When they reached her ankles, she held onto my arms as she stepped out of them.

The bruises on the inside of her thighs had completely faded now, but the burn marks would always be a permanent reminder of what she'd gone through, what she'd survived. I longed to kiss each and every inch of her skin, but I held myself in check this time. Instead I took her shorts and bent down to help her put them on.

Once she was fully dressed for bed I asked her if she needed to go to the bathroom. She nodded, and I stepped back, letting her know I wanted her to go ahead. I watched as she slowly walked across the room and disappeared into the attached bathroom.

While she was gone I waited patiently on her bed. Looking

around the room I noticed that even though she had been living here for three weeks, the only evidence of her habitation, besides the slept-in bed, were the two books on her nightstand. Everything else was exactly as it had been before she'd arrived. It was like she would only occupy the space temporarily, a room, a place to sleep, not a home.

Brianna didn't take long in the bathroom, but when she returned she looked uncertain again. I stood and motioned for her to come to me.

Her walk was slow, but eventually she made it back to my side. I pulled back the covers and helped her lie down. This time her eyes didn't leave me.

After tucking the sheets around her, I leaned in and placed a kiss on her forehead.

"Good night, Brianna," I whispered against her flesh.

"Good night, Master," she whispered back.

The next morning, I called Jamie and asked her to see if Brad could stop by my office around midday even though I knew he would come anytime I asked. That man was more than predictable. I honestly thought he'd jump off a cliff if I asked him to.

Sure enough, at twelve fifteen Jamie knocked on my door to let me know Brad had arrived. "Tell him I'll meet him in the gym in five minutes."

I changed quickly and headed down the hall. Brad was standing near the stack of weights against the wall but turned when he heard me come in. "Mr. Coleman," he gushed.

Brad was a great personal trainer. He had a way of creating targeted workouts for his clients but changed things up often enough to keep it challenging. "Hello, Brad."

He moved toward me. "Was there a problem with your workout, sir?"

It was no wonder he thought there was a problem. We normally met once every six weeks to go over and change things. I was two weeks early. "No. The workout is fine," I said as I walked over to the mat to begin my routine. "I wanted to talk to you about how things are going with Brianna."

"Ah," he mused as he watched me move. It never escaped my notice that he paid a little too much attention to certain areas than others, but he'd never been inappropriate. I was a valued client and he treated me as such. "The beautiful Anna is doing very well. The treadmill has been hard for her to master, but everything else has been easy enough. Did you wish to step things up?"

Anna? Why did he call her Anna?

I shook my head, looking at him in the mirror. "No. Not exactly. I wanted to see what you thought about adding some self-defense moves to her program. Nothing too complicated, but something she can add to in the future."

He nodded. "Some lunges and general agility would be a good starting point for her, I think."

I agreed. Anything more would overwhelm her.

I stepped onto the treadmill, pressed the buttons, and began my warm-up. "Are you having any trouble getting her to communicate with you?"

My pace picked up to a run as he answered. "She doesn't talk much, but if I ask her something, she answers. If I tell her to do something differently, she does her best to correct it."

I nodded and continued my run while he watched. Brianna's interaction with Brad hadn't concerned me too much. Given he did not find females in the least bit attractive, I doubted Brianna would fear him as she did most males. He wasn't a threat.

Brad didn't comment until I slowed back down to a walk. "Looks like we are going to be increasing your cardio soon. That was way too easy for you." He laughed.

"Speak for yourself," I said, stepping off the machine.

He walked toward me and placed his fingers at my pulse point to check my heart rate. I noticed his pulse beat a little faster at the contact and had to suppress a laugh. After a few seconds, he lowered his hand and nodded. "It's within the acceptable range, but I'd still like to increase it."

I wouldn't argue with him. Walking over to the weights, I said, "Have Jamie set up a two-hour block in two weeks, and we can rework the specifics for both Brianna and myself."

"I'll see you in two weeks," he said as I saw him take one extra-long look at me in the mirror before turning to leave.

I shook my head and finished my workout. I wasn't sure if I should be flattered or cringe at the fact that my personal trainer was very obviously attracted to me.

Thursday night I decided not to push things with Brianna. We'd already made such progress this week, and I wanted to reward her. After dinner we just sat in my chair and watched television while I held her. All the while my mind kept returning to what Brad had called her today. Anna. Why had he called her Anna?

One o'clock on Friday I received a call from my lawyer. Oscar informed me that his secretary received a call earlier that morning from someone claiming to be from the sheriff's department, inquiring about a Brianna Reeves.

He assured me that no information had been given and that the person had been told none could be released without a court order. Apparently the person on the other end of the line hadn't liked that answer and had then become rather forceful in their requests to the point where Oscar himself had had to take the phone and inform the caller that he would file an official grievance should this persist.

The man had quickly ended the call after that. And after talking with his secretary, Oscar realized that they had not even gotten the man's name.

I, however, had a pretty good suspicion as to who it had been. My only question was why now, after eleven months, was Jonathan Reeves looking for his daughter?

Brianna

This week was full of mixed emotions for me. It had been filled with so many ups and downs.

Master seemed to be happy with me, even though I had embarrassed him in both the restaurant and the store on Monday. He'd been kind to me Tuesday as we'd talked again about the man at the store and then again after he'd stalked toward me like some kind of animal.

But he'd been right. The look in his eyes had been the exact look that had been in that man's. Master hadn't said anything about it after that night, but I had no doubt that he would at some time. It seemed he liked to talk about things, especially the things that scared me.

Wednesday I'd had more time to myself than usual since both the house was clean and I didn't have to work out. It left me a lot of time to think, and my mind wouldn't stop returning to what Lily had said. *No. I was never his slave. And neither are you.*

So I decided I'd try to watch him closer than I had before. But by Friday night when he'd come home from work, I was still as confused and unsure as I had ever been.

A part of me just said to ask him. But what if Lily was wrong and I was his slave? I liked the way things were now. What if asking him changed things?

After dinner on Friday he told me that we would be going over to his aunt and uncle's house again on Sunday. I wasn't sure how I felt about that, but of course it wasn't my decision. We would go wherever Master wanted.

Saturday morning I woke up to find Master in the kitchen making eggs. I went to kneel, but he stopped me. "Set the table, please, Brianna."

I moved to get the plates, silverware, and juice out on the table quickly. He brought the pan over with the eggs and divided them up on our plates. Then he walked back to the stove, and brought back with him a plate full of bacon and another with four slices of toast.

Master laid everything down and took a seat. "Sit and eat," he ordered.

Breakfast was very good. I noticed Master kept things simple when he cooked, but what he made was always tasty.

About halfway through, he spoke up. "It's a beautiful day today, and we are going out. Make sure to wear shoes you can walk in. When you're finished, do what you need to do and meet me by the door."

That was all he said as we finished the rest of the meal in silence. He stayed seated until I was finished before getting up and removing our plates. I did as he'd instructed and went to my room to get ready.

My mind was racing as to what he might have in store for us today. Truthfully, I was both scared and excited. Would we go to a restaurant again, the mall, a store? Or would we go somewhere completely new?

Minneapolis was a big city, so it really could be anything. I just had to remember that he would take care of me. He would protect me. I would be fine.

When I came out of my room, Master was waiting for me. I

walked to him with my head down, and he took my hand. We left our jackets at home and headed down in the elevator. This time, however, we didn't go to the parking garage.

The elevator stopped and opened into a large lobby with marble floors. We walked down a short hallway toward a set of doors. But before we reached them, a man behind a large desk off to the right called out a greeting to Master. "Good morning, Mr. Coleman."

"Good morning, Tom." The man, Tom, smiled at my Master like he knew him well, and Master smiled back before leading me out the doors.

Master had been right. It was a beautiful start to a spring day. The sky was overcast, but it wasn't raining, and the air felt warm against my skin.

We began walking briskly down the city streets. If I hadn't been doing my workouts, I would never have been able to keep up with him.

There were people everywhere, but Master didn't let go of my hand. We walked for over a mile before stopping in front of what looked like a bicycle shop. He pulled us both inside and after a few minutes we had a scooter and two helmets.

I'd never ridden a scooter before, but it turned out to be rather fun. My arms were wrapped around Master's waist, and I was able to see so much of the city as he drove.

Soon we were driving out of the city. The number of buildings lessened, and the number of trees increased. I lost track of how long he'd been driving and just enjoyed the ride.

Once we left Minneapolis behind us it wasn't too much farther before Master turned onto a side road that led to a park entrance. He followed a winding road through the trees that created a canopy above us. The road opened up ahead, and Master parked the scooter in one of the marked spots.

The scooter had a compartment under the seat where he placed the helmets before grabbing my hand and pulling me forward. We walked toward the trees, and I felt myself start to panic when I realized where we were going. The sign ahead gave little doubt as to what we were going to do. Hiking.

I was a horrible hiker. Trees literally came up from out of the ground just to trip me whenever I attempted it.

But even as the thought crossed my mind to tell him I couldn't do this, I pushed it away. It didn't matter where we were going any more now than it did before. This was what Master wanted, so this was what we would do. All I could attempt to do was not fall on my face.

It only took about fifty feet down the trail for me to trip over a root. Master was still holding my hand and felt me stumble. He made sure I was stable again before moving closer and placing his arm around my waist.

I still tripped a few times after that, even though I kept my eyes on my feet the entire time. But with Master's arm around me, I never came close to falling.

We walked for what seemed like hours before he guided me off the path. The going was slower now. There were fallen trees and plants everywhere.

Suddenly the area opened up again and there was another trail before us. This one was different than the other. The overgrowth along the edges indicated it had not been used very often.

Then we stopped. He released me and reached into the back pocket of his jeans. When his hand reappeared he held a long black piece of fabric. I just stared and felt my panic begin to rise when he came to stand behind me.

Master's arms appeared on either side of me. One hand held the black . . . scarf?

"I'm going to put this over your eyes, Brianna." I swallowed and tried to remember to breathe. He didn't say anything else as he took the free end of the material in his other hand and brought the middle level with my eyes.

And then there was nothing but black as he pulled the scarf and tied it securely behind my head. I was in total darkness.

Chapter Twenty-Four

Brianna

The utter lack of light was making me uneasy. It reminded me of being in Ian's dungeon. But then I felt Master's arms come around me, and I was able to calm myself. I was safe. With my Master.

Instead of wrapping around me, his arms only touched my sides. "Put your arms in front of you and take my hands, Brianna," he instructed.

Blindly, I reached out using what I could feel as a guide. It took some work, but eventually I found his hands and laced my fingers with his.

Master's hold was firm. "We're going to walk together. It isn't far, and I've got you so you won't fall. Take your time and try to feel what is under your feet."

I wasn't sure I could do this, but I was willing to try. He wouldn't let me fall.

I lifted my right foot and cautiously moved it forward. The ground was farther away than what it seemed without the blindfold.

My next step was just as unsure, as was the one following. I had no idea how long it was until he finally told me to stop. But even though we were no longer moving, he didn't remove the covering from my eyes. Instead, I felt him move away from me.

As much as I tried to stop it, I felt the panic eating at me. Logic told me that he wouldn't just leave me alone, but did I really know that for sure?

I did. Didn't I?

Without being able to see, I could hear so many things. I knew we were still in the forest. There were birds everywhere, surrounding me. I could hear other noises, too, but I couldn't quite define them.

I was so lost in my thoughts that I jumped when he spoke again.

"Today we are going to work on your focus," he said. His voice was moving as if he was circling me. "I want you to walk forward. You may go as slowly as you need. Your hands are to remain at your sides," he said, pausing as if to let that sink in. "I want you to tell me about your childhood. Your mother. Your pets. Your teachers."

I took a deep breath. Talking about my mom, although making me sad, wouldn't be that hard.

But then he continued. "I do not want you to stop talking until I tell you to. Do you understand?"

"Yes, Master," I said with confidence.

"Good girl," he said from behind me.

Then I felt something touch my hip. "While you're talking, I'm going to periodically touch various parts of your body like this," he said, giving my hip a light tap with what felt like a stick about the thickness of a pencil. "When I do, you will stop what you are saying long enough to say what part of your body I'm touching and then go back to your story. Can you do that?"

I nervously swallowed again but answered, "Yes. I think I can."

"You think you can, Brianna?" he said, his voice taking on a slightly harsher tone.

I took a deep breath and gave him what he wanted. "Yes, Master. I can do it."

"That's better," he said with a clear smile in his voice.

Then the pressure on my hip disappeared.

"Begin."

He'd asked that I talk about my mom, so I focused my thoughts only on her. I took the first tentative step and started talking. "Mom had me when she was only nineteen. She wasn't ready to settle down and get married, so she decided to move the two of us to Dallas."

As soon as I said the word *Dallas*, I felt the slight pressure of the stick again. "Shoulder," I said, before continuing with my story.

It seemed like I had talked for hours, telling him about my mom going back to school to become a teacher and how she'd gotten me a dog we'd called Rusty because of his red coat. I told him about Cliff. How mom had fallen head over heels for him and married him after only knowing him a month, but that when she was diagnosed with cancer, he'd taken off and served her with divorce papers not long after.

I hadn't fallen, although it had been close a few times. Only once in the story did I miss calling out when he'd touched me. His response had been a harder tap to my thigh that left a light sting in its wake. I didn't forget again.

Stephan

After contemplating Brianna's reaction to the man at the store, I decided that it came down to focus. She had lost all knowledge of her surroundings when she saw him looking at her with primal hunger in his eyes. Her panic had set in because she could not rationalize that she was safe in the store with me rather than in danger.

We needed to work on getting her to stay focused even when her mind was on other things, especially if school was going to happen. This had seemed like the perfect place to start.

As she'd talked about her mother, her dog, and even her stepdad, I had moved around her, changing both my position and the angle at which the thin branch I'd selected made contact with her body. Keeping the touches unpredictable.

She'd done well. Four times she'd lost her footing, but in each instance she kept herself from falling. Only once did Brianna not immediately pause her story to do as I'd instructed. And after the small reprimand she seemed even more determined not to make the same mistake twice. Brianna had a stubborn streak. That thought made me smile.

I learned a lot about her as she talked. Brianna had grown up quickly, especially after her mother got sick and her stepfather abandoned them. I'd known she was strong and smart already, but this just made me admire her more.

And as much as I wanted to end today on a positive note, I knew that the time had come to get some real answers from her. The phone call from Oscar meant that her father was looking for her, and I needed to know how she would feel about that.

But before delving into a subject I suspected would be difficult for her, I told her to stop moving and let the stick drop to the ground as I stepped closer. I stopped just inches in front of her. And even though her eyes were still covered, she knew I was there.

Her breathing picked up, but there was no sign of panic. I leaned in and let my breath brush the hair behind her ear. "Not bad, Brianna. Only one slip."

It took her a few seconds before I heard a soft, "Thank you, Master," fall from her lips.

Keeping my face just a breath away from her skin, I moved my mouth down the line of her jaw so that my own lips were hovering just above hers. I could tell she was waiting for me to kiss her, but I wanted to see if she'd ask. I was hoping she would ask.

It took one hundred and forty-two seconds before I heard the words from her that I had wanted to hear. "May I kiss you, Master?"

I moved my lips directly in front of hers before I answered. "You may," I whispered back.

Brianna's mouth blindly sought mine. Our lips came together, and I followed her lead.

Her mouth glided with mine. It was so innocent that it was difficult not to plunge my fingers into her hair and kiss her the way I wanted.

I controlled myself, though, and waited until she pulled back slightly.

The look on her face was one of happiness that I was beginning to see more and more.

This time when the impulse to touch her came, I didn't stop it. My hands came up to thread through the hair at the base of her neck. "Are you ready to continue, Brianna?"

"Yes, Master."

I allowed my fingers to linger at her neck for a moment then took a step back and retrieved my makeshift cane from the ground. As quietly as I could, I moved to stand behind her. And just to make sure she was paying attention, I placed the tip of the stick at her lower back. Obediently she said, "Back." My only response was a

Slave

smile, which she couldn't see.

It was time to get to the information I really needed. "Now, Brianna, I want you to tell me about your father."

Her intake of breath was so sharp she almost choked. "I know you lived with him after your mother died. Tell me about him."

This time when she didn't talk or move, I brought the stick down on her behind with a slight flick of my wrist. She responded immediately. Slowly she took a small step and began to speak in the same monotone voice she used when she was distancing herself. "My dad came to my mom's funeral, and then he took me back to Two Harbors, Minnesota with him. He's the . . . leg . . . county sheriff.

"J . . . John. He . . . my father . . ." I brought the stick to the top of her breast and it seemed to bring her out of the haze she'd started to fall into.

After answering with the appropriate body part, she continued her tale once again in the same lifeless tone. "Living with John was different. He worked and I went to school. I made dinner, did homework while he watched television. We didn't . . . ankle . . . talk much.

"Mom was outgoing. John . . . hip . . . was . . . leg . . . reserved. Mom always wanted to get out. Do things. John insisted we stay . . . home."

I hadn't missed her hesitation or the fact that she'd stumbled as she'd forced that last word out of her mouth. Leaning in, I once again pressed my lips close to her ear. "Where is your father now, Brianna?"

And then I heard a whimper escape her throat. "I don't know, Master. Please don't . . . I want to stay with you. I . . ." When I came back around to her front, the tears were streaming down her face.

I tossed the stick aside, pulled her into my arms, and lowered us to the soft ground. With her tucked into my chest, I reached up and removed the covering from her eyes.

She blinked several times, but instead of calming she cried harder and clung to my shirt. I wrapped my arms around her and just let her have a moment to release what had been building inside. Although I didn't have all the answers yet, I did know one thing. Brianna had no desire to see her father.

We sat for a long time before her tears began to ebb. "Are you

201

ready to talk to me?"

She nodded and burrowed her face even deeper in my chest.

I let a little chuckle escape me at that. "Love, I think it will work better if you talk to me rather than my shirt."

She stiffened a little, but I rubbed her arm in reassurance. I wasn't upset with her, and I could only imagine how difficult this was for her.

Brianna shifted slightly in my arms so that her cheek was resting against my shoulder. I brushed her hair back from her forehead and placed a soft kiss there, letting my lips linger. "Tell me how you came to be with Ian," I said softly.

Again she nodded. "It was a Saturday. I was home . . . alone." She swallowed and readjusted her grip on my shirt. "J . . . John." I felt her lean into me when she said his name. "He'd gone to Minneapolis for . . ."

She paused. I felt a drop of moisture land on my hand and knew she was crying again. I held her tighter. It was all I could do at the moment. "He said he was going for . . . work."

I had her folded against me with my arms around her waist. Her right hand wiggled its way out of its place between our bodies and gripped my hand. I gladly laced my fingers with hers.

After taking another deep breath, she continued. "I'd just finished cleaning up after lunch when the phone rang. It was . . . John. He told me that he wanted me to join him for dinner at a friend's house in Minneapolis. That a car was on its way to pick me up. To be ready by three o'clock. To . . . dress nice."

She held my hand tighter. "At three, a black car pulled up to the house. A man got out and opened the door for me."

Brianna stopped for a minute, but not like before. This time, she appeared to be thinking, considering her next words. With more caution, she continued. "John was a simple man and . . ." She paused. "I don't know much about cars, but I knew this one was expensive."

And then, as if she was talking to herself, she quietly added, "Maybe if I'd . . ."

"No second-guessing yourself," I said. "Just tell me what happened next."

She seemed a bit startled at my response to a comment she'd obviously not meant me to hear. But after a minute she continued her story. "He never spoke to me. Even after I asked him how much farther it was.

"I didn't start to get nervous, though, until I looked out the windows and realized we were heading back out of Minneapolis. When I tried the doors, they were locked. I . . . started to . . . panic, but I knew . . . I knew it wouldn't do any good," she said as the tears starting flowing fresh. "There was nothing in the car or my purse I could use to get out, even if I thought I could."

I felt her breathing begin to pick up and knew we must be nearing the part in her story where things went horribly wrong for her. My thumb rubbed softly over her knuckles trying to offer her what comfort I could.

"Then the car . . . stopped. The man, he opened my door and told me to get out.

"I was so scared," she whispered, her whole body trembling. "I moved as far away from him as I could. My back hit the other door . . . Then I was falling."

She paused again, but this time she looked up at me. The look on her face was a strange one. "That was when I met Ian," she whispered.

I was so very proud of her. She'd made it through the entire story without having a panic attack. A first.

My hands came up and cupped her face. "Brianna, you did so well today. I know it was difficult, but you stayed focused and didn't let the panic overwhelm you. Next time it will be easier."

Her eyes held mine with a look of pride. "Yes, Master."

With a swift kiss to the top of her head, I asked, "Are you getting hungry?"

"Yes."

I stood and offered her my hand. "Let's get back into town and see what we can find, shall we?"

It took us a while to make our way back to the scooter I'd rented. The return trip was filled with just as much peril as going in. I'd had to hold onto her every second in fear of her falling.

We made our way back into Minneapolis and went straight for the bike shop to return the scooter. Once that was done, we walked two blocks to my favorite pizza place.

Tony looked up at the sound of the bell over the door and smiled when he saw me. "Ah, Stephan. How are you this evening?" he said, coming out from behind the counter.

"I'm good, Tony. How about you?"

"Ah, I can't complain," he said. Then he noticed Brianna. "And who is the lovely lady?"

I smiled and pulled Brianna closer so that she was standing directly beside me. "Tony, this is Brianna. Brianna, this is the owner of the best pizza shop in town."

As expected, Tony blushed a bright red, and I chuckled. What I hadn't expected was for him to turn his total attention to Brianna. "You have to watch out for this one. He's quite the ladies' man, you know," he said winking.

Brianna just flushed and lowered her eyes while holding tighter to my hand. I squeezed it back. "Do you think you can spare a table for us, Tony?" I said, looking around at the near-empty restaurant.

"Of course," he said and turned to direct us over to a table in the corner.

We took a seat, and this time I placed Brianna opposite me. I wanted to see how she'd do since there was only one other couple besides us there. It was a little early for dinner, although most of Tony's business came from deliveries.

Tony disappeared for about thirty seconds and returned with menus. "Can I get you something to drink?"

"Just water, Tony."

"And for the lady?"

"She'll take water as well," I answered for her.

Brianna hadn't moved since sitting down. I knew she was nervous, but I was hoping she'd be able to work through her fear.

Tony left us to get our waters. I glanced over my menu to look at Brianna. "Do you want pizza or something else?" Instead of answering me, I saw her swallow hard. I was not going to ask her again, so instead of commenting I raised my eyebrows and gave her a pointed stare.

It worked.

"Pizza's fine," she said cautiously.

"Very well," I said putting my menu down.

Tony returned to the table and placed the glasses in front of us. "Just a large pizza with everything except onions, peppers, and anchovies tonight," I said, smiling.

"Coming right up." He winked at Brianna again.

I took a slow sip of my water before setting the glass back down. "You can calm down, Brianna. Tony is a big flirt, but he won't hurt you."

"Yes, Master," she whispered.

"Brianna," I said lowering my voice. "You will refrain from addressing me like that when we are in public." Her eyes widened, but she nodded in understanding.

No other words were exchanged until the pizza arrived. After thanking Tony, I let Brianna know she could help herself.

I watched her take a few bites of her pizza before bringing up the subject I wanted to try and discuss with her. "Tomorrow we will be going to my aunt and uncle's again. Do you have any questions for me?"

She shook her head. "No, M—" She caught herself. "No."

After taking another bite, I pressed forward. "I will stay close to you tomorrow, but I may leave you alone once or twice."

I saw her stop eating. At first I was concerned that she would begin to have another panic attack, but she just gripped her napkin tighter for a minute and then released it.

Once I was sure she was again in control of herself, I continued on. "Nothing has changed from the last time we were there. You're safe within the house, and you are to speak freely with the exception of how you address me," I said, meeting her eyes with that last part.

She just nodded instead of answering verbally.

Now that business was out of the way, I wanted to steer her to a more relaxing subject. "Have you been reading your books this week?"

"Yes."

"And what do you think so far?"

All at once her shoulders relaxed and her face lit up. For the rest of dinner we discussed characters, plots, and writing styles. It was the most I'd seen her open up outside my home since she'd arrived.

Chapter Twenty-Five

Brianna

My eyes fluttered open to the soft light of the morning coming from the window, and I couldn't help but smile. I didn't know the last time I'd felt so relaxed.

With that thought, I felt a moment of panic and glanced over at my alarm clock. Seven fifty. I took a deep breath and let the tension leave my body. Somehow I'd managed to wake up before the alarm.

And the alarm was set. I'd watched as Master had done so last night just after I had climbed into bed.

I was still trying to wrap my mind around yesterday. When he'd had me talk about John and what had happened, all I'd wanted to do was to please him. And although I was nervous as to his reaction, I had known that I had to be honest. He'd made it very clear that he prized that above all else.

But, as something I was becoming more able to accept from my Master, he had comforted me. He hadn't gotten upset that I'd tried to get away from my captors.

Master's arms had held me tight as I'd told my story, grounding me to the present and not letting me fall into the past.

Master had kept his arm around me the entire time we walked back to the scooter, and it had calmed me. I knew he wouldn't let me fall.

Once we'd gotten back into town and he'd returned the scooter, I thought we'd go home, so I'd been surprised when Master had led us into a restaurant. The man, Tony, had made me nervous as all men did, well, except for Brad. I still didn't understand that really, but he didn't frighten me at all. With Tony, I tried to remember that Master was with me and that he wouldn't let anyone hurt me.

As I remembered our dinner, I groaned. I couldn't believe I'd slipped and called him Master. I was very lucky he didn't punish me for it once we'd gotten back home.

Today was a new day, though, and we were going to have lunch with his aunt and uncle again. Diane was nice. I liked her.

Dr. Cooper—Richard—still made me nervous. Last time he and Master had gotten into an argument, and I knew it had been over me. For some reason he must not like me. Or maybe it was that he didn't want Master to have me.

Before I could go further with that thought, the alarm went off. I turned it off and made my bed before getting dressed in the clothes Master had laid out.

After a quick clean up in the bathroom, I walked out into the main room. I'd expected Master to be upstairs in the gym waiting on me as he usually did, but instead he was standing in the living room talking to someone on the phone.

I wasn't sure what to do, so I slowly walked into the room toward him. Thankfully, he saw the movement and looked up. My momentary good mood faltered when he didn't return my smile.

Master asked the person on the other end of the line to hold on before addressing me. I was trying very hard not to let my nerves get away from me. "You can go on upstairs and get started, Brianna. I'll be up shortly."

He went back to his phone call, and I hurried past him and up the stairs to the gym. I had no idea who was on the phone, but Master was obviously not in a good mood this morning.

Almost twenty minutes passed before he joined me. The look on his face told me nothing. He walked over to the mats and began stretching without glancing at me.

It was another ten minutes before his eyes met mine. They were guarded but not angry. I took a deep breath and relaxed a little. Whatever it was, it didn't appear to have anything to do with me.

We finished our workouts and went downstairs for breakfast. Master was quiet until we sat down at the table. "My aunt called this morning. That is who I was talking to when you came in."

I didn't comment or react in any way. I just waited. His mouth went hard as he said the next words. "Diane has invited some friends to join us." At his words I dropped my fork, and it made an awful sound as it first hit my plate and then bounced to the floor.

Master picked up my fork, wiped it off, and then laid it on my plate as if nothing had happened. "Although I'm not thrilled about it, it's not my decision. I've asked Diane if I may invite Logan and Lily along, and she has agreed."

Then he stopped and reached for my hand. I hadn't realized it was shaking until he held it in both of his. "You'll be fine, Brianna. Nothing has changed. You will be perfectly safe inside the house."

I didn't move or even know how to respond. Today I would not only have to face his uncle again, his uncle who didn't like me, who'd picked a fight with my Master, but I was also going to meet people I'd never met before.

The knowledge that Lily would be there was comforting, but what would these new people be like? Would they be nice? Or would they hate me? I was a slave after all. Or was I? Why did this have to be so confusing?

Suddenly I wasn't in my seat anymore. I felt him pick me up, and then I was sitting in Master's lap. As his arms surrounded me, my breathing became easier. I leaned into him and felt his lips brush against my hair.

"Are you all right?" he asked.

I nodded. "Yes."

His hand ran up my arm before coming up to cup my face. He turned my chin so that I was looking at him. "I know the news was unexpected, but why did you start to panic, Brianna?"

I swallowed. "What if they don't like me?" I whispered.

Master's eyes widened at my question. "Why do you think they won't like you?"

Without thinking about it I looked down, and I immediately felt his hand tighten. My eyes snapped up to meet his again. Instantly his grip relaxed.

"Your uncle doesn't like me," I stated.

He closed his eyes briefly before meeting mine again with a sad look. "Richard doesn't dislike you." He sighed. "He's worried about you." Then his hand came up to brush through my hair. "He wants to make sure that I am taking care of you."

My brow wrinkled in confusion. This didn't make sense. Master was so very good to me. How could his uncle think that he wasn't?

My thoughts came up short as he asked, "Would you be willing to talk to him? Without me in the room?"

I swallowed hard and knew my face had to show the apprehension I felt. "If that's what you want me to do, Master."

He sighed again, but this time it was in frustration. "Brianna, this is not an order or a command or even a request. It is a question. I think he might feel better about things if you were to talk to him, but I will not force you into that situation if you do not wish to do it."

So many thoughts ran through my mind as I considered talking to his uncle. He had been nice when he'd examined me. But Master had been right outside the door then. Would he be the same if we were completely alone? Did I want that?

Master must have seen the confusion in my eyes because his hand found my chin again, and he made me look at him. "You don't have to decide right now. Think about it, and you can tell me your decision once we reach the house, okay?"

I nodded. "Thank you, Master."

He smiled and patted my thigh. "Now get back in your chair and finish your breakfast."

For the rest of the morning I couldn't think of anything else. A part of me wanted to talk to Master's uncle. I didn't want to cause problems between the two of them.

But I couldn't shake the fear. No matter how much I tried to convince myself that I shouldn't be afraid, I couldn't make it completely go away.

We pulled up to his aunt and uncle's house at twelve forty-five. Master shut off the car but didn't move to get out. Instead he continued to look ahead and asked, "Have you made your decision, Brianna?"

I took a deep breath, closed my eyes as tightly as they would go, and said the words. "I will talk to him, Master." I paused. "If . . . he wishes to speak to me."

Master didn't comment on what I'd said. He just nodded and got out of the car before walking around to open my door.

We walked inside just as we had two weeks before and headed straight for the kitchen. The only difference was this time a deep voice I didn't recognize stopped me in my tracks halfway there.

Master noticed that I was no longer moving and walked back to me. His free arm circled my waist, and his lips brushed softly against my forehead.

"It's fine," he whispered and waited for some of the tension to leave my body.

I took a deep breath and let the scent of Master relax me. He didn't move or say anything more until I had once again calmed down.

"Are you ready?" he asked.

"Yes," I said, remembering not to call him Master. He stepped back and squeezed my hand before walking again.

Once we entered the brightly lit kitchen, it took everything I had not to run from the room. There was a man standing by the counter a few feet away from Diane, and he was huge, at least twice the size of Master. He was laughing so hard it shook his entire body. It was only the smile on Diane's face as she talked to the man that kept me from running in the other direction.

I stepped closer to Master and gripped his hand tighter. He seemed to know how nervous I was because he didn't try to move away from me to greet his aunt. "It seems I'm missing out on a good joke," Master said with a chuckle.

The large man turned his attention to us. A grin lit his face as he strolled over. I stepped back and angled myself behind Master.

Before I knew it, the man had Master wrapped in a hug.

Although Master was enveloped in an embrace that looked almost painful, he never let go of my hand. I was very grateful because the feel of his hand in mine was the only thing keeping the panic from taking control of me.

Then the man turned in my direction. He moved toward me. Master stopped him and the man looked puzzled.

Instead of answering his expression, however, Master said, "When Diane called to tell me they were inviting friends for dinner, I had no idea it would be you."

The man laughed again, appearing to forget his confusion from a moment ago. "Good to know I can still keep you guessing, Stephan."

Master laughed this time, too.

"So do I get an introduction to the girlfriend?"

That was when a blond woman I hadn't noticed walked toward us. She extended her hand to my Master. "Maybe if you weren't so excited to see Stephan, you wouldn't have scared the girl half to death, Jimmy."

The man, Jimmy, looked hurt for just a moment and then laughed. The woman ignored him and turned to Master. "How have you been, Stephan?" she asked with an air of formality.

"Fine," he answered her with the same overpoliteness. "And you?"

"Can't complain," she answered with a smirk. Then her eyes fell to me. "*Do* we get an introduction?"

He turned a little to look at me and tugged on my arm slightly, bringing me more to his side. "Brianna, I'd like for you to meet Jimmy and his wife, Samantha. We went to high school together."

Be polite. Be polite. "Hello," I said sheepishly.

"Oh and she's shy," Jimmy commented and then laughed, causing me to cringe against Master again.

Samantha just shook her head. "Please excuse my husband. He's a little overexcited today. He's not normally this . . ." She seemed to be searching for a word. "Insufferable."

"Hey!" Jimmy acted offended, but just as quickly he pulled Samantha into his arms and kissed her soundly.

When they broke apart, the doorbell rang. "That must be Logan," Jimmy said as his excitement from earlier returned. I watched as he hurried past us in order to greet the new arrivals.

Logan and Lily followed Jimmy into the room along with Richard. Logan greeted Stephan and me before turning his attention to Diane and Samantha.

Master kept hold of my hand as we all stood around talking for several minutes before Diane began handing plates and bowls to everyone for the dining room table. I was handed a beautiful bowl filled with mashed potatoes.

As we all took our seats, I realized what had been bothering me since Lily and Logan had arrived. Lily hadn't said anything. Not one word. She'd smiled at me briefly when Logan and Master had been talking with Jimmy, but she wasn't her normal energetic self.

Now, as I watched her take a seat beside Logan, I noticed that her demeanor hadn't changed. Something was wrong.

The food was passed around the table, and I put food on my plate as Master handed me each dish. My eyes never left Lily, though. Twice Logan had not handed her something going around the table. Instead he had given the bowl to Jimmy who was sitting on the other side of her.

My confusion continued as everyone started to eat. I waited for Master to begin before I did, as usual, but noticed that Lily also didn't start to eat until after Logan had taken his first bite. What was going on?

Most of the conversation throughout the meal was directed toward Samantha and Jimmy. Apparently they had been living in Boston near her family but had decided to come back to Minneapolis so he could start his residency. He was training to be a surgeon.

I was only half paying attention because of what was happening just across from me. Every now and then Lily would glance up at me, but she never spoke. About halfway through dinner Diane asked if everything was all right, and Logan had just said that her throat was bothering her and she was resting it. When Richard offered to take a look after dinner, Logan waved his hand and said he was sure it would be fine by tomorrow.

After that Master changed the subject. The dinner continued with Lily still not saying anything, and my worry was increasing. She just wasn't being Lily.

When Diane disappeared into the kitchen, Master leaned over to whisper in my ear. "What's troubling you, Brianna?"

I turned my head so that I could speak to him quietly without anyone overhearing. "I'm worried about Lily. She isn't acting like herself."

Master glanced quickly to where Lily and Logan were sitting and his lips turned up in a smirk before he turned back to look at me. "Lily's fine. I will explain later if you wish."

I looked over at Logan and Lily myself and then nodded to Master. "Yes, please." She was the closest thing to a friend I'd had in almost a year. Lily wasn't being Lily, and I wanted to know why.

After dessert, we all sat around the table talking. Well, everyone except Lily.

Somewhere along the line, Richard and Diane got up and disappeared into the kitchen. Master told me he'd be right back and followed them.

I tried not to be nervous as I awaited his return. Logan asked me if I was getting excited for school to start, which brought on more questions from Samantha. The more I talked, the easier it was. But still Lily didn't say anything.

Master returned, but instead of taking his seat again, he held out his hand and helped me to stand.

"Excuse us," he said politely to everyone sitting at the table. I heard Jimmy mumble something, but I couldn't make out what it was, and Master chose not to acknowledge it at all.

With his hand on the small of my back, Master ushered me down the hall to his uncle's study. We paused outside the door, and he looked down at me, his eyes searching mine. "I will be just in the other room should you need me," he said as he leaned down to place a kiss on my forehead. "Richard won't hurt you, I promise." He pulled back and took one last look at me before walking down the hall and back into the dining room.

I stood staring at the door in front of me, knowing that eventually I'd have to go inside. He'd offered me a choice. Why had I agreed to do this again?

With a shake of my head, I pushed all the questions aside. I knew the exact reason I'd said that I would talk to Richard. This was something simple that I could do for my Master, and I would do it.

Slowly I turned the doorknob and pushed open the only thing separating me from Master's uncle. There, standing across the room, was the man I was to talk to.

His eyes were very different from Master's. They were softer and seemed to hold so many questions. There was also uncertainty in them. That was something I'd never seen in Master's eyes.

"Hello, Brianna," Richard said, breaking me out of my musings.

"Hi," I said meekly.

Richard motioned to a set of chairs over by the window. "Will you come in and sit down?" I hesitated, taking one last look out into the hallway before taking the final steps into the room and closing the door behind me.

He moved slowly as he took a seat in the chair farthest away, allowing me the one closest to the door. I was trying to stay calm. To remember that if I yelled, Master was close enough to hear me. Master had assured me that I was safe with his uncle, and Master wouldn't lie to me.

Finally I sat down on the edge of the chair. The panic was pushing forward, but I was doing everything I could to push it back. My hand came up to touch Master's collar. *I am always with you, Brianna.*

He was always with me. I could do this.

It was Richard's voice that brought my head up. He cleared his throat, and I met his eyes.

"Thank you for agreeing to speak with me. I know you must be nervous, but I assure you that I mean you no harm."

I wasn't sure how I should respond so I just nodded.

Richard cleared his throat again and leaned toward me. Instinctively, I pulled away. He seemed to notice my reaction and sat back in his chair. "I believe Stephan has told you that I'm concerned for you. He tells me that he is not being inappropriate and that he is treating you with care."

He ended there, leaving his words hanging in the air. I realized he was waiting for me to comment. I briefly debated how I was to refer to Master in his uncle's presence, but then realized that Richard knew what I was, so I didn't censor my words. "Master takes very good care of me."

Tilting his head, he looked me over very carefully. "I know this is going to sound like an odd question, but I feel I need to ask it. Are you and Stephan having sexual relations?"

My head fell. "No, Sir. Master doesn't require that of me."

"Are you happy, Brianna?"

That brought my head up again. "Yes, Sir. As I said, Master is very good to me."

He nodded.

When he didn't immediately ask another question, I decided to take a chance and ask one of my own since I was told I could speak freely. "Will you be nicer to Master now?"

Richard looked surprised, but he didn't answer right away. Instead he gave me a searching look. "I am concerned about you, Brianna. I am not sure that Stephan is what's best for you."

His words upset me. It was a mixture of panic and wanting to defend my Master. "You don't understand. Master saved me! He took me from that awful place," I said, feeling the memories and the panic once again beginning to rise.

I brought my knees up to my chest and tried to force the things I was seeing from my mind. Ian couldn't hurt me anymore. He couldn't hurt me.

Stephan

Ever since I'd left Brianna with my uncle I couldn't concentrate. I was largely unaware of the conversation around me.

Diane had brought Lily a cup of tea to help "soothe her throat" while trying, without success, to include her in a discussion she was having with Samantha. Jimmy wanted a day of fishing out on the lake with Logan and me. He'd tried to engage me in the conversation, but was having about as much luck as Diane was with Lily. After I'd given him nothing but vague, noncommittal answers a few times, he just carried on the conversation with Logan and left me out of it.

It had only been fifteen minutes, but I had to force myself to stay in my seat and not go and hover by the door. I kept looking at the clock on the wall every thirty seconds.

Then I heard Richard call my name. It wasn't panic filled, but I knew that something must be wrong.

I didn't bother to excuse myself or acknowledge anyone at the table before taking my leave and hurrying down the hallway to my uncle's study. What I found there wrenched my heart.

Brianna sat in one of Richard's high-backed chairs with her knees to her chest, her arms wound so tightly around her legs that her knuckles were white. She was chanting to herself something that sounded like *he can't hurt me* in a barely audible voice.

I said her name before reaching out and trying to loosen her fingers. Somewhere in her mind she must have registered my presence because, although she didn't look up, she did stop chanting the phrase she had been saying and changed it to the word *yellow*.

Before she'd said her safeword, I knew that she'd been at least at an eight given our experiences together so far. I was still happy that she had used it, though.

Once I'd released her hands from their death grip on her legs, I placed both her hands in one of mine and used the other to cup her face. "Focus on my voice, Brianna. You're safe, love."

It took repeating these words three times before I finally began to feel her calm. She looked at me and that was when the tears started to fall. I didn't hesitate picking her up into my arms and then sitting back down with her in the chair.

After settling her in my arms I looked up and found that although Richard was still the only one in the room, everyone else, including Lily and Logan, were standing in the doorway. I gave Logan a pointed look. He whispered something to Lily, and then motioned for everyone to move away except for Richard and Lily.

With everyone else out of view, Lily moved into the room and came to kneel in front of Brianna. Her hand came up to where Brianna's hand rested in her lap. It didn't take long for Brianna to recognize the gesture and for her to take Lily's proffered hand.

We sat in our little bubble until Diane returned with a glass of water. I took it and thanked her before offering it to the fragile woman in my arms. Brianna surprised me as she had so many times by reaching out, taking the glass from me, and drinking.

Diane reluctantly left the room, leaving the four of us alone once again. I looked down at Brianna. "I need to speak with Richard. Are you okay here alone with Lily?"

"Yes," she whispered. Slowly, I lifted both of us from the chair and placed her back into its comforting depths.

I waited until Richard and I were out in the hall before leveling a look at my uncle. "What happened?" I snapped.

"I was honest with her. I told her I wasn't sure her being with you was the best thing for her. She defended you and started spiraling into a panic attack, which is when I called for you."

"You were just supposed to make sure she was okay. That was it. Why did you force her into having to defend me?" I hissed.

"Stephan, she is in very real danger of developing—"

"I don't care what she's in danger of developing. It's not your concern. She is *my* responsibility." Without letting him say anything else, I marched back into the study.

Lily was still kneeling on the floor, but now so was Brianna. As I walked into the room, what I heard Lily say brought me up short. "You're not a slave. Talk to Stephan. He'll explain everything."

Chapter Twenty-Six

Brianna

I watched as he left the room to go speak to his uncle. There was a part of me that wanted to call him back. To ask him to never leave my side, but I couldn't.

Lily's voice brought my attention to her. "Are you okay?" Instead of answering her, my arms flew around her neck, nearly toppling her over, and I started crying once again.

Her hands came up to rub comfortingly on my back. "It'll be all right," she said, trying to soothe me as she regained her balance.

She didn't understand why I was crying. "You can . . . talk," I choked out.

Arms squeezed me tighter before she pulled me back and wiped the tears from my cheeks. I sat facing her on the floor, watching as she looked at me with a strange expression on her face. "I need to apologize to you, Brianna."

"Lily—"

"No. I did something very wrong, and I need to tell you that I'm sorry."

"But . . ." And then a fear went through me. "You're not . . . leaving. Are you?"

"No. I'm not leaving. I'll be here as long as you want me to be."

With her reassurance, I was finally able to release the breath I'd been holding. "I don't want you to leave." She smiled back at me, but it held a hint of sadness.

"Last weekend when we were in your bedroom you asked me a question, and I didn't fully answer you or encourage you to talk to Stephan like I should have." Swallowing, I tried to remain calm. I knew exactly which conversation she was talking about.

"I told you I was never Stephan's slave and that you weren't either. But I should have stayed and made sure that you understood, that you knew that you could talk to me and to Stephan about anything. I failed you, and I'm sorry."

"But he bought me," I whispered. My voice sounded weak even to my ears.

Her hands gripped mine tighter. "You are not a slave. Talk to Stephan. He'll explain everything."

I didn't know what to say. Denial rang through my brain, and I wanted to scream. I was a slave. It was what I was. I'd accepted that.

But then the doubt I'd had since last weekend began to push its way in. What if Lily was right? What did that mean exactly? Why . . .

There was movement in the doorway, and my head came up. My eyes met the worried ones of my Master.

He entered the room with slow, steady steps and crouched down beside me. His left hand came up to brush the side of my cheek, while his right slid into the strands of my hair. A level of calm that was only present when he touched me had me leaning into him. He pulled me closer against his chest, and I wrapped my arms around his waist.

At that moment, I didn't want to think about what Lily had told me. There were obviously things that I didn't understand. She knew my Master much better than I, and I trusted her almost as much as I did him. I would do as she said and talk to him. Just not right now. Right now I needed to know that he was here and that I was safe. That no one was going to take me away from him.

All too soon we got up and joined the others waiting for us in the sitting room. Everyone looked at me huddled into Master's side.

Master thanked Diane for dinner and told everyone that I wasn't feeling well so we were going home. Diane came up to us and asked if she could give me a hug. I felt Master's arms hold me tighter, but for some reason I didn't feel panicked at his aunt's suggestion, so I nodded.

Her arms surrounded me, even though I never released my hold on Master. The hug was brief and not nearly as forceful as the first one I'd experienced from her. I felt bad that everyone seemed to feel they had to handle me with kid gloves but grateful at the same time. She turned to Master and gave him a much tighter hug, whispering something in his ear that sounded like *take care of her.*

Once Diane walked back across the room to stand beside Richard, the awkwardness increased. No one seemed to know what to do, and Lily was standing by Logan's side, back to not acting like herself.

Master said a final goodbye to everyone, and as we walked out the door, I heard Logan say they should be going, too. It seemed that I had ruined the dinner for everyone.

Stephan

I was teetering somewhere between rage and the overwhelming desire to hold on to the creature at my side and never let her go. The dinner had been going so well. I thought giving Richard a chance to talk to her alone would be a good thing. I had been beyond stupid.

And then there was Lily. She had been quiet all throughout dinner. Punishment, I suspected. But then the first words I heard out of her mouth left me trying to remember how to breathe.

I thought that we were making headway. That she was starting to see herself as a person again. An individual. But that was obviously not the case. Brianna understood nothing, and it was entirely my fault.

As I pulled into my spot in the parking garage, I could see Logan behind me. I had a feeling they would be coming to make sure Brianna was all right. It wasn't as if we could speak openly about the situation while at my aunt and uncle's house.

All the way home I'd tried to provide what little comfort to Brianna that I could with my touch. We needed to talk. She needed to understand once and for all what had happened and what I wanted from her. For her.

I didn't wait for my friends before going up to my condo. Even if I only had a minute alone with Brianna before everything started, I wanted it.

We walked into the open layout of my home, and I wrapped her in my arms. Her hair brushed against my lips as I took in her scent. I knew what needed to happen now, and I could only hope that she didn't run away from me screaming. That she would understand what I was trying to do, and that she would allow me to help her.

All too soon, Logan and Lily made their presence known. I released my hold on Brianna and let them in.

We all walked over to the living room. I went directly to my chair and had Brianna sit on my lap while Logan and Lily took seats on the couch.

My best friend was one of the most levelheaded people I knew and got to the point quickly. "I know that you and Brianna need to talk about some things, but I felt that Lily needed to explain herself first."

He looked over at Lily, and she began talking.

"When we were in Brianna's room last weekend, she asked me if I was ever your slave. I told her I wasn't and that neither was she." Lily's eyes lowered. "When it was time to go, I should have asked for a few more minutes or something other than what I did, which was nothing."

I had had no idea that Brianna had asked her if she was a slave last weekend. Looking at Logan's face while Lily told her story let me know that this was why she had not been speaking today at dinner. Lily should have said something. To Brianna. To Logan. To me. Instead she had kept it to herself and allowed the woman in my arms to suffer even more confusion than was necessary. Brianna had opened up to Lily and had gotten silence in return.

Lily finished by apologizing again for her poor judgment and fell silent. Apparently her punishment wasn't over. I couldn't say that I disagreed with Logan.

My best friend then stood and walked over to stand in front of us. Brianna looked up hesitantly, and he smiled at her before turning serious again. "My deepest apologies, Brianna."

Then he looked at me. "Please call if you need anything." I nodded and they left.

Brianna sat unmoving in my arms. I knew that she'd heard

every word that Lily and Logan had spoken, and I knew she had to have many questions floating in her head that she was probably afraid to voice. Everything in me rebelled against letting her go, but I knew that I must.

I patted her arm and told her to stand. Then, taking her hand, I led her to the couch and had her sit down beside me. We hadn't been here since the time I told her she didn't have to end every sentence she said to me with *Master*.

She sat with her head down, holding tightly to my hand as if she thought I might let it go. I wouldn't. I was too selfish for that. Some part of me had to be able to touch her while we talked.

My thumb moved lazily on her knuckles as I stated, "There's something you want to ask me."

She didn't answer me, so I waited. If it took all night for her to talk to me, we would wait here.

And wait we did. After five minutes she began picking with her free hand at the slacks she was wearing. After ten she began moving her legs. Fifteen minutes passed, and she opened her mouth, but no sound escaped. This went on for several more minutes before small sounds began emerging.

But even after that it took another three minutes before a definable word came out. "You . . . bought me."

It wasn't a question, but I answered anyway. "Yes. I did."

Her head fell lower, and her shoulders fell forward slightly. "I am your slave," she whispered, clearly not talking to me but herself.

"Look at me." She did as I said, albeit slowly. Her eyes were fearful. It was something I'd noticed gradually fading when she looked at me. I didn't like seeing that it had returned.

"Would you like to know why I bought you?" Brianna's eyes widened and her breathing picked up. I both saw and felt the signs of her anxiety. She wanted to know, but she was scared of the answer.

"Maybe I should have told you that first night. I don't know," I said to her honestly, pleading with her to believe me. "You didn't believe anything I said back then." I shook my head as I remembered what she'd been like that first night. So fragile and completely broken. "I didn't know how you'd react."

She didn't say anything so I continued. "A friend of mine came to me." I tried to pick my words carefully. "He saw you at a party."

Her hand loosened around mine. The fear was turning into

panic. As much as I wanted to keep space between us, I just couldn't be physically separated from her anymore. I couldn't just watch her crumble before me.

I released her hand and wrapped my arms around her, pulling her flush against my body. My forehead rested against hers as I looked into her eyes, almost forcing her to concentrate on nothing but me. "Daren told me he didn't think you were there because you wanted to be. He had asked Ian"—she shuddered when I said his name—"if you were for sale. He knew I had the means to buy you. That's why he came to me."

Brianna's eyes were still fearful, but they were no longer unfocused. I softened my tone as I said the next words. "I didn't buy you to own you. Not like you think I did."

More minutes passed in silence. "Say something. Please," I begged.

"Why?" she whispered.

"Why what?" I said back just as softly. We were so close that our noses were almost touching.

Her eyes changed to pleading, but I wanted her to say something. Anything. "Do not be afraid, Brianna. You can ask me anything."

Brianna's words were still weak as she spoke them. "If . . . if you didn't want to . . . own me," she choked, "then why did you . . . why would you buy me?"

I closed my eyes and took in the scent of her. My next words could change everything for her. And for me. "There are people out there who enjoy what Ian does. Alex, for example. But if you weren't that type of person . . . well, I couldn't just not do something. I had the means to help you. I couldn't just walk away and leave you there if that wasn't what you wanted."

She blinked up at me. There was still so much confusion in her eyes, but I was glad to see the fear was retreating. "Then I saw you," I said, bringing my hand up to caress her face. "I knew without a doubt that this was not the life you wanted. But you were so broken, so scared. I wanted in that moment to help you above all else."

Brianna's eyes were full of questions now. I knew I still had so much to explain. "I was selfish, though. When I brought you into my home I knew that I wanted to keep you." She stiffened, and I strengthened my hold. "Not as my slave, Brianna."

I released a deep breath and dropped my hand back down to her side. "I'm a Dominant, like Ian. But unlike Ian, I do not believe in forced slavery. I want a woman to submit to me because she wants to serve me. Not because she is forced to."

I paused and looked into her eyes, trying to convey all the emotions, all the love that I had for her. "I want you to want to serve me, Brianna. I want you to let me take care of you. To show you that you don't have to be afraid of me or anyone else."

She didn't say anything for too long. I could hear the minutes ticking away and with every one my fear grew. And with her next words I had to force myself not to react. She couldn't see how much I feared her leaving.

"But I can't leave?" She phrased it as a question.

"If leaving is what you desire, then I won't stop you," I said as calmly as I could manage. "I don't want you to leave."

The confusion was back. "I can . . . leave?" she asked.

I closed my eyes, trying to keep the pain out of my voice. "Yes. If you wish."

Obviously I didn't do a good enough job. Her hand came up to my face, and she hesitantly traced the worry lines on my brow. Fingers followed the line of my nose and traced my lips.

Brianna's hand dropped back into her lap, and at the loss of her touch my eyes opened to search hers. But instead of what I'd been expecting, she surprised me. "What's wrong with Lily?"

It took me a moment to change gears. I'd been so worried, so sure that she'd get up and leave that I hadn't been prepared for anything else.

As quickly as I could, I answered, "Lily is Logan's submissive. She did something wrong, so she was being punished." I couldn't help but smirk. "Lily likes to talk, so taking that away from her has quite an impact."

Again, Brianna's eyes were full of questions. I waited until she settled on one to ask. She didn't disappoint. "I'm your submissive?"

I sighed. "Yes. In a way, you are. Although not in the traditional sense."

She looked confused again, but for some reason this time it made me laugh. "When you were with Ian, Brianna, you had no say. He controlled everything you did. It was what you were used to, and I thought giving you a whole new set of rules, a completely different way of doing things all at once, would be too much of a shock to you."

I looked at her, trying to will her to understand what I was saying. She could still choose to walk away from me. "So I decided to start slow. Keep structure in your life while trying to get you to open up to me so that I could help you."

My hands came up to cup her face lightly. "It was working. You started to relax, to talk to me, to trust me."

Her nose scrunched up as if she was deep in thought. "If I stay here, what will happen?"

I couldn't stop the excitement that was pounding through me. She wasn't bolting for the door. "That will depend on you," I replied honestly. Her eyes were questioning again. "It will depend on what you want. If you want to be my submissive or not."

"If I don't?" she asked.

Fear gripped me again at the thought of losing her, but I pushed it into the far corner of my mind. I'd deal with it later.

"Then I will help you in any way that I can. I have access to resources all over the city. I'd still like to see you finish your schooling, but I'm sure that eventually you would want to have your own apartment and a job."

Again she was quiet for way too long. Then she whispered, "If I do?"

Once again I framed her face with my hands. I leaned in close, making sure she could feel the sincerity of my words. "Then we have a lot to talk about."

Over the next two hours there was little talking done. She looked so lost that I ended up pulling her onto my lap and just holding her.

Brianna did ask me about the collar I'd given her. I explained that it had more to do with her safety and security than a traditional one given by a Dominant to his submissive. It signified, as I'd said, that she was my responsibility. She was under my protection. I had not wanted her to think that anyone would just come and take her away from me. My commitment to her hadn't changed.

When dinnertime came, I decided to order in, rather than having either Brianna or I make something. She was distracted and rightly so. The last thing I needed was for her to hurt herself in the kitchen by not paying attention. I also wanted to keep an eye on her.

About the Author

Sherri spent most of her childhood detesting English class. It was one of her least favorite subjects because she never seemed to fit into the standard mold. She wasn't good at spelling, or following grammar rules, and outlines made her head spin. For that reason, Sherri never imagined becoming an author.

At the age of thirty, all of that changed. After getting frustrated with the direction a television show was taking two of its characters, Sherri decided to try her hand at writing an alternate ending, and give the characters their happily ever after. By the time the story finished, it was one of the top ten read stories on the site, and her readers were encouraging her to write more.

Since then Sherri has published several novels, many of which have hit the top 100 in their category on Amazon. Writing has become a creative outlet that allows her to explore a wide range of emotions, while having fun taking her characters through all the twists and turns she can create. You can find a current list of all of Sherri's books and sign up for her monthly newsletter at www.sherrihayesauthor.com.

All throughout dinner I kept watching and waiting. I told her earlier that she could ask me anything she wanted, and I would answer her honestly. So far, she hadn't asked any more questions.

Once our food was finished, I stood to help her clean up. She froze. "Is everything all right?" I asked, coming up to her side.

"Yes." She nodded and then seemed to shake herself out of wherever her mind had been.

It didn't take long to clean up the takeout, and once the leftovers were put away, she seemed lost again. Her eyes couldn't find a resting place. First she would look down and then at me. I even caught her glancing over to her bedroom door a few times.

Not wanting to cause her any more distress than what she was obviously in, I walked over to my chair and sat down just like I always did after dinner. I turned on the television and waited to see what she'd do.

At first, she did nothing. She stood unmoving behind me. I had to force myself not to react, not to do something. Brianna needed to make the next move.

Finally she did move. Her footsteps were slow and hesitant as she drew closer to me. She paused beside my chair for several seconds. I didn't move from my position.

Then in a flash she sat in the middle of the couch just to my right. I glanced over and gave her a small smile to let her know everything was all right, but she didn't return it. She wasn't even looking at me.

The smile I'd been wearing turned into a frown as I noticed her hands begin to fidget and then shake. My discontent deepened as she pulled her knees up to her chest and began to rock. This was not what I'd been hoping for.

I closed my eyes, took a deep breath, and said, "Brianna, look at me." She didn't respond. "Brianna," I said more firmly. This time her head snapped up, and she looked at me. "Would you like to sit with me?" She nodded, and I opened my arms in invitation.

For the rest of the night, we sat in my chair holding on to one another. I had no idea what the future would bring for us, but for tonight she was still in my arms, still mine.

For up-to-date news about Sherri Hayes' books, subscribe to her newsletter athttp://eepurl.com/J4vDb